ALL __
AND
JEST

by

Kate Harrad

GHOSTWOODS

THIS IS A GHOSTWOODS BOOK

2nd Edition
6 7 8 9 10 11 12 1 2 3 4 5

Text copyright ©2011, 2016 Kate Harrad

ISBN: 978-0-993507-70-0

This edition published June 2016 by:
Ghostwoods Books
Maida Vale
London, United Kingdom

http://www.gwdbooks.com

All Lies and Jest:
Saving the World For Fun and Profit

by

Kate Harrad

Author's Note

Every person and event in this book is imaginary. Some of it is inspired by real internet sites and conspiracy theories, hence the chapter headings. But I really did make it all up.

Contents

Chapter One
Finding Stefan

"Being a vampire is difficult in today's society."
vampiredungeon.iwarp.com

Search terms:
real vampire craving, vampire pathology, vampires among us

Saturday, September 20th

I fell into London face first, like a child with a box of sweets. I wanted to gobble it all up, the sticky, delicious, dangerous city. I wanted to do everything, meet everyone, make my mark, disappear into the night, leave an impression. But I didn't understand what I really wanted, not fully, not till later.

It started when I met Stefan. There was a party and a murder: there were drugs and sex and insanity and death. There was blood on Naomi's lips, fervour and guilt in her eyes, and I stared into the dark alleyway where the body lay as if drunk, wondering how I'd come so far so quickly when two weeks earlier I'd never even met any of them.

Two weeks earlier, in fact, I hadn't really known anyone in London at all, and that had become a problem. I'd been in the city for a couple of months by then, but it had turned out that London wasn't an easy place to meet people. Though having spent my previous twenty-three years in Middleswithin, a small town in Somerset where I knew the names, ages, tastes, opinions, ancestry and golf handicap of everyone within a three-mile radius, I was in many ways thoroughly enjoying the anonymity of being a stranger.

My home was a tiny studio flat, reluctantly paid for by my parents because it was the only way they could get me to leave. I told them I needed time to repent. I told them I would pray for my sins daily. I told them I had a job to go. None of it was true. But they wanted to believe it, and they wanted rid of me, so before you could say 'excommunicated' I was living in Morden as a free woman. Free from parental authority, free — at least partially — from the Resurrected Church of England, and free to find something to do on a Saturday night. In Middleswithin, as in most British towns, if the Resurrected Church cast you out, your social life went with it. So I'd spent my time playing with my iTem, plotting the destruction of organised religion and dreaming of the big city, where they had social events that didn't revolve around Jesus.

And now here I was. As I'd suspected, I had had no trouble getting temp work. If you can do repetitive administrative tasks competently for minimum wage and manage not to stab anyone in the process, the world is your very dull oyster. But that wasn't what I'd come for.

It was the iTem that sparked things off. In those days, they'd just started testing the real-life Find a Friend application (introduced after concerns that people were beginning to lose the ability to interact on a face-to-face basis) and not that many people had signed up. Nevertheless, I'd played with it obsessively at home, trying to find if my town had anyone interesting in it—it didn't—and eventually I decided I needed to use it in London. I hadn't managed to make friends by talking to work colleagues. I was too menial to be invited out for drinks, or by striking up random conversations in pubs. Possibly I shouldn't have handed out questionnaires as an opening gambit. My sense of liberation from my claustrophobic adolescence had begun to sour into isolation tinged with loneliness. So, one Saturday afternoon, I found my way to Oxford Street and tried out some search terms.

I don't know exactly why I chose to search for 'vampire'. Blame those long Somerset Saturday nights, letting my imagination run wild about London and mystery and adventure and excitement. I wasn't expecting to get any results.

But I did.

One hit. A photo stared up at me: dark eyes, pale skin, brooding expression. "Stefan Drayton. Sound engineer, goth and creature of the night" said the description. Did that mean he had a sense of humour, I wondered, or that he really didn't? In any case, with an impressive lack of care for his own privacy, he'd provided an email address and had even signed up for the GPS option. In other words, if I wanted to find out where he was at that very moment, I could.

I wanted to.

Some people, I reasoned, joined evening classes to make friends. Some got involved in political parties, or environmental activism, or — shudder — religious movements. I needed to meet people somehow. Interesting people. Weird people. People who didn't belong to the Resurrected Church. And, maybe, people who believed they were vampires. What was the worst that could happen?

I tapped the screen and an address appeared: a bar, it looked like, on a side street off Oxford Circus. Even the idea that people might spend their Saturday afternoons in a bar gave me a frisson of excitement. I was there within five minutes.

It was a basement bar: wobbly tables, low ceilings, lighting that could more accurately have been described as darking. It had several goth-type people in it, but as I'd suspected, spotting Stefan Drayton wasn't hard at all. In a corner sat three goths, one of whom was clearly the original of the photo on my screen. He was a boy around my age, tall with dark hair and very white skin and eyes you could drown — or at least paddle — in. He was sitting with two friends, and all of them were wearing black as if there were no other colour in the world. I leaned around a corner from them for a moment, to gauge whether it would be a good idea to introduce myself. I could hear their conversations easily. Actually, I could have heard the conversations of everyone in the bar, had I wanted to. The small room resonated with voices as if they were competing with each other for my attention.

If they had been, then Stefan would have won easily. Everyone else I could hear was discussing mortgages. He was talking about blood.

"Finding donors isn't easy," he was saying sternly. "I won't feed from anyone unwilling or unworthy."

"I can see that narrows it down, yeah," said the girl sitting opposite him. She was short, curvy and displaying more cleavage than I'd realised anyone even had.

Unlike Stefan, she wasn't pale. In fact, she was black. I was uncomfortably aware that I found her skin colour exotic, not in the sense that I thought she came from outside the UK — her accent was pure South London — but in the sense that I'd lived my entire life in a more or less all-white town. I'd barely even met anyone with black hair, let alone black skin. I told myself firmly that if and when I introduced myself, I would not be embarrassing about this. I hoped I was right.

The third person was a short stocky boy with ginger hair and cheerful freckles, who nevertheless managed to pull off an air of gothness through the determined application of black eyeliner, black velvet, and a serious expression. He said, in what I felt was a slightly disappointed tone, "So no hunting young girls down dark alleyways and sucking them dry, then?"

Stefan raised an eyebrow. "I am a vegan, Simon."

"Heroin!" said the other boy sharply.

Odd, I thought. Was he calling for some, like ordering another beer?

Stefan went on. "Life is sacred and consent is all. As with animals, so with humans."

His black lace top was quite see-through. This observation wasn't relevant to anything, but I just happened to notice it, and once I had, I couldn't stop myself leaning forward slightly to see if his nipples were visible. They were.

"But you need blood to live?" asked the goth girl. I noticed that she was keeping her tone carefully neutral, and deduced that she didn't believe Stefan, but did find him attractive.

"Ultimately, yes. Not all the time, of course. I can absorb pranic energy from other sources, but sooner or later, the Thirst begins again. It's a craving within my veins — lust and hunger and longing combined. And then I have to submit to the demands of my nature." I was impressed by his ability to capitalise Thirst, and also by the way his tone of voice managed to make his words sound almost sensible. Almost.

"What's pranic energy?" asked Simon. Stefan looked annoyed. I got the impression that he would have liked a minute's silence while his words resonated in the air.

"It is not an easy concept to explain."

"It's like spiritual energy, from the air and from people and from other stuff," said the girl helpfully. "You know breatharians, those people who say they don't need to eat? It's what they use instead of food. Or so they claim. Bunch of wankers." She added hastily: "But that's different from vampires, of course. You just use it as a top-up."

"Indeed," said Stefan authoritatively, regaining his control of the conversation. "Vampires like myself take energy from human emotions. We feed on fear, or desire... or hate." The last sentence was said in a lower, darker tone. I winced.

"Do all emotions work?" asked Simon. "Like irritation, and cheerfulness?"

Stefan ignored him. "However, stealing emotion is just as immoral as non-consensual blood drinking. Unless I have active consent to absorbing human energy, I absorb pranic energy in more ethical ways."

"Like...?"

"For example, eating lettuce."

There was silence for a moment. Stefan clearly realised that his announcement had been less than impressive.

"You can assimilate pranic energy through material sources," he elaborated. "When I eat salad, I am not merely assimilating its normal protein and calories, the way humans do. I am absorbing its spiritual energy into my body, and it gives me strength. Afterwards I feel... strong. And more spiritually aware."

"Wow," said the girl, again carefully balancing her tone. "Um... can you get energy from sex? I mean, I'm just wondering."

"I am celibate," he said aloofly. "I feel that sex wastes valuable energy. It drains me."

"So you'd need to eat lots of lettuce to recuperate?" she said innocently. In the battle between sarcasm and libido, sarcasm was clearly beginning to gain the victory. I mentally applauded her.

So then, a vegan vampire, I thought. Even weirder than I'd expected.

Still, in spite of Stefan's conversation, I was starting to like him. Or possibly I was just giving in to his pale-skinned, brunette good looks and the gently enticing movement of his long slim hands on the red plastic tablecloth. But no, there was more to my attraction than his looks. After all, he was certainly interesting. And he might be the passport to other interesting people. Since the US had gone all fundamentalist, a lot of alternative cultures had set up shop in London. One of those dark, mysterious little back-alley shops, presumably.

The bar was getting emptier and the goths had gone quiet for a moment. Now was the time to introduce myself. I smoothed my hair, currently a bright auburn, bit my lips, and plunged.

In the time it had taken for me to do that, Stefan had started explaining about the occult significance of green beans. As I moved closer he looked at me for a moment, then registered me as 'not a goth' and his eyes lost their gleam of interest. I was dressed in black, as a matter of fact, but faded jeans and a tee-shirt rather than anything you could do serious moping in, and I hadn't managed to apply make-up. Attempts to put on eyeliner usually ended up with my contact lenses smeared in black goo. One of the many reasons why I couldn't do the image full-time, despite my fascination with it. (Another was the fact that I was a John Denver fan. There are no goth clubs that play country music. Maybe I would set one up and become famous.)

I stood by the table until Stefan was forced to look up. "Yes?" he said, in a voice the word 'hauteur' could have been invented to describe.

I pulled out my iTem and showed it to him in an explanatory manner. It was glowing blue now, since I was standing next to him. Its screen showed the words:

"Results for search: 'Vampires in London'.
1. Stefan Drayton. Currently in: The Bar Noir."

The eyes reacquired their gleam. "Oh, I see. Yes, I remember registering for that. You were looking for a vampire, then?"

"The iTem directed me to you, yes," I said noncommittally. "So, are you *really* a vampire?" It seemed wisest not to reveal that

I'd been listening in to their conversation for the last ten minutes.

Despite a credible attempt to disguise it, he looked flattered. "I am, yes. Greetings." He smiled slowly and enigmatically, long black eyelashes sweeping down modestly over his eyes, waiting for breathless, embarrassed acknowledgement of his status.

Half of me fought the urge to giggle. The other half found that my knees had gone a bit weak. The combination made me feel slightly dizzy. The goth girl looked at me with sympathy.

I said, "My name's Elinor Rosewood. Can I offer you a drink?"

An elegant hand reached out to grasp my wrist. He looked carefully at the veins between it and my elbow, and nodded. "A willing donor? Certainly you may. Shall we do it here, or would you prefer a little more ritual? I have a flat in West London."

"Actually," I said, "I wanted to *buy* you a drink. From the bar."

Simon and the girl failed to repress giggles. Stefan's foundation failed to conceal his blushing. I failed to hide my pleasure — I'd successfully got him off balance.

He recovered quickly, though, and said, "Espresso, please," in a neutral fashion. I nodded and went off to get his coffee. Up close, Stefan had perfect skin and his eyes looked even bigger than I'd imagined. Wow.

I sternly reminded myself that he was very, very silly, and that just because he was cute didn't mean I should give credence to a word he said.

When I returned, all three of them were quiet, clearly waiting to interrogate me. I didn't mind. I would have interrogated me. (Sometimes I did, late at night when bored. I always confessed in the end and took my punishment like a man.)

"So, who are you then?" said the girl in a reasonably friendly tone, starting things off straightforwardly.

"Apart from being Elinor?" I shrugged. "I'm twenty-three, I'm from Somerset, and yes I know I don't have the accent. I moved to London a few weeks ago, and I want to meet new people. The iTem seemed like a good way of doing that." I shrugged again.

"So you searched for vampires? Why?"

"All of the people I've met at work talk about house prices or church politics. I'm very bored of the mainstream, so I thought I'd take a dive into a subculture. I've been to a few groups and clubs and stuff but I thought I'd try this too. Be proactive. So," I added, "who are you?"

"I'm Joanne, this is Simon. He was calling himself Heroin for a while, but he seems to have got over it now."

Simon (Heroin) frowned at her. "I still think it would be cool, actually," he said, "but I can't get these two to go along with it, so..."

"I'll call you Heroin if you like," I said helpfully.

"Really?" He gave me a grin that might well have got him thrown out of some of the cooler goth clubs. "I like her. She can stay."

"I should clarify that Simon has not actually ever taken any drugs, let alone that one," said Joanne, "but he doesn't seem to feel that disqualifies him from adopting it as a name."

"Oh, it's the *drug* you named yourself after?" I said innocently. "I assumed you meant heroine, like hero. It's good to be in touch with your inner five-year-old fairy princess."

Joanne snorted and even Stefan gave a half-smile. Simon looked genuinely taken aback. "No! I — no! Oh shit. Maybe I should be Cocaine instead. Or Ketamine."

"How about Illegal Drug of Choice?" suggested Joanne. "That way you can be everything to everybody."

"Fuck off," said Maybe Cocaine (but basically Simon), with no particular aggression. Obviously a well-rehearsed argument.

"Anyway," said Joanne, reverting to the introductions, "this, as you know, is Stefan. Our vampire god and entry ticket into the world of blood drinking. In his spare time he works as a sound engineer. Tonight he's munching us."

"Sorry?" It seemed to me that Joanne was almost certainly too sarcastic to be welcomed into the vampire subculture, unless it was a lot more able to laugh at itself than I imagined.

"He's taking us to a vampire meeting," explained Simon (drug name to be confirmed). "They're called munches. We might be donors."

"Donors? Really?"

Joanne shrugged. "It's something to do on a Saturday night. And I have a thing for cute brunette boys with sharp teeth."

I tried not to nod too hard in agreement. I really didn't want Stefan thinking I'd set this up in order to pull him. I really hadn't, The fact that I now wanted to was something I'd sort out later.

Stefan gave up being aloof and decided to get the conversation back. "Joanne, you have to realise that there is *far* more to this than just sex. It may be the most meaningful thing that ever happens to you. Embrace it. Appreciate it. That's assuming," he added meaningfully, "that someone agrees to do you the honour of accepting your blood as an offering."

"Wait, wait, wait. I thought vampires were supposed to be desperate for blood? I was working on the assumption that I'd be doing *them* a favour." Joanne raised an artificially dark eyebrow.

"It's true that we do need willing donors, of course," conceded Stefan with reluctance. "But it's still an honour."

"I'll try to feel honoured," said Joanne levelly. "But there'd better be some sex in this somewhere."

Simon nodded in emphatic agreement. I got a quick flash of the kind of vampires he was almost certainly visualising. The image was mostly composed of breasts and full pouty lips. I hoped he wouldn't discover that all the blood drinkers at the munch were elderly men with bad breath.

"So, Elinor." Stefan gazed down at me. His own lips were quite full, come to think of it. And pouty. Nice hair, too. And those eyes, so dark, so full of apparent depth... Oh, was he saying something? I tried to remember how to listen, a faculty I appeared to have suddenly lost.

"Would you like to come with us? You seem to have some interest in our lifestyle, and a certain amount of understanding. More than some others I recently introduced to it," he added with a meaningful glance at Joanne. "Might you be interested in donating?"

"Er, blood? I'm not sure. I'm anaemic, I'd probably taste all washed out and pale, like really diluted juice. But yeah," I added quickly, "apart from the blood aspect I'm on for it. Let me just check my diary." I checked my calendar on the iTem, just to make sure I looked as if I had other options, which I didn't. "Yes, I'm free. I'd love to, thanks. Cool. Excellent. Thanks." I decided to stop talking.

"Very good. We shall depart for King's Cross in one hour." Stefan sipped his espresso with a poise that was either ridiculously pretentious or disturbingly sexy. I hadn't decided which yet. I was finding that the more I stared at his eyes, the less I wanted to laugh at him.

"Cool," I said again.

Something had begun.

Chapter Two
Marianne, Suspender of Disbelief

"A lot of clubs have themed nights where you can pervert something more mainstream into an outfit. They can also create a lot of scope for something different and interesting. At a Sci Fi theme night I saw a wonderful 'borg' outfit made out of rubber car mats cut up with old computer parts stuck onto them worn over a black catsuit. Very effective and inexpensive! ... One gentleman made up a wonderful outfit for his first club out of a thong and a pair of L Plates."
http://www.londonfetishscene.com/newsdesk/ViewArticle.asp?ArticleID=405

Search term:
"Torture Garden"

Saturday, September 20th — evening

Before I talk about the rest of my evening, I want to talk about someone else's. She was in King's Cross that night too, but I didn't meet her, not then. Perhaps we passed each other on the street. I like to think we didn't though, because I want to imagine that I would have remembered her.

Anyway. Her name was Marianne Swift, and tonight she was going to a fetish club for the first time. Like many other things, fetish clubs had recently become illegal as pressure increased for Britain to become a theocracy like the CUS. But being driven underground had, if anything, increased the clubs' popularity. Why don't religious fundamentalists ever learn this lesson, I wonder? Adding an aura of Prohibition glamour to something is never going to make people want it less. So they flourished, particularly around King's Cross, which had just the right air of urban seediness to provide a suitable context.

The place to which Marianne was headed had chosen to masquerade as a members' club dedicated to the advancement of French cuisine, called Le Pain. If one arrived at the entrance dressed normally and pronounced the name 'le pan' in correct French style, one was directed to a small room in which a very dull woman gave a lecture on the history of baking in Provence, calculated to ensure that listeners were not encouraged to return. If one pronounced it Pain, looked interesting, and was prepared to hand over a largish entrance fee to the dour receptionist, then the door down to the basement was unlocked and one descended down rickety metal stairs into a dark underground world of black leather, shiny rubber, and pleasures beyond imagining. Well, probably not beyond imagining. In fact, if you were the sort of person who wanted to go to Le Pain, you'd probably more or less imagined them already. But there was definitely decadence with a capital D and one of those little curly flourishes.

Unlike most of its patrons, Marianne had not imagined what Le Pain what would be like. This was because she hadn't heard of its existence before three days ago, which was when she had met Martin. Martin was an unassuming man in his early thirties who she'd started chatting to in the pub while waiting for her date to arrive. By the time the date had arrived, Marianne had lost all interest in him and was instead committed to joining Martin in his lifestyle of deliciously forbidden BDSM. (Bondage! Discipline! Dominance! Submission! Sadism! Masochism! Never had four letters stood for six concepts in such an alluring way.) Martin had told her that she was a born Domme and, once he'd explained what that was, she was convinced he was right. Tonight he would be her slave and she would grind him beneath her heel. Yes.

In pursuit of that image, she had done some shopping. An afternoon in Camden had resulted in a short red leather dress (short enough that she had needed to buy matching red knickers as well), black fishnet hold-up stockings (which were failing to hold themselves up and kept falling down, but never mind) and red knee-high boots with a heel that made her a good four inches taller. Which, started from five foot two, was not to be despised, although she did keep nearly tripping over things. Perhaps next time, she thought, she would get Martin to show her where you bought the comfortable fetish clothes that fitted you and stayed on.

Still, waiting outside the station for Martin, she felt she looked the part, or would do once they got inside. Currently, of course, the outfit was concealed by a long black coat, partly because it was autumn and partly because the club was a secret. A secret club! Marianne hugged herself with excitement, then remembered she was supposed to be an icy, dignified mistress of pain and adjusted her expression accordingly. When Martin arrived, he found her gazing haughtily at a London Transport poster. She gave him a stern look.

"You're late."

He wasn't and they both knew it, but he apologised anyway. "I'm so sorry, Mistress. Let me make it up to you by paying for entrance and all your drinks tonight."

"Very well." Marianne nodded graciously, perfectly well aware that such had been the arrangement in any case. "Let us go."

Le Pain was situated in one of those buildings that could have been anything: grey stone pillars flanked wide steps up to a large anonymous door. Martin rang the doorbell and said "Pain, please," to the narrow-faced woman in black who answered. She nodded, accepted three crisp notes, and let them in.

Tottering down the stairs to the basement, Marianne regretted not having spent more time practicing how to walk in heels. However, she managed to avoid breaking any ankles and having successfully negotiated the last step, she spotted a chair and sank gracefully into it — first removing her coat, though, to give Martin the opportunity to admire her outfit. He gaped gratifyingly at the expanse of cleavage revealed by her dress.

"Gin and tonic," she ordered, thrusting her coat at him as well.

He nodded, collected the coat and went to get drinks, leaving her to take a proper look at her surroundings. The club consisted of one long dark room with several even darker spaces opening off from it. There was a small bar along one wall and a small dance floor in one corner. Images were being projected onto the wall above the dance floor, old Victorian black and white photos of plump-bottomed girls being spanked by tightly corseted governesses with severe expressions. Apart from that the room only contained chairs, bar tables and bar stools, and various items of equipment whose function Marianne was currently unsure of, although she was instantly determined to educate herself.

The room was about two-thirds full of people, mostly sitting at tables and watching each other either covertly or openly. Apart from the usual leather and rubber (Marianne was half-consciously pleased with herself for managing to be world-weary about fetishism on her very first night of exposure to it) there were an impressive variety of materials, though not much of a colour range — black PVC, black lace, black nylon, black fishnet. The men seemed to be wearing either all-over black clothing, from wrist to ankle, or virtually nothing. A man crossed Marianne's field of vision clad only in a transparent jockstrap. It hardly seemed worth it.

The women offered more of a choice of colours. One wore bright red feathers, another what looked like gold cling film, another was in a rubber Star Trek uniform that must have cost a fortune. *How often,* wondered Marianne, *would you get to use a fetish science fiction costume?* Nobody was doing anything much, just standing about at the bar, or sitting in corners, or wandering from area to area without catching anyone else's eye. The latter group was mainly composed of single men, and they occasionally glanced at her, along with the other women in the room, with a quick movement that was furtive yet clearly meant to be noticed. None of them were wearing more than a square foot of clothing over their bodies.

On cue, Martin returned to kneel by her feet and hand her drink to her, with a nice little dip of the head to indicate absolute subservience. Marianne took the drink without a word and thrilled to the feeling of control. There was nothing especially difficult about this dominating thing. She patted her slave on the head and he looked pleased. On a whim, she ran a sharp fingernail down his back and he shuddered, actually visibly shuddered, and let out a soft yelp. As if attuned to the sound — which of course they were — all the single male heads in the room swivelled round to stare at her.

Marianne grandly ignored them all and sipped her G&T, enjoying the rush. She could do anything she liked with any of these men and they would not just let her do it, but plead for more. She could break their hearts and they'd thank her for it. The smile she gave then made several of the watching men groan involuntarily. This was a *great* club.

Chapter Three
Munch Time

"Recent surveys suggest that one in every thousand people is a vampire, which means everybody probably knows, or has met one."
http://www.sanguinarius.org/vampsupport/articles/brownie.htm

Saturday, September 20th — evening

I hadn't been to King's Cross before, apart from the station. Most places in London had struck me as a lot less scary than I expected. Soho, for example, appeared to be mainly full of tourists and gay couples, rather than being the hell-dimension full of pimps and rapists that my mother had warned me about. Though possibly that was more to do with her feverish imagination than anything else, given that the most dangerous place in Middleswithin was the patch of ice by the parish church.

But King's Cross looked genuinely dodgy, which was exciting. The dimly lit streets were full of women in very short skirts, men selling a variety of semi-legal substances, and buildings that looked as though they had once been respectable and were now being used as impromptu dens of iniquity. I stalked along the pavements with my new friends and practised an expression of blasé detachment while I thought about what I wanted from the evening.

Would someone on the street offer me drugs? We didn't have drugs in my home town — or at least, if there was a seedy underground crack scene, nobody had told me about it — and I was fairly sure I'd like them. As we walked up York Way, I tried to look receptive to offers. Surely the goths would be like catnip to drug dealers? But we didn't stop to find out. Oh well, perhaps someone at the munch would shower me with grated cocaine. (I was a little sketchy on how these things actually worked.)

Did I want sex, I wondered? I had had some of *that* before, at least. Even in church-infested Middleswithin, teenagers remained teenagers, and several of the boys in my youth group had succumbed to my charms. As had a couple of the girls, although it was that which had tripped me up. One had an attack of religion and reported me to the vicar for deviancy. Cue a rather embarrassing public exorcism and a ducking in the town pond. It was after that incident that I'd persuaded my parents to fund my move to the big city.

Stefan's long black cloak flapped in front of me as he strode gorgeously toward wherever it was we were going. I tripped up on it a couple of times but I didn't mind. I was with cool people, they seemed to like me, I was out on a Saturday night for the first time since I moved to London. And most importantly, I was going to a place where nobody was going to talk to me about mortgages.

* * *

"So, have you bought a place yet?" said a short plump man wearing a black lacy cloak and an expression of genuine curiosity. "Interest rates are down, you know."

This was not promising.

The venue had looked good — a dark underground bar in the middle of some disused warehouses behind King's Cross station. Very Creatures of the Night. But the people had so far not proved to be everything I had hoped. This was my third conversation about property. Why did everyone in London have this house obsession? I made a mental note to rent for the rest of my life, if this was the alternative.

I smiled vaguely in a sorry-didn't-quite-catch-that way, and sidled off back to Joanne and Simon, who were huddled in a corner trying to decide who to donate to.

"I think I'm just going to mingle," Joanne mused. "Nobody's flinging themselves at my feet begging to be allowed to drink my menstrual blood."

"You were expecting that to happen?"

"One can hope. I took my tampon out specially." Simon stared pointedly into the distance, making a not-hearing-this humming noise.

"How long have you two known each other?" I said.

"Oh, since college," said Joanne airily. "Of course," she added, "we're both still at college, so in fact we've only known each other a year or so."

"She picked me up," said Simon.

"Did not! I saved him from one of my friends who's a notorious man-eater, or in this case boy-eater, and he latched on to me. Just couldn't get rid of him."

Simon raised his eyebrows in mock-shock. "You invited me to your birthday party, gave me a goth makeover and then tried to shag me!"

"I may have invited you to my birthday party, but I swear I'm not responsible for the gothness. And I refuse to even discuss your third accusation. You know we've always been just good friends."

"Apart from that one time..."

"I remember nothing. Nothing, I tell you. I must have been extremely drunk, if anything happened, which it didn't. La la la la, there's no point you saying anything further about it, I'm not listening."

"Anyway," Simon said, waving at the room, "I refuse to save myself for you as you so obviously want. I'm out there, exploring my options. Like that woman in crimson and black over there." He stared lecherously across the room.

We looked around. The room was dense with crimson and black dresses, all filled with busty dark-lipped women. "Which one?"

"That one. There. With the cleavage."

"Still not making it easy."

"Wearing really dark lipstick."

"You're just not trying to help, are you?"

"OK, fine." He took Joanne by the arm and marched her towards a dark-haired woman in her thirties who did indeed have a lot of both cleavage and makeup. I watched him introduce himself to her and wondered what name he'd chosen to use. Judging by the way he was pointing at his own neck, I thought he'd probably missed out the small talk and gone straight for the killer chat-up line. Joanne was rolling her eyes at me, but I noticed she was also scanning the room for likely male candidates. Would she be able to keep quiet long enough for anyone to bite her?

I had to admit, though, that some of the vampire people were cute. Stefan was chatting to a goth even taller and thinner than he was, who was wearing a large cross that appeared to have blood dripping from it. I went to get a drink and managed to brush casually past them, wishing I was wearing higher heels. I'm five foot eight and a size fourteen, but next to them I felt like an obese gnome.

"Hi, Elinor." Stefan touched me lightly on the shoulder. I jumped, but luckily he seemed to mistake it for fear rather than uncontrollable lust. "This is Justin, leader of the Jesus' Blood church."

Church? Fuck, not here too. My face fell. I was reluctantly impressed, though, when Justin bent down, took my hand and kissed it.

"Always good to meet a new recruit," he said gravely, with a precise intonation. His accent was soft Southern American. It wasn't hard to guess why he'd left, or been thrown out of, the Christian United States. Whatever the Jesus' Blood church was, it clearly wasn't the same as the Resurrected Church of America — and anything that wasn't the RCA (or its British equivalent, the RCE) was blasphemy.

Wait. Recruit? Oh no. Please don't let this evening end with me being told to accept God into my life, I prayed. (Not to God, of course, that would be silly. Just a general prayer.) If they all turned out to be evangelical Christians I was going to have to kill myself, or, preferably, them.

Justin saw my expression.

"Don't worry, Elinor. I take it you haven't heard of us? We don't take pains to be noticed." He smiled, exposing fangs. Well, that would explain the careful way he spoke. They were stainless steel — must have been implants — in the shape of tiny crosses, sharpened at the end. The cross part was on the canines, with the long end as the fangs. My mouth was hanging open rather unattractively, but he seemed pleased at the reaction.

"We worship Jesus as the first and greatest Vampire," he said. I could hear the capital V even through the pointy teeth. "Jesus said 'Whoso eateth my flesh, and drinketh my blood, hath eternal life.' And his disciples drank his blood and were given eternal life. And — two thousand years later — so were we."

"Given eternal life?"

"Indeed."

"So, when were you born?" I made sure to say this in an interested, rather than disbelieving, way. I was getting lots of practice with that today.

"Nineteen eighty." He must have seen this wasn't quite as impressive a date as I'd been expecting. "But I don't look like I'm in my thirties, do I?"

It was difficult to tell under the foundation, to be honest. "No, you look, er, twenty-five at most. So, have you met any of the original disciples? Presumably they're still around somewhere?"

"Sadly not. In a typical example of Christian vampire persecution, they were all staked, set afire or decapitated before they had the chance to enjoy their immortality. However, they had time to turn others, and those others are our blood ancestors." At the word 'blood', he touched his cross, which didn't, I noticed, actually have blood on it. It was made of a rust-coloured metal though, with metal drops hanging off the arms. "When we pass on the gift, we are passing on the blood of Jesus himself."

"Wow."

"Indeed. The vampire church is an old and active one."

I involuntarily pictured a vampire church, stalking the night dragging its graveyard behind it, wearing the world's largest black cape. "Does it drink the blood of other churches?" I said. "There must be a bit of a problem with the holy water."

Justin looked sternly at me. I tried to keep a straight face.

"As a matter of fact," he said, deciding to forgive me, "holy water and crosses do not affect us. As Christians, albeit of an unusual type, we are immune."

"How handy. Um, is it a big church? I mean, I can see that the vampire community is quite large." I glanced round the crowded room to make my point.

"The church has a substantial membership, yes. Mainly Americans like myself. Indeed, many of the people in this room are American. Hardly surprising."

"No," I agreed. The population of London was something like twenty percent American these days.

Stefan was only half-listening to the conversation. Clearly he'd heard it before. I found that I was very aware of him, though, and I could still feel the exact spot on my shoulder where he'd touched me.

"You seem very ready to tell me about all this," I said tentatively. "I mean, it's fascinating, but should you reveal all this to a stranger?"

"Why not? We do nothing illegal. Which is more than you can say for some others of... our kind." He glanced briefly across the room and I saw his eyes catch those of a serious-looking woman about my height with very pale eyes, dressed in black from neck to wrists to ankles and standing alone. She shuddered at his glance, and turned away.

"Let me assure you, we're quite harmless. We oppose the non-consensual taking of blood and we are extremely choosy about our membership policy. Stefan himself cannot —" He paused, then seemed to change his mind, and went on: "So, Elinor, tell us about yourself. Stefan says you are working in temporary administrative positions at the moment?"

"For a while, till I get my one of my ideas going and become rich and famous. I'm not the world's most enthusiastic temp, to be honest. But I have lots of ideas for other ways to make a living. For example, I'm planning to design Adult Lego."

"Interesting," said Stefan noncommittally. "More complicated Lego, you mean? Or bigger blocks?"

"No, no. Adult Lego, as in 'adult shop'. Anatomically correct Lego people you can fit together, like blow-up sex dolls in small plastic form. You could have whole conga lines of little Lego gay men. I think they'll be a huge hit."

I was possibly not addressing my target audience. Stefan and Justin both made identical 'hmm' noises and then turned the conversation to the care and maintenance of velvet shirts. But I wasn't put off. After all, I still had to let the Lego people know of my plans, so the idea was very much in the early stages of development. I also didn't know how you made Lego people, but that was just a detail. Admittedly, a lot of my plans foundered on my lack of attention to detail, but I was sure I'd get better at that. The important thing was to make one's mark on the world.

I looked around. Joanne was talking enthusiastically to a slim man who waved his hands around a lot, and Simon — where was

Simon? Oh yes, in a dark corner with the woman he'd been chatting up earlier. All I could see of her was a shining white V of breasts held up by a dark red, underwired velvety top. And even that was a little obscured by Simon's head being buried between the V. Well, good for him. I allowed myself a small shiver of excitement. This was the kind of London I'd wanted to find. My search for excitement, adventure and really wild things was going somewhere. Now I just needed to persuade Stefan to sleep with me, and all would be well.

For the moment, however, it was time to go back to the rest of my life, such as it was. There were a series of night buses to be navigated before I could get home, and all of them would probably contain someone very drunk who would want to either kiss me, throw up on me, or both. I needed to leave while I was still awake enough to push them away.

During goodbyes, I gave Stefan my email address and he unexpectedly invited me to a party at Joanne's in a fortnight's time. Joanne overheard us and detached herself from the enthusiastic man to come over and give me her address — a shared house in Crystal Palace. She'd invited everyone in the room, she said.

"Bunch of wankers, but I quite like them all so far," she said cheerfully. "And I can't wait to see my housemates flee in terror when this lot show up. Bet you a fiver they lock themselves in the bathroom for the night."

"See you then, Elinor?" said Stefan, waving a languid hand in my direction. I thought he was pleased I was coming to the party, but it didn't necessarily sound as though his life would be meaningless if he never saw me again. Still, I could work on that.

Chapter Four
Not Peace, But a Whip

Search term:
"Christian BDSM"

Sunday, September 21ˢᵗ

Marianne remembered reading somewhere — some self-righteously healthy women's magazine, probably — that an hour's sleep before midnight equalled two hours afterwards. Since she'd got to sleep at something like 5am the night before, that must mean she'd had no sleep at all, mathematically.

Well, that explained why she was feeling so vacant. The next thing she needed to establish was where exactly she was. Not her flat. Martin's flat? But that wasn't Martin in bed with her. This was a new flat, with a new naked man beside her who looked only vaguely familiar. Marianne sat up and squinted down the length of the bed. His lower half looked really quite familiar, actually. It had long red marks on bits of it. There was a riding crop lying on the far side of the bed. Suddenly, everything swam into perspective. This involved an actual swimming feeling, which made her sway a little, but at least she remembered last night now.

She had beaten Martin with the riding crop. She had demanded to be told how to use the pieces of equipment, all of them, and half the club had begged to be allowed to show her. She had ridden high on a dizzy sense of triumph, feeling the kind of self-confidence that normally took her several lines of cocaine to achieve. (Several lines of cocaine had in fact been offered to her and accepted by her during the evening, but she was sure that had had nothing to do with it.) Men had literally queued up for her services. She had been bought so many drinks that she'd started just pouring them over the heads of the men kneeling around her.

Wow.

At some point, Martin had respectfully reminded her that he was her date for the night. Which, now that she thought about it, wasn't actually an unreasonable thing to have said, but she had been high on her new-found power and suddenly Martin had seemed far too pedestrian for her tastes. So she had told him he was rude and presumptuous, and he had left looking disconsolate, and she had ended up going home with the man who was currently lying beside her. Um, Giles, was it? Or Gerald? They had presumably come back here and she had inflicted some damage on him, or possibly just fallen unconscious the moment her head hit a soft surface; she had no idea. Oh well, she was the Mistress, she could do what the fuck she liked. In fact she seemed to remember telling several people that last night, accompanied by emphatic strokes of a crop.

However, what she would currently like was breakfast in bed, brought to her by her new acquisition. Whose name she would doubtless remember before long. She prodded his shoulder experimentally.

"Urgle…" he muttered, and curled up, stealing all the duvet in the process.

Well, fuck him then. Marianne, feeling rather naked and a lot more awake, crawled out of the bed and found some clothes on the floor that looked like they might be hers. When she'd finished dressing she had a feeling that she'd put some of them on upside down and/or inside out, but she left the bedroom anyway.

The Unidentified Sleeping Man appeared to live in a smallish two-bedroom flat with both bedrooms opening into a long, thin, pale living room. In the living room, she discovered, were two people. They looked as though they could be left over from last night's fetish club, more or less: they were wearing black leather, covering most of their bodies, and around the necks of each hung a large fish symbol. One was male with short dark hair, one female with long dark hair. Apart from that they looked remarkably similar, and were both watching Songs of Praise with quiet concentration.

"Hi," offered Marianne, momentarily thrown by the choice of TV programme. The man and woman looked up, and then straight down again.

"Hello," said the woman with an impressive lack of any tone whatsoever. Their attention returned to the TV set.

After the triumph of the night before, Marianne found this lack of interest extremely disconcerting. Admittedly she was dressed rather more randomly this morning and her make-up was probably on the back of her head by now, and she wasn't wearing the heels, but still, she deserved attention. And respect. And, preferably, deference. So she didn't walk back into the bedroom, but sat on a chair next to the sofa and said, "My name's Marianne Swift," in an assertive twang. As an afterthought, she asked, "And can you tell me the name of the guy I just woke up next to?"

The couple managed to make their shiver of disapproval chill the entire room, but the man said, "I'm Daniel, and this is Patricia," in a not unfriendly tone.

It occurred to Marianne at this point, though, that there was a very definite gap between 'not unfriendly' and 'friendly'.

"And that's Mark," he added, with a nod at the bedroom she'd just come from.

Mark. Right. Yes.

"Thanks." Marianne smiled at them and settled a little more comfortably on the wooden chair. "So, were you at the club last night?"

"No, we weren't at any club." Patricia's tone, like Daniel's, was definitely on the cooler side of 'not unfriendly', and they were both looking with clear disapproval at the cleavage she'd exposed. It was impossible, she thought, to imagine them ever being referred to as Pat or Dan.

"Oh, OK. Sorry, I don't remember that much about it. Not the end of the evening, anyway." She tried out a wider smile. It made the atmosphere, if anything, chillier.

"You'd been drinking?" said Patricia, in a tone that made it breathtakingly clear how she felt about people who drank a lot and then turned up half-naked in her flat the next day.

Marianne bridled. "I was drinking, yes. It's a perfectly normal thing to do in fetish clubs, and I assume you are familiar with the concept of fetish clubs. Given what you're wearing." She was still assuming that anyone who had that much leather on had to be *some* kind of kindred spirit.

She'd said the wrong thing again.

"Certainly not!" squeaked Patricia with indignation. "Those kinds of places are a haven for drinking and drugs and depravity and debauchery..."

"...And swearing and immorality and fornication," said Daniel, proving that he at least was aware of sins that didn't start with the letter D. "We would never set foot in such a place."

"OK, look," said Marianne, who felt that something needed to be cleared up. "You're Christians, right, I get that, with the Songs of Praise and the fish symbols and everything."

"We do indeed worship Jesus as our Lord and Saviour, yes," said Daniel, unbending a little.

"But the leather? And you choose to share a flat with a guy who, not that I know him at all, obviously goes in for BDSM in a fairly lifestyley way. Plus," she added, "your bedroom door is open and I can see a wide range of whips hanging on your wall above the bed." Both her new acquaintances flicked their heads towards the bedroom, then back at her, then nodded briefly in unison. They'd clearly been together for a long time.

"Like many people," said Daniel, turning the volume down on the TV, "you see but you do not understand. The use of implements such as whips is not incompatible with a life dedicated to Jesus, far from it."

"Oh, like monks wearing hair shirts?" said Marianne brightly, feeling that she'd got a handle on the situation now. "And nuns flagellating themselves?"

"No, no!" Daniel sounded horrified. "Those were Catholics, not real Christians. God is not found through pain, but through faith and true belief. And love for one's fellow man." The love in question was presumably being saved up for someone who wasn't Marianne, as little of it was coming through in his voice.

"So, er, the whips are what? Decoration?" She raised an eyebrow.

"Is this really any of your business?" snapped Patricia. "We *were* watching Songs of Praise."

Marianne shrugged. "Fair enough. I'll get myself a coffee, then." She wandered deliberately across their line of sight to get to the kitchen, which was small and very clean. Her curiosity was growing intense, but she made herself a cup of coffee and stood in the kitchen, deciding that she'd better let these strange people finish watching Songs of Praise.

Which, she now remembered, lasted for a good three hours, enough to fill in the gaps between morning service and mid-afternoon communion for those who needed non-stop godliness on a Sunday. She'd just have to interrupt again, then. First, though, she redid her clothing to reduce the amount of visible flesh and wiped off as much makeup as she could, peering into the cloudy silver side of a kettle to assess the effect. She was pleased to discover that she looked significantly more respectable.

The existence of her erstwhile pick-up Mark was now as far from her mind as the existence of Martin. Marianne was all about the present, with a hefty dollop of the future. The past dissolved in her mind like the steam from the coffee she was holding. In her twenty-seven years, a lot of people had been taken aback, and in some cases quite upset, by her blithe inability to be interested in anything longer ago than yesterday. In this case, even yesterday was too far back, since in Daniel and Patricia she had encountered people who were both resistant to her charms and apparently in possession of a knowledge she didn't share. They had come into focus for her, and Mark's attractions, whatever they might have been, had become merely a blurred backdrop.

When she went back into the living room, therefore, she was not the sarcastic dominatrix she had been half an hour earlier, but a shy, anxious girl, keen for enlightenment.

"Hello again," she said with a bright smile. The couple looked up, and appeared mollified by Marianne's demeanour and lack of cleavage. She even won a small smile from Daniel and a relaxation of the eyebrows from Patricia, which was probably as close as she got to friendliness. Good. She decided to try to establish some common ground.

"The thing is," she said, perching on a stool, "that club last night was the first time I've done anything like... that. And it was fun, but this morning I felt oddly hollow inside when I woke up." (I'm fairly sure that this was not in fact true, but when Marianne switched roles she did it thoroughly, and she certainly now believed what she was saying.)

Patricia nodded. "You see, you made the mistake of practising BDSM outside the proper context. Just like sleeping around, it might feel good at the time but it leaves you empty afterwards."

Marianne, who had slept around plenty of times and felt perfectly fine afterwards, said: "Oh yes, I know what you mean. It's just meaningless, isn't it?"

"Whereas," said Daniel, "*within* the proper context, BDSM can be a fulfilling and spiritual experience."

"And the proper context is...?" said Marianne, who had a feeling she was expected to work that out for herself but was worried she'd get it wrong if she guessed.

"It's very simple, really," said Daniel, with the air of one who had explained this before. "*For the husband is the head of the wife, even as Christ is the head of the church.* Ephesians 5:23. I have a God-given duty to guide Patricia and she has a complementary duty to submit to me as her husband. Particularly in bed."

"Oh. I see."

"*Likewise, ye wives, be in subjection to your own husbands.* 1 Peter 3:1," said Patricia. "To put it another way, Jesus wants Daniel to spank me."

"The fact is, the Bible sanctions dominance and submission — within a lawful wedding relationship — and also sanctions the husband beating the wife on a regular basis, both as punishment for misdemeanours and, er, for fun."

Marianne waited for Patricia to give chapter and verse for that one, but she merely smiled and wriggled a little on the sofa.

"I see. So you whip her and she has to do what you say." Suddenly Marianne realised why the kitchen was so clean. "And you have to tell her what to do?"

"Indeed. The black leather and the riding crops aren't ordained by God as such, but they're not actually forbidden, and we like leather. Though we only wear it in the privacy of our own home, to avoid inciting other people into thoughts of sex."

"Thoughtful of you."

"Thank you," said Daniel, with no apparent sense of irony.

"What if you want to swap, have a day when she beats you and tells you what to do?"

"That would be forbidden by the Bible," said Daniel smugly.

Not a switch, she guessed. Patricia looked resigned. Clearly it was an idea that had occurred to her before and had not gone down well.

"And God's happy about all the beating?"

"The important thing," said Patricia firmly, "is to remember our primary purpose in life and honour the Lord with our every action. Each of our whips has a Bible verse written on it, and when Daniel beats me I thank Jesus with every stroke."

"Yeah, I tend to use God's name during sex as well."

There was a pause.

"Whereas you, you see, are damned." Patricia's tone went cold again, and Marianne jumped slightly. "You practise fornication, you swear, you use drugs —"

"You don't know that," protested Marianne.

"Well, do you?" asked Daniel.

"Well, yes..." Marianne felt she'd lost a point she should have won.

"You have not given your life to the Lord, so the leather you wear is a symbol of your devotion to Satan, whereas ours proclaims our salvation." They nodded grimly at each other.

"What, this leather? But I'm a good person really. I give money to charity..."

"I'm sure we don't need to quote you the Bible's stance on good works not getting you to Heaven, do we?" said Patricia sharply.

"I gave people pleasure last night..."

"Sinful pleasure. You're sending all those people further on the road to Hell. Including Mark, who may be a sinner but has some potential for grace. If you go on as you doubtless have been doing for the last thirty years —"

"Twenty-seven!" said Marianne, hurt.

"You see? Your life of evil has aged you before your time," said Daniel triumphantly. "I would have taken you for at least forty, myself."

"Forty? Really?"

The events of the previous night now seemed bathed in an altogether more unpleasant light. Patricia and Daniel were so *sure* of themselves. Marianne experienced the feeling — a not unfamiliar one, though never fully analysed by her — of being a moth in the presence of a very intense flame. Being a Mistress was all very well, but having this kind of certainty — being, as it were, submissive to God Himself — caught up in the heat of His loving strokes, mute and helpless before His overwhelming, controlling presence — it was irresistible. Marianne looked at Daniel and Patricia, upright and forthright and well, *right*, on their sofa, and knew with complete certainty that she had found her soulmates.

Half an hour later, all three of them were down on their knees fervently praying.

Some time later, Mark woke up briefly, glanced into the living room, groaned, muttered, "For fuck's sake, not another one," and went back to bed, vowing to find new flatmates at the earliest possible opportunity.

Chapter Five
Shopgirl

Search term:
sneezingbeauties

Friday September 26th

Although I managed to keep myself busy, the fourteen days between the munch and Joanne's party crawled by like a series of heavily drugged tortoises. Even work had started going downhill. My temping agency had told me the market in office admin roles was slow at the moment — or possibly they were just being tactful about my 30 word-per-minute typing — so I'd taken a temporary job in my local chemists instead.

It was a small shop sandwiched, as it happened, between two sandwich shops. A little dusty, a little out of date, not too demanding. There were so few customers that an assistant wasn't really needed at all, but I presumed the manager had wanted to give himself plenty of time in the back office to pursue his true vocation, surfing the net for lesbian sneeze fetish sites. I'd wandered in one afternoon, looked over his shoulder, and read: "...Heather took a deep breath through her swollen nose. The sensitive membranes of her nasal passages quivered with that deep tickling, her nostrils flaring with each shaky breath..." I left him to it. Possibly he had been hoping for a temporary assistant with a cold.

The shop being mostly quiet was good, because I couldn't really be bothered to sell people things, and when someone did wander in I quickly developed a habit of muttering under my breath in rudimentary Spanish and making random hand movements in their direction until they went away again. However, the lack of custom also gave me time to think about the fact that I was working there instead of changing the world, which was bad. And to stare at tubes of haemorrhoid cream to see if I could make them spontaneously combust using sheer willpower. It appeared not.

I was not a natural shop assistant. I wasn't not sure what I was a natural at, but this wasn't it. The worst thing about it though, I reflected, was having my name written on my breast. Nothing makes you feel more vulnerable than having your identity sprawled across a sensitive erogenous zone.

The thought of erogenous zones reminded me again about the party. I had to admit I was inordinately excited about going — but that was fine, since I reasoned that getting all the bounciness out of the way in advance would drain it out of my system, thus ensuring that by Saturday the fourth I'd be totally blasé and laid back.

I leant on the off-white plastic counter, drably festooned with Whistle Pops and packs of decorated tissues, and thought up schemes for improving people's lives, or at least making my own more interesting. Adult Lego clearly wasn't going to take off. My letter to Hamleys suggesting they add a sex-toy shop to their premises (just a little one, at the back somewhere, like a crèche for adults) had gone unanswered. My new plan was to change the world through performance art. I was going to buy a pot of white paint and a brush, and paint pairs of open scissors on the dotted lines in the middle of roads, like 'cut here' signs. I wasn't sure exactly what effect it would have on the world but I assumed it would at least cheer some drivers up, and perhaps cause a couple of amusing accidents.

So after work on Friday, I went for a bus ride in search of a) paint and b) roads. I like buses. You got to work out how bits of London connected up to other bits of London, which was something tubes didn't really help with, and you could see the city from further up than usual. There's a large marble cow above one of the hotel entrances on Berkeley Square that I would never have known about if it weren't for the number eight bus.

It is often said by smokers that the way to get a bus to arrive is to light up a cigarette. Not being a smoker, I decided to try seeing if I could trick the universe by using candy sticks instead. The local newsagents sold packs of them — the kind that used to be called sweet cigarettes before people started questioning the wisdom of making five-year-olds believe that tobacco was sugar-flavoured. Leaning against the bus shelter, I started sucking one while holding it between my fingers. The universe refused to fall for my ruse, but I certainly confused passers-by, especially when I got halfway through and ate the rest.

When the bus did arrive, it illustrated another problem with buses as a form of transport, even apart from their lack of response to sugary sweets; i.e., the way that they frequently attracted people with a shaky grip on reality. Some of them had lost said grip altogether and were in happy freefall down the cliff of delusion. Of course, this wasn't really a problem for me, since I was on a mission to explore people with unusual beliefs anyway, but ideally I preferred to choose my own times and places for those encounters. On this particular Friday night trip, there was a woman on the seat opposite me who was muttering about sodomites and sinners in a way that made me very nervous.

"...the time is at hand. They shall burn, yes, in the fires, and those who support them shall burn with them, all of them screaming, screaming in the pain of their sins..." Her hands were wringing in a way I'd thought was confined to novels. Over and over, like kittens fighting. I made sure not to look up at her. Once you do that you're stuck with them till you get off, and I wanted to get to Clapham without having to politely agree with madwomen, if possible. I stared at the floor and thought about whether performance art would make the world a better place or not. Couldn't really tune her out, though.

"...fear none of those things which thou shalt suffer: behold, the devil shall cast some of you into prison, that ye may be tried..."

She seemed to have moved off burning and into Revelations. Was she just religious or actually insane? Not that I considered there to be much of a difference between the two, these days.

She got off at the same stop as me, Clapham Common. I watched her head off down a side street, still muttering, and went off to find a paint shop. Though I had already had a better idea: make a series of naked aerobics videos. Get fit and watch beautiful women jumping up and down with no clothes on; who would say no to that? I'd be a millionaire in no time.

Or maybe... A variety of ideas broke into my head and set up residence, like presumptuous burglars. I stared at a party shop on the corner, open and enticing, filled with early Halloween tat of startling kitschness. You didn't get a lot of Halloween celebration these days. Too Satanic. I approved.

I glanced in the other direction. If I squinted down the side street, I found, I could just see the madwoman from the bus furtively entering some kind of church building. I couldn't help wondering what she was up to.

Chapter Six
CULT — Creed and Credulity

"...Holographic projections of the "CHRIST IMAGE" have already been seen in some remote desert areas..."
http://www.trunkerton.fsnet.co.uk/blue_beam_project.htm

Search term:
"Project Blue Beam"

Friday, October 3rd — evening

They met weekly in the local Resurrected Church of England hall, which was on a small road near the common. It wasn't cover, particularly, it was just a useful place and time to meet: every Friday night, after the youth group meeting. At eight-thirty, Carol and Himmler Cingin cleared up the tea things and ushered the polite cluster of fifteen-year-olds into their parents' waiting cars. Sometime a shy girl or lanky boy would try to stay late and ask advice on how to speak in tongues, disprove evolution or resist the evils of masturbation, but they were quickly disposed of with a selection of leaflets. The other adults sat in the small kitchen drinking more tea and discussing church gossip in whispers until the teenagers had gone. The youth group thought they were there to organise the church's country dancing evenings.

Tonight none of the teenagers even tried to stay late, and the meeting began promptly at nine. A fresh pot of tea was brewed in the crucifix-shaped teapot and the members of CULT, Christians Under the Lord's Thrall, gathered round in a businesslike fashion around the table, which now held seven cups and a Bible. Apart from the Cingins, they comprised two elderly ladies called Mabel and Hannah, a shy middle-aged man called Pete, and a fervent boy called David who had been promoted from the youth group when he'd turned eighteen a few weeks previously. The seventh member was a black-haired woman in her twenties who looked entirely unremarkable, except for the fact that the pupils of her eyes were white. It was her second meeting.

Carol and Himmler (Himm, for short) were the leaders and founders of the group, and prominent members of the Resurrected Church. They had also founded the youth group, which was called Teens for Christ, along with others, including Toddlers for Christ, Babies for Christ, and Pensioners for Christ. They liked groups. But Christians Under the Lord's Thrall was different from the others, and not just because of the new title format. It was invitation-only. It discussed issues that the normal members of the Church would find difficult to understand. And it had a mission.

Himm was the official chair, as Carol disapproved of women putting themselves forward. The role of the others, as far as the Cingins were concerned, was mainly to agree with Carol. Carol found that being disagreed with disagreed with her.

She rattled her cup to still the chatter of conversation, and the room was immediately quiet.

"Welcome," she said, smiling round. "Well, this is our seventh meeting and I'm sure we're all very excited about the way our discussions have developed. I know I am! But before we get going, let's all bow our heads for a moment and thank our Lord for this day, and for giving us the power to help Him in this crazy, forsaken world."

Seven heads bowed. There was silence for a moment, then Pete, the middle-aged man, began to mutter to himself, *"Jesus faz bolinhos encantadores da uva-do-monte..."* (*Jesus, who makes the lovely cranberry muffins...*). His quiet babbling was soon lost as one by one, everyone began to speak in tongues. The new recruit watched quietly but did not attempt to join in.

The sound died down and Pete finished off, quieter and quieter, with *"Para não mencionar seu creme de gelo do bolo de queijo e seu cabelo bonito..."* (*Not to mention His ice-cream cheesecake and His beautiful hair...*) and it was silent again.

"OK," said Carol cheerfully but efficiently bringing the meeting back to the matters at hand. "Time to start! A warm welcome to our newest recruit, Ruth, who joined us last week. Do we all remember where we finished at the end of the last meeting?"

David, the lanky teenager, brought out a slightly tattered piece of paper from his pocket; he liked to make agendas. "Um, last week, we talked about, er, how to prevent the New World Order. And how Mrs Adder's new baby could be the Antichrist because she's called it Damon, like demon, and Adder's like snake, so it's kind of a demon snake..."

"And we made fairy cakes," said the rounder of the two elderly ladies helpfully, "only we called them angel cakes because fairies are unnatural abominations."

"Yes. Thank you, David and Mabel. Well," said Carol, beaming, "I'm pleased to report that Mrs Adder has bowed to pressure from the Church and agreed to name her baby Paul instead. And she's also going to persuade her husband to change their surname to Ander, so they won't have any connection now with the Devil and his works."

Everyone applauded. "Carol, how on earth did you do that?" said Hannah, the less round of the two elderly ladies.

"Mr Ander works under one of our church wardens," said Carol. "So clearly it was his God-given duty to refuse Mr Ander promotion unless he renounced the name of Satan."

Impressed smiles all round. David carefully crossed off the Adder item off his agenda and looked up expectantly.

"And now..." said Himm after a nod from his wife, "we should talk about the Project."

It almost looked as though the room had got slightly darker. The expression on everyone's faces now was serious, reverent. This was important work they were doing. Last week, when the Project had first been mentioned, Carol had assured them that they would go down in history. It seemed unbelievable to them that this small, dingy room in South-West London could be so essential to world events, but they knew that all revolutions started in small, dingy rooms like this. Carol had explained that. One person could change the world, she said; therefore, seven people could change it forever.

"Let's start with a reading from the Bible, shall we?" Carol picked up her large, heavy, we-mean-business King James from the table in front of her, and opened to a very well-worn page.

"*I come to bring not peace, but a sword,*" she read, then closed the book again. That had been the reading last week too. It was all the encouragement they needed. Everyone quivered with anticipation.

"OK. So, last week," said Carol, "Ruth joined us and told us how she'd been looking for a group just like us to help combat the conspiracy she'd discovered. Which is brilliant, isn't it, because we've been trying to decide how we're going to fulfil our mission to turn

Britain into a properly Christian country just like the Christian United States, and now we have a way to do it! Now, who remembers what the conspiracy is called and what it's about?" Hands flew up so fast that a couple of people hit their arms on each other's chairs and grimaced. "David?"

"Er, Project Rupture?"

Carol nodded encouragingly. Ruth clasped her hands together and leant forward. David took the reactions as encouragement to continue.

He took a deep breath. "Right. So the New Word Order —"

"World Order," corrected Carol patiently. David looked flustered.

"World Order, sorry, I meant that. Is very powerful and trying to take over the world so that Satan can rule. And they've been doing lots of little things for ages to make that happen, like putting the number 666 all over the place. *But,* since the Christian United States was formed, they've been really scared, because God's people are seriously winning the battle between good and evil. So now they're looking for a way to crush us utterly beneath their demonic heels in one fell swoop." He made a sweeping gesture to indicate crushing.

"Very good, David. Hannah, would you like to carry on?"

"Certainly, Carol." Hannah's hands rubbed together excitedly, as they had a habit of doing. "Ruth has discovered what the New World Order is up to, and I'm sure we're all very grateful to her for that. They're going to subvert the Rapture with their holographs." Hannah smiled, pleased with herself for remembering the unfamiliar word. "And it's up to us to stop that happening and to save the world from Satan." She paused. "And to send the sinners into the pit of fire to be burnt for all eternity," she added. She liked fire.

"Excellent." Carol decided to switch to Pete next; she wasn't sure Mabel had any real grasp of the technical aspect of the Project. (She wasn't entirely clear on it either, but she was hardly going to admit that to them.) "Pete, could you explain to us how exactly it's going to work?"

Pete took out some notes, squinted, and began to read. "Holography is a technique for obtaining three-dimensional images, involving an interference pattern between two sets of single-wavelength light waves." Hannah and Mabel's eyes instantly glazed over, though Ruth's white pupils still stared intently at the man. "When combined with mind-control weapons that beam radio-frequency waves into the brain, this technology is capable of projecting an image into the sky and convincing people that they're seeing the second coming of Christ."

He paused.

"So in simple terms," said Carol kindly, "it will *look* to people as though Jesus has returned to us, when in *fact* it will just be a Satanic deception."

"Exactly," said Pete fervently. "The sky will become a movie screen with laser projections showing across the world, everyone getting an image of Jesus. There'll be computer animation and sound effects which seem to come from the depths of space. And everyone will think the Lord has returned, even the atheists and Muslims and so on."

"Wasn't there something about telepathy too?" asked Himm with absorbed interest.

"That's the next part," said David, his face lighting up. "It's electronic telepathy, it goes inside people's brains and gets mixed up with their own thoughts to form artificial thoughts, which will mean people believe God is speaking to them from within their own souls. And then, an electronic universal, er, manifestation will make Christians believe a rapture is about to happen."

"Excellent, David." Carol looked round the circle of intent faces. "So you see the plan? They want to make us *think* that the Rapture is coming and that we'll be lifted up into heaven. We'll even see footage on TV of people being lifted up. But it won't be real, so of course, it won't actually happen to anyone. And when all the Christians in the world start thinking that the Rapture's happened and they've been left behind, there'll be a global wave of disillusionment and loss of faith, and the atheists and Muslims will be laughing at us. Which will mean the New World Order can take over and destroy the world by turning it into a home for demons and homosexuals."

There was a hush as everyone took all this in. They had heard the basics of it last week, but it was still a lot to absorb.

"So, how are we going to stop this happening? When is it due?" This was David, youthfully eager.

"Well, we'll go into that in more detail next time, but I can tell you that it's planned for this year. Which means soon, as it's already October." She paused for this to sink in. "As for how to stop it, I'll remind you of the text that started our meeting. Don't forget it. Read your Bibles. We have become the chosen ones, and we must do what the Lord commands. Our personal feelings must not be allowed to interfere. Ruth gave a very inspiring talk on this last week, I thought."

Ruth bowed her head modestly. "Thank you, Carol. I explained that obedience to the word of God is the only absolute we have. Abraham was ready to sacrifice his son Isaac on the altar. Can we do less?"

There was an emphatic nod from Pete, who had never liked his son much anyway, and more excited hand-twisting from Hannah, who liked the idea of sacrifice in general, particularly if burning was involved.

Ruth continued: "I personally am willing to follow the will of God wherever it leads, regardless of what our unsaved brothers and sisters might think. Human laws apply to us only as far as they reflect the will of God and not a moment longer." There were thoughtful nods all round and approving smiles from Carol and Himm. Ruth sat back, looking humble but satisfied.

"So — action points!" said Carol cheerfully. "Has everyone got their edible paper pads?" Everyone produced rice paper notebooks and non-toxic pencils. When they had carried out their action points, she had explained, they would eat the relevant parts of the notebooks, thus preventing discovery.

"David — I need you to find out more about holograms and sound effects, how that's going to work. Ruth, you're our double agent — you said you could find out who's in charge of this?"

Ruth nodded. "It's a London-based group, I know that much. I've already started the process of infiltrating it — I'll report more next week."

"Hannah and Mabel, I'd like you to work on the church congregation. They don't know exactly what we're doing, obviously, but it would be nice to feel they're behind us in general. Start a few conversations about the Book of Revelations and see where that gets you." They smiled and nodded; it was what they did anyway, and Carol knew it. "And Pete, continue with what we talked about last week, please. How's it going?"

"I've got contacts," he said mysteriously. "Shouldn't be long now, and I can get you as many as you need."

"Wonderful!" Carol said, looking around brightly. "Himm and I are in charge of general recruitment and supervision, as usual. I've heard rumours of a Christian group that could provide us with a convert or two — it's called Hitting For Jesus, which sounds broadly in line with our own views on the need for Christian violence where appropriate. So, everyone happy with their roles?"

Smiles all round.

"Right," said Himm briskly after a glance at his wife for approval, "I think that wraps up this week's meeting. Any questions?"

Mabel raised a tentative hand. "Are there any angel cakes left?"

Chapter Seven
What Doesn't Kill You Makes You Stranger...

"This lifestyle is not for everyone. Take care in who you choose to bring into it. Those who are mentally or emotionally unstable have no place among us. They are dangerous and unreliable and may betray us in the future. Make certain that those you choose to bring in are mature enough for this burden."
http://www.sanguinarius.org/13rules.shtml

Search terms:
breatharian, sanguinarian, sanguinarius.org

Saturday October 4th

And then, finally, it was Saturday night.

I decided to wear what I'd normally wear to a party: black trousers, purple silk shirt and a look of interested intelligence. I was ruefully aware that I wanted to impress Stefan, but I refused to spend the day dyeing my hair black, filing my teeth and applying industrial-sized quantities of eyeliner. Anyway, I didn't want to be one of them, exactly. I wanted to be a semi-detached observer, looking on, finding out their deepest motivations, moulding them to my will.

Or, you know, making friends. Whatever.

An email from Joanne had informed me that the party was starting at nine. I left home at seven because that's how long it usually takes to get across London, and picked up a bottle of absinthe on the way on the basis that that couldn't possibly be a bad idea. Of course, according to ancient London transport laws, the only time it's possible to reach a destination quickly is when you don't want to, so I arrived on Joanne's doorstep at half-past eight, clutching my absinthe and feeling extremely uncool.

The door was opened by a girl who looked familiar — very pale grey eyes, face like depressed thunder. Then it clicked into focus: she'd been at the munch two weeks ago. She was the woman Justin had glanced at when he'd said his church did nothing illegal. Interesting.

"Hi, I'm Elinor," I said, with a cheery grin to balance out her glum look. "Sorry I'm early. Is Joanne in?"

She stared at me as if I'd arrived clutching a bouquet of decapitated children. "Turn away," she said bleakly. "Turn away from these demons. Escape before you're drawn into this web of deviance."

Joanne appeared behind her. "Elinor! Hi! Nice to see you!" She sounded a little desperate. "Please do come in. Please. Naomi, could you let Elinor in?"

The girl moved aside with an air of resignation. "You're doomed, you know," she said.

"OK," I said, patting her on the shoulder for want of anything better to do. She flinched. I stopped.

Joanne made frantic apologetic faces from behind Naomi's left shoulder.

I stepped in and handed her the bottle. "Oh, thanks. Er, this is Naomi? From the vampire munch?"

"Yes, I think I saw you there," said Naomi.

Joanne ushered us down a corridor and into a large living room. Nobody else had arrived yet.

"So, do you go to the munch often?" I said, genuinely curious.

"Every time. They're all going to Hell. So am I." Naomi turned away and sat down on a wooden chair, staring into space.

"Why don't you come through to the kitchen and tell me what you want to drink?" said Joanne to me with forced jollity. I followed her down the corridor into a narrow, elderly kitchen piled high with crisps, dips and alcohol. Both of us ignored the food and headed towards the whisky.

"She turned up at five this afternoon," said Joanne, abruptly abandoning the fake cheerfulness. "She's been sitting in my living room, drinking vodka and telling me about how awful her life is and how I'm going to burn in a pit of fire. I think she may have exhausted all my hostessy instincts before the party's even started. God, I hope they're not all going to be like that."

"I doubt it," I said. "She seems... unique. Why is she so upset, anyway?"

"Don't ask. Or rather, if you're going to ask, ask her. I've blotted it out of my mind. It's all Stefan's fault, anyway," she added, mixing herself a rum, gin and tequila cocktail. I quietly poured myself an absinthe and Coke.

"Why?"

"She'll tell you. Believe me, she'll tell you. When he turns up I'm going to hit him with something."

"So, Stefan's definitely coming tonight then?" I said with the most casual of casual intonations, or so I thought. Joanne looked at me wearily.

"Yeah. Don't bother to affect indifference, I know you fancy him. I do too, apart from the fact that he's a pretentious idiot." I opened my mouth to disagree, then realised I agreed, so I shut it again.

"Anyway, yes. He's coming. So are the vampire church lot and a selection of others from the munch, I think. And Simon, of course. And some of my other friends from college." She looked a bit more animated. "That should be fun. They're all nice little emo gothlets who write poetry about trees at midnight and don't know what the word fellatio means. Subculture meets subculture. Can't wait."

"I'm sure," I said politely. I was dying to go and find out what terrible wrong Stefan had done to Naomi. "Tell you what, shall I go and keep your depressing guest company while you get yourself back in a party mood?"

"Would you?" Joanne looked ecstatic. "Welcome to my top ten list of favourite people. Here, have some gin. I'll be here if you need me. Please," she added, "don't need me." She cut herself a very large slice of chocolate cheesecake.

I accepted the gin and moved cautiously back into the living room. Naomi was muttering to herself, stopping only to swig vodka from a large bottle. She looked up as I entered and shook her head with glum resignation.

"Doomed," she said. "Doomed. All of us. Especially me."

I'd come across plenty of gloomy puritanical Christians before, but they had all believed that they, at least, were immune from damnation. Naomi intrigued me. I sat down next to her on the sofa.

"So," I said, "Doomed, then?"

Her disturbing eyes swung round to my face and fixed there. "He damned me to hell. Now it doesn't matter what I do. I can't escape my destiny. I hate him. But I can't stop myself wanting to see him," she added, the note of self hatred creeping up one notch further.

"Stefan?" I guessed. She nodded, staring at her shoes. I noticed that she was wearing dark grey this week, not black, but it was a similar outfit to the one she'd had on at the munch: a long-sleeved rather shapeless dress that reached her wrists and ankles.

"Stefan... ruined you?" It was a Victorian turn of phrase, but looking at Naomi it seemed apt.

She looked up again. "Yes. He made me evil, and I can't ever be redeemed. I'm one of them now. I come to these events to remind myself of my damnation, and their damnation."

That must make her popular, I thought. "Don't you ever just come along to have fun?"

"My only pleasure is in contemplating the fact that Stefan the Antichrist and his cohorts are bound to an eternal hell," she said.

"Oh."

"And in drinking the blood of the devils," she added, standing up.

I turned sharply to look at her, but she was walking out of the room.

It was about nine o'clock now, and people were starting to arrive. I hung around in the kitchen mixing people drinks — always a good way to start conversations at parties. So far the guests were mainly Joanne's more normal friends, who seemed relieved to find that I wasn't about to tear their throats open and eviscerate them. I wondered what Joanne had told them about her new acquaintances.

Around ten, the vampires started arriving. First was Justin and a small coterie of the Jesus' Blood group. They installed themselves in the living room, making occasional sorties to the kitchen to get more absinthe and enjoy the naked terror on the faces of Joanne's friends. Later more random vampires drifted in, mainly staying in the living room too since it was darker. The bright light of the kitchen made them wince, even behind the sunglasses most of them wore. There was no sign of Naomi. Joanne informed me that she'd gone upstairs to lie down for a bit, and added some uncomplimentary (but justified, I thought) remarks about people who couldn't take their drink. I still wanted to know exactly what Stefan had done to her and why she was so weird, but Joanne clearly didn't want to talk about it. A few cocktails had put her into a party mood, and she was having fun mocking her friends, then wandering into the living room and mocking the vampires. Nobody seemed to mind much.

I also wandered between the two groups, feeling not quite included in either, but in a way that didn't bother me. It was a cool, on-the-edge, impartial-omniscient-observer kind of thing... or possibly it was the effect of the bit of cocaine Joanne had given me as a thank-you for occupying Naomi. Finally, someone had offered me drugs: I mentally crossed off item #3 on my Things to Do list.

I'd expected cocaine to have a violent impact, but instead it just ironed out all the insecure undercurrents of my personality — if you can iron an undercurrent, which I'm aware you can't — and left just the confident, outgoing facet. I hoped I didn't get to like the effect too much. I couldn't afford an addiction at this point. (Maybe later, when I'd saved the world through paint or whatever, and had been officially assigned a free lifetime supply of the finest hard drugs.)

I recognised most of the vampires from the munch. Justin gave me a smile that I think he intended to be friendly, but with the crucifix fangs, no smile of his was ever going to be anything but horrifying. I wondered what he did for a living. Presumably it didn't involve much contact with the general public. Computer programmer? Stefan was a sound engineer, I remembered. That didn't sound like it included much customer service, either. Did most vampires work in behind-the-scene jobs? My guess was yes.

Justin introduced me to a couple of his church members, one of whom was the woman whose breasts Simon had been buried in at the munch. (He hadn't turned up yet, but was apparently expected later.) Her name turned out to be Viola and I was a bit surprised to find she had an East End accent. The long black flowing gown, long dark hair and dark red lipstick had prepared me for something more Eastern European. I asked her about Simon.

"Oh yeah, him. He was sweet." She grimaced.

"Is that bad?" I asked, confused.

"Sweet as in sugary. Must have been eating chocolate that day. Made my diabetes flare up."

"Oh. It must be tough being a diabetic vampire," I offered.

"She's a gluten for punishment," said Joanne cheerfully, passing by.

"Don't you mean glucose?" I said.

"Don't be pedantic."

"Sorry."

"Anyway," said Viola, wincing, "I was a bit shaky after that. I had to hunt up a health freak I know who likes a bit of pain now and then, to regulate my sugar levels."

"I'd never realised drinking people's blood could be so complicated," I said, fascinated.

"Oh yes," said Justin. "Another member of the flock is an alcoholic. He only drinks from drunk people. Seems to work. Then there's the junkies... Oh, and the girl with nut allergies. That takes some organising."

"Wow. Do you all, er, drink a lot of blood, then?"

"Not really," said Viola. "Once a week or so. None of us are stupid enough to use it as our only source of nutrition. After all, Jesus ate food."

"Actually," said a random, rather emaciated vampire who was listening in, "some people believe Jesus didn't eat at all and that we don't need food to keep us alive. Just, and you'll find this interesting, our own fresh urine."

I nodded intelligently.

We took a mutual, tacit vow to ignore him and never mention his existence again.

"And, of course, we only drink from willing donors." Justin seemed keen to get that point across.

"So, if you knew of a vampire who took from... unwilling donors — would you go to the police?" I tried to make it sound like the most hypothetical question ever.

Both Justin and Viola looked shifty. "Well, in theory, yes..." he said slowly. "But of course, one does not normally see another vampire drinking illicit blood — I mean, you might not necessarily know it was going on. You might suspect, but if you were not *sure*... it would do so much damage to the community as a whole if one of us got in trouble. We would prefer our image not to become any worse than it already is."

"Yes, I do see that. But presumably the community has, you know, gossip? You'd all know if someone was, er, attacking people or anything?"

"Oh, we know," said Viola, breaking in. "We don't talk to her. It's not our fault if she keeps turning up. It's not our fault that Stefan... anyway. I'm not blaming Stefan. But she isn't normal."

I tried to pretend I was taking a wild uneducated guess. "Naomi?"

"Yes. She's insane. We don't know what she does, really, but she doesn't seem to have any ethics at all. Like I said, we don't talk to her usually. Sometimes we have to... I mean, Stefan's our friend, so if he needs helping out... but we don't like her."

Justin glanced at her. "It is certainly true that we tolerate her for the sake of Stefan's conscience," he said smoothly. "However, I'm sure Elinor is not interested in the intricacies of vampire politics. Tell us, Elinor, what do you do? Do you work in IT?" He and Viola started a discussion about the pros and cons of Unix. Both of them, it appeared, were programmers.

Clearly, I really needed to talk to Stefan.

He turned up at eleven, in roughly the same outfit that he'd worn two weeks earlier: black, black and black, with a lacy white shirt that could have been stolen from Lestat. He looked as pretty as I remembered.

"Elinor," he said softly, kissing my hand and then Joanne's. Both of us blushed and avoided catching each other's eyes.

"Would you like some wine?" offered Joanne with an evil glint in her eye. I think both of us were a little surprised when he said, "Yes, please. Red if you have it." She poured him a large glassful without further comment, and began chatting to her gothlets. He leant against the kitchen counter, took a sip of wine and smiled at me. "It is good to see you again, Elinor. Are you enjoying the party?"

"Er, yes." I could have sworn I'd had some witty repartee stored up for our next meeting, but apparently not. "I've been talking to a friend of yours. Well, I say friend, I think I probably mean enemy."

"Oh?"

"Naomi."

"Oh." His face went blank. "Naomi. She is a very troubled young woman."

"Nobody's arguing with you there, but what did you do to her?" Oh, very subtle, Elinor, I thought. What happened to the fifteen minutes of small talk before you worked your way round to the Naomi topic?

Stefan looked away. "She was already troubled before I met her. I was wrong, though, very wrong. I thought I could help. No, I wanted... I don't know. Perhaps I thought I was helping, perhaps I simply wanted to hurt her. Certainly the effect I have had on her has been... unfortunate."

"What could you have done that would have helped and hurt her at the same time?" A thought occurred to me. I didn't like it much. "God. You *turned* her? Into a, you know, vampire?" I couldn't believe I was even saying those words.

"You could say that, yes."

I stared at him incredulously. "Against her will?"

"Very much so. She had... annoyed me." I stared into his eyes. They suddenly seemed colder.

The kitchen was getting crowded and the conversations around us were dying out as people abandoned their various chats and started openly listening to our discussion instead. Perhaps we should move into the front room with the other vampires, I thought; but I didn't want them listening in, either.

There was a small, dark and unoccupied spare room next to the living room. I dragged Stefan in there and sat him down on a two-seater black leather sofa, casting a glance at the door to make sure Naomi wasn't hanging around. I sat next to him, for once not caring that our legs were touching. My curiosity is almost always stronger than my libido.

"Look, Stefan..."

He looked at me. "I know exactly what you're thinking. One, I had no right to make her a vampire without her consent, and two, it is not possible to turn someone into a vampire."

I was taken aback. "That's more or less it, yes. Sorry for not believing in your lifestyle choice —"

"Well, as a matter of fact," he said uncomfortably, "I am not able to turn people."

I was further taken aback, and actually moved slightly backwards to indicate this. He was being surprisingly honest. "Why can't you?"

"I am not a member of the Jesus' Blood church, and they are the only ones who have the power to create others of our kind. I rarely even bite people. I prefer to absorb energy through other sources such as —"

"Lettuce, yes, I overheard you in the bar when we met. So, what happened? Did she really piss you off?" Someone put their head round the door and I glared at them. I had no intention of being interrupted till I'd found out the full story. But they were one of the vampires, and impervious to glares.

"Stefan," they asked, "did you want a drink?" The voice revealed them as female.

"I have one, thank you, Willow." Stefan held up his glass.

Willow's eyes widened. "Oh. Oh, I see."

"No, no, it's just red wine," he said impatiently. "I am not Dracula, you know."

She backed away, muttering apologies. Stefan appeared to have a certain amount of cachet in this community. Was it because he'd turned Naomi? Maybe, though personally I would have been inclined to lynch him. Why add a miserable Puritan to the community if you didn't have to? It wasn't like she fitted in.

I got up and pulled the door ajar — closing it completely would have been tantamount to posting a sign saying 'We're Having Sex In Here!' — and turned back to Stefan. He stretched out his long legs on the small sofa and sighed.

"So. Did Naomi tell you that she was a Christian?"

"I worked it out for myself, thanks, what with her constant references to everyone being doomed." He nodded wearily.

"Oh —" A light bulb went on in my head. "— I understand something she said now. You made her a vampire, or whatever it was you did, and now she thinks she's going to hell?"

"Yes. She believes she's damned for eternity along with the rest of us, and she thinks she can't appeal to God for mercy because she believes she's lost her soul. I do feel rather guilty about that."

"Oh, I don't think you should blame yourself," I said briskly, not being sure if I really believed it, but wanting him to tell me more. "She sounds like a very silly woman. And also mad as a brush."

There was a pause as Stefan arranged his thoughts. I stayed quiet and stared at the slightly-too-pastel shade of green on the walls. You could tell this was a rented house; these were colours only used by those who knew that someone else would have to live with them.

He sighed. "She tried to convert me, you see. It was about a year ago. She came along to a munch looking for what she called sinners, and attached herself to me because I was the only one willing to talk to her. I believe in being open about vampirism. That was why I listed myself on the iTem directory. So I told her what I was, and she told me I was evil, and we argued for a while. Or rather, she talked at me and I tried to listen politely, then I left. She must have followed me home, because the next night she turned up on my doorstep."

"Eeek."

"Indeed. I wasn't sure what to do."

I noticed that his style of speech was becoming more informal, and grinned to myself: he couldn't keep up the pseudo-old-fashioned idiom for an entire conversation. Thank goodness.

"She kept ranting about how I needed to turn to God and let him save me from my wicked blood-drinking habits. Then she just kept talking about the blood, and the biting, and the evil... I decided that what she really wanted was to be one of us. Or perhaps I just wanted to frighten her."

"Maybe you thought it would be funny," I suggested.

He gave me a stern look. "I do not do things because they would be funny."

I sighed. "No, I suppose you don't. I would have. Anyway, so…?"

"So, she came round one night and talked at me for three hours without stopping about my need to call on Jesus' name and beg for salvation. I tried to be nice to her for a while — she seemed troubled — but at the end of that rant I just couldn't manage it any more and I told her to leave. She said she would leave when she had seen me change. She meant change and accept Jesus, of course, but I pretended to misunderstand. I asked her to excuse me for a moment, went to the bathroom and put my fangs in. I hardly ever wear them. They're very sharp and I tend to cut my lip."

He was getting more human all the time.

"I did my makeup and put in my red contact lenses as well. I wanted to scare her away, I think. Then, with the fangs in, I went back in the room and snarled at her."

"How cute!"

"Sorry?"

I backtracked quickly. "Er, I mean that must have been scary."

"I could have sworn you said 'how cute'."

"Figment of your imagination. Get on with it."

"Well, she screamed. That triggered something in me, I think. And putting in the fangs had already — you know, switched me into vampire mode. I know you do not necessarily subscribe to my beliefs, but I really do identify as a vampire, and I do have a physical need for energy, not always blood, but something… Anyway, something in my head, and in the situation, suddenly altered. Naomi is such a natural victim, she really seems to ask to be ill-treated somehow, and she was mad, you know. Even before. I looked into her eyes, those empty, grey eyes, and I knew that she was convinced I was going to Turn her."

"And suddenly I wanted to. And I did." He dropped his head into his hands, slightly theatrically.

"You turned her into a vampire? I thought you said…"

"I know. But… it was so powerful, the feeling — I could have done anything to her. She was terrified. Do you know how *incredible* it can feel to have someone that scared of you?"

"Actually, no. But I think I know where you're coming from." I did, as a matter of fact. I could hear it in his voice.

"So I took hold of her, drank deeply of her terror and her helplessness, and bit her throat." Did I hear a trace of guilty pleasure behind his words? "There was blood... she fainted. When she woke up, she believed that she was a vampire. I did not undeceive her."

I asked the obvious question. "Why not?"

He looked at me. "Why should I? She had entered my house, inflicted her beliefs on me, told me I was evil. To have her believing that she was damned... I think the phrase is poetic justice."

I sighed. "So now, she's going to spend the rest of her life tormented because she thinks she's going to hell and can't do anything about it? Surely you've had your revenge?"

"Oh, I had no intention of continuing the deception indefinitely." He shrugged. "But it is too late. I tried to talk to her a week or two later and to explain that I had not Turned her, that I could not Turn anyone, but she didn't believe me. And then I found myself wondering if... perhaps, she was right." He looked thoughtful. "I was never able to Turn before, but these things can change. Perhaps Naomi is my first triumph." The thoughtful look acquired an edge of something else, possibly pride.

"Triumph?" I said incredulously. "The woman's a mess!"

The pride instantly disappeared. "You don't know the half of it," he said, taking a deep draught of wine.

"I've heard some. Justin and Viola think she kills people."

"They may be right. I'm not sure," he said vaguely. "She certainly drinks unwilling blood. She thinks it doesn't matter, you see."

"Because she's already damned anyway? So hurting or killing people doesn't make any difference?"

"Yes. I told you she was mad."

I'd managed to prick his brief bubble of success. Not that I was feeling too guilty. The story I'd just heard was not one that Stefan came out of well, even if I did think Naomi was certifiable, self-righteous and generally depressing. And an evangelical Christian, my pet hate. Actually, I didn't find myself that unsympathetic to Stefan now that I thought about it properly. He had behaved badly, true, but Naomi really was stupid. People who were stupid enough to believe in God deserved to be damned.

Joanne's voice floated in from the hallway, startling us. "You two, stop being all couply and get back out here!" She sounded like she'd thoroughly cheered up.

The room seemed very dark. Couply? Suddenly, I became very aware of Stefan's leg against mine.

Chapter Eight
Hitting For Jesus

Search term:
"1 Timothy 2:9"

Saturday October 4th, 7pm

"A bit harder. Good. Hmm... a little further down is probably better, or it won't be quite painful enough, will it? Excellent." The sound of rhythmic hitting echoed flatly through the small, dingy room. Ten people sat in wooden chairs attentively watching a man hit his wife with a paddle. Both husband and wife were fully clothed in sensible beige suits, and the atmosphere was serious and attentive. " OK, well done, very good Tim and Helen. Let's pause there for a moment and discuss what we've seen."

Daniel came forward to retrieve the leather paddle from the nervous couple at the front of the room and to hand it to Patricia, who placed it carefully on the table in front of her. The table also held three whips, a pair of leather handcuffs and something called a spreader bar, which was a length of silver metal with ankle restraints attached. Daniel had explained to the group that it stopped women closing their legs, thus reminding them of the way that they couldn't stop themselves from letting God into their lives. All the BDSM explanations so far had included a discussion of their Christian significance. The handcuffs represented the fact that Christians voluntarily surrendered their free will to God. The three whips were the Trinity, and each apparently had a slightly different effect on the human body which were similar to the effect of the Father, the Son and the Holy Ghost on the human soul. Or something.

Marianne was fascinated. She had been sitting in a corner at first, just watching, but by degrees she had edged further into the room and started asking questions. She had even earned an approving nod from Daniel for her suggestion that Tim's pain at having to hurt his wife was similar to the pain of the Father, giving his only son up to be killed. She was finding the combination of sex and religion heady and exhilarating. It lacked the obvious glamour of the fetish club, but the very drabness of the surroundings focused her attention on the people, and on the actions being performed. Though the people were quite drab too, actually. She would never have picked them as being BDSMers.

But then, this was a different kind of BDSM. This was Hitting For Jesus, the monthly Christian BDSM workshop for husbands and wives. It was held in the neutral space of a small North London pub's function room, since Daniel and Patricia's local church had politely refused to allow their church hall to be the venue, and of course they would never go to a gay or fetish place. Daniel had said Marianne could come along even though she wasn't married, because sometimes single Christian men came along looking for future spouses who understood their needs.

There weren't any of those tonight though, just couples, and one other woman on her own. Marianne had chatted to her briefly before the workshop started and had found out that she was called Carol. Attempts to draw her out on the subject of BDSM had been entirely unsuccessful, so Marianne had talked about herself instead, mentioning the fact that this was her first Hitting For Jesus experience.

Apparently it was Carol's, too. She didn't say why she'd come. She'd seemed nice, though, in a schoolmistressy kind of way. She spoke briskly and appeared to be sure of everything she was saying. Marianne was sure of herself too, naturally, but sometimes these little doubts crept in and they were so unsettling. She glanced down at herself and was reassured by the sight of her sensible brown shoes and sensible long brown skirt. Christian BDSM had necessitated buying a whole new wardrobe, but it was worth it to fit in. Her black leather had been unceremoniously relegated to the back of her chest of drawers.

"Now, did you all pick up on the difference there?" said Daniel cheerfully. "That was punishment. On Tuesday night, Helen confessed to Tim that she'd drunk alcohol at her Women's Institution meeting — only half a glass of white wine, she said, but we know where that leads, don't we? The downward spiral is fast and inexorable! In a week's time she'd have been on the streets begging passers-by for mouldy heroin!" He raised an admonishing eyebrow at the blushing Helen. "As her husband, Tim naturally wanted to prevent that happening, and as his Christian wife she accepted that she deserved punishment both for its own sake and to stop her from drinking again. Since he consulted me on the subject, I persuaded him to postpone her beating until tonight, so that it could form part of our workshop."

He paused to drink some water, and to allow time for people to mutter, "Thank you, Daniel", which some did quietly, on cue.

"The workshop tonight," he resumed, "is of course on the topic of "Punishment versus Pleasure". So what we are talking about here is the difference between beating one's wife because she has done something *wrong*, and beating her because you both *enjoy* it. Let me recap what we've talked about so far. If you are punishing your wife, it should not involve any element of pleasure, so you need to make sure you do it in a way she doesn't enjoy. Use a part of her body that she doesn't like to be beaten on. You saw there that Tim was beating Helen's legs, which he knows she finds painful and unpleasant. Use an implement she hates — Helen is vegan, so to be beaten with a leather paddle was especially uncomfortable for her. Good thought there, Tim."

Tim beamed shyly.

"Don't show any affection during the punishment, and don't indulge in anything sexual. Obviously once it's all over and a suitable amount of time has passed, you can start to show sexual interest again, but please do let some time pass or you will confuse her. It is crucial to establish that this is not a reward, or she will be encouraged to repeat her bad behaviour."

Marianne nodded thoughtfully. It all felt so right. Now that she had Jesus in her life, she understood the relationship between pain and pleasure and power and God. People who had power over you inflicted pain on you. You took pleasure from this because the power came from God. God was, in effect, the one beating you with a leather paddle. "I am Jesus' submissive," she thought with pride and a sense of peace. No more dominance, no more having to work out what to do and how to behave. These people would tell her how to behave. She would find a nice God-fearing man to marry and have his children. It was a shame Daniel was taken already.

She returned from being lost in her thoughts to discover that Daniel was on the subject of how much pleasure a wife should be allowed in a non-punishment context, such as normal marital intercourse. He was suggesting that it could be made contingent on the number of Bible verses she could recite from memory. The men were nodding; the women were nodding slightly less enthusiastically.

Marianne glanced round and saw that Carol had put her hand up. She had an odd expression on her face.

"Yes, Carol?" said Daniel. "You're new here, I know. Anything troubling you?"

Carol took a deep breath. "Well, yes. There's the fact that you're all damned to Hell. There's the fact that what you're doing is evil in the eyes of the Lord, and doubly so because you're using His name in vain and invoking His authority to do it. There's the fact that you're using blasphemous words to promote your twisted, perverted idea of marital love. Not to mention the way that this woman here is shamelessly wearing pearls in defiance of 1 Timothy 2:9!" She pointed dramatically at Helen, whose hand nervously went to her tiny pearl necklace.

"And then," she said climactically, voice rising a pitch or two, "there's the way you're dragging sweet, innocent girls like this one —" she waved a hand in Marianne's direction "— into this *filth*. I'm leaving now. Come along, Marianne. This isn't the place for you. Join my group. We're going to save the world."

She stood up, looked sternly round the room, grabbed Marianne's hand and swept out majestically. Daniel started after Marianne, but she didn't even look back. Her eyes were fixed firmly on Carol.

The room was silent for a moment. Daniel sighed and nodded to Patricia, who got up and closed the door behind her. The group exchanged glances.

"Another one. Honestly, if every meeting's going to be ruined by these people..." Daniel waved an irritable hand.

"She's gone now," said Patricia. "What did she mean by blasphemous words?"

"'Sexual', I suppose." Daniel sighed again. "And she took our new recruit, too."

"Good," said Patricia. "She'd never have stayed, anyway. I know that type."

"That woman was right about the pearls, though," said Daniel, with a thoughtful stare at Helen. "I suppose we really should read our Bibles more often, instead of just using them to beat each other with." He beckoned to Helen. "Come on — throw your necklace away and get back up here for your next punishment. There's a good girl."

Chapter Nine
...What Does Kill You Makes You, Well, Dead

"The prohibition of drinking of blood is one of the few commandments of the Lord which cuts across the time of Noah, the Mosaic Law (Lev. 3:17, 7:26) and even into the New Testament church (Acts 15:20, 29). God did this because He knows that there is something compelling and darkly exciting in vampirism, for 'The blood is the life.' (Deut. 12:23)."
http://www.christiangoth.com/vampires.html

Saturday, October 4th— evening

Joanne appeared in the doorway.

"Sorry to interrupt darlings, but we need the room. We're going to play Truth or Dare and I thought this would be good, neutral space, try to bring the vamps and the gothlets together. You know how it is. There's a spare bedroom upstairs, I think, if you want to carry on, you know, *chatting.*" Joanne's speech had become noticeably more slurred in the few minutes since Stefan and I had been talking.

"We're fine," I said, getting up. Stefan stood too, touching me briefly on the shoulder as he left the room.

"I'll see you later," he murmured. The touch made me tingly. Apparently being made privy to some of his darker secrets hadn't put me off.

"How's it going?" I said to Joanne. "Good party?"

"Lovely, sweetie." Who would have guessed, I pondered, that a sarcastic goth would transform into an Ab Fab character when pissed? "Everyone's having a *wonnnderful* time," she continued, dreamily leaning against the doorframe for support. "Everyone's so lovely. Lovely, lovely people. Even the ones who keep asking where I'm from."

"Where you're from? Aren't you from London?"

"Of course I am, but if I say that they say 'no, where are you from originally,' and I say 'still London,' and they look all confused. Happens all the time if you're black, unfortunately. People are very stupid. But lovely," she added, reverting to her good mood. "I'm having a lovely party and I will not let anything get to me. Even that bitch Naomi."

"Oh, is she still here? I haven't seen her for a while."

"Well, you haven't been, er, *around* for a while, have you, my love?" slurred Joanne. "Off with your gorgeous bloodsucker here, who I would be fighting you for if I wasn't blind, blind drunk. Yes, the little Christian's here. Not talking to anyone and a bit covered in blood, but definitely present and correct, no problem there. Now, out you go. Shoo!" She gestured vaguely in the direction of the stairs. "Go and do stuff in my bed, I don't care. Just don't leave any blood on the mattress, it's new."

"Blood?"

"Well, if you're going to screw a vamp I think you should be prepared for blood, Elinor, my sweet." Joanne pushed herself off the doorframe to make her point with a finger that I assumed was intended to touch my neck. Instead she managed to poke me in the nipple.

"No, no," I said, gently batting her hand away, "That's not what I meant. Did you say Naomi was covered in blood?"

"Oh. Yes. Not to worry. She probably caught one of my gothlets or something. Or maybe it's hers. She looked a bit out of it — maybe she ran out of victims and starting biting herself. Hahahahaha. Hahahahaha." I caught hold of my hostess, as she seemed about to collapse under the weight of her own drunken laughter, and sat her down on the sofa.

Other people started trickling into the room and discussing Truth or Dare rules. Clearly it was going to be an interesting game. The gothlets were discussing whether it was fair to make the participants improvise blank verse; the vampires were arguing whether it would be necessary to get consent before ordering people to commit oral sex on each other.

I left them to it and started searching for Naomi. There had been too many hints that evening about her potential for causing damage. If she had blood on her, I wanted to know whose it was. Why I'd decided to appoint myself guardian of the vampire group I had no idea, but it felt like they were mine now, and if something had happened, I felt I should at least know about it.

I checked the kitchen and living room first, but she wasn't there, of course. Stefan had wandered back to the living room and was chatting to Justin in a melancholy sort of way. Joanne was in the kitchen slurrily expostulating to her friends about Simon's many character flaws, in his absence.

"Posturing little poseur," she muttered, poking a nervous gothlet in the arm for emphasis. "Las' week he was all over me, begging me to find him a nice fanged girlfriend. Well, he can fuck off. Didn' even ring to cancel, just totally, totally failed to put in an appearance. Fuck him 'nd the horse he failed to ride in on." She noticed a couple of the other gothlets exchanging disapproving glances, and added belligerently, "'S my party and I'll bitch if I want to. Bitch if I want to, bitch if I want to..." The rant died out as Joanne pirouetted around the tiny kitchen, gestured grandiloquently towards the gothlets and fell slowly out of the back door.

So, Simon was missing. Had never turned up, in fact. Hmm.

Upstairs, there was still no Naomi, just a collection of bedrooms which featured a) a sleeping housemate of Joanne's, b) a pile of coats and a couple of startled naked students who had managed to scatter their clothing over an impressively wide area, c) a trinity of vampires ceremonially cutting each other with small sterile scalpels and d) a quintuple of really hardcore vampires who were engaged in some kind of blood bonding ritual which appeared to include both shooting up *and* penetrative sex. I apologised to them all for interrupting, checked the bathroom queue briefly and unsuccessfully, and decided to seek Naomi, and possibly Simon, outside.

Joanne's house was in a very typical East London street, if by 'typical' you meant 'grey, a bit scruffy and somewhat dodgy at night'. Some of the street lights were working, so I wandered up the road a bit, peering into gardens and cars to see if anything looked odd. Nothing did, particularly. I wandered back down to the house and tried exploring in the other direction. Round a corner, I discovered a small alleyway off to the right with no lighting at all. A rapist's dream. Had Naomi been raped? Was Simon involved? He'd seemed quite sweet, but that didn't mean anything.

I stood on the fairly dark street at the entrance to the *extremely* dark alleyway. Faintly menacing orchestral music had started playing in the background, or more probably just in my mind. Either way, I wasn't keen to go any further in. I took a tentative step forwards and my left foot touched something.

Someone.

I moved my foot back and then, after a panicked pause, forwards again. My boot was providing enough padding that I couldn't actually tell what I was pushing against, but I got a general sense of flesh — soft flesh. Whoever it was didn't say anything. Guided by an impulse I couldn't precisely define, I drew my foot back and kicked the flesh hard. No sound.

"Naomi?" I said quietly? "Is that you?" Nothing. Oh fuck. She'd killed herself or something. Or she'd been hit by a car and crawled in here to die. What a way to end a pretty miserable life. "I'm sorry," I said aloud.

"What for?" said Naomi from behind me.

I jumped and my heart did a somersault, or at least I think it was that way round. I skidded round and there she was, standing under a street light, bathed in an orange glow and looking frankly demonic.

"Why are you out here?" I put a hand against the brick wall behind me for stability. She really did look scary.

"I needed to think," she said. "I needed to think about my evil. About my devil-driven need for blood and death. Sometimes, when I think about it, I can almost manage to embrace my destiny. I can almost accept what I've become, this creature of darkness. This thing." Her face twisted and she stepped back against the lamppost. "They say it's important to accept yourself as you are. I do try."

I glanced back at the indistinct form in the alleyway. " Naomi?" I wasn't at all sure how to form the next sentence. "Naomi, how do you express this acceptance? What do you do to accept your... darkness?"

She stared at me levelly. "They won't do anything. They didn't before. They protect me, because they're evil too. All damned together." She flung her head back and said again, dramatically, "All damned together." A very small part of my mind expected her to laugh insanely, but she didn't, not even a short giggle. She just let her head drop again and stared at the pavement.

Weary and more than a little irritated, I turned back away from her. I really didn't want to do what I was about to do. But I crouched down, took a deep breath and pulled the limp, dead body of Simon — aka various Class A drugs, surname unknown to me — out of the little alleyway.

* * *

"No."

"Seriously, no?"

"Seriously, no. I know how it sounds..."

"I should hope you do."

"Of course, you are not a member of my church and you are not under my jurisdiction. You are not compelled to obey me. But none of us are going to betray Naomi's connection with this death, and I would very much appreciate it if you did not do so either."

"What are you going to do?" I said. "Just leave him there and pretend it's nothing to do with you?"

"I know it's not much of a plan, but yes." Justin shrugged.

I stared at him and said, "Aren't the police going to track her down anyway?"

"They didn't before," said Viola from the bed.

The three of us and Stefan were upstairs in the bedroom formerly occupied by the three vampires with scalpels, who had apparently finished cutting and were downstairs showing off their pretty scars. Nobody had talked to Joanne yet. I didn't care who did, as long as it wasn't me.

"So you did know she was capable of this," I said. "You kept hinting it to me, earlier."

Viola looked away. Despite their surface bravado, it was clear that she and Justin were genuinely shaken. "OK, yes, we knew. At least, we know she's attacked people before. A few. They all survived it, though. This is new. She must be getting madder."

"But how come she's never been caught?"

"Her dad's a policeman. Fairly high up. I'm not saying he's been using his influence, but — well, she's never even been questioned, so you have to wonder."

"And all this happened since Stefan...?"

"The attacks only started then, yes. She wasn't exactly mentally stable before — she'd been coming along to events for ages and trying to convert us all to the Resurrected Church by handing out handwritten pamphlets. Featuring little cartoons she'd drawn of us being impaled by demons in hell." A faint smile. "But she used to be harmless. Until he got involved."

She shot a hard glance at Stefan, but he avoided her gaze. He looked very tired. He'd been in charge of getting Naomi indoors, upstairs and lying down. She'd gone quietly and done as she was told, but I got the impression Stefan would almost have preferred her to scream.

I sat in the corner, curled up in as close to the foetal position as someone who's five foot eight can get. I hadn't seen much of Simon's body, just the leg that I'd grabbed to pull him out of the alley. Then I'd left him where he was, and dragged Naomi back to Joanne's house, since I couldn't think what else to do. But seeing and touching that leg was easily enough to keep me huddled in that corner for a good while yet, and that wasn't even taking into account the fact that the woman who'd murdered the body belonging to the leg was in the room next door.

She was asleep. I could hear her snoring though the wall.

I wished I could sleep. I wished I could lie down without getting dizzy. I wished I could think coherently, but I couldn't move forward. I wasn't sure I could move at all. My body no longer seemed set up for it. Maybe I would have to spend the rest of my life in the corner, hugging my legs, trying not to think. Trying not to think about legs. My mind was a spiral going up and round and up and round, and the spiral ended where it began — with Simon's dead leg, lying across my thoughts and deadening them too. I was being suffocated by a leg. I giggled briefly, and that made me remember the others were there. They were still talking. I didn't have the energy to talk much, so I stayed quiet in the corner.

I didn't have a lot to contribute, anyway. It was looking as if I didn't have much choice but to keep quiet about Naomi, what with the potential cover-up from her dad, and the fact that it would be my word against hers, and the fact that all the vampires would support her. And if that happened then I would lose all my new friends at a stroke and be back to square one. I knew perfectly well that I shouldn't be considering any of those things as important. I should be doing the right thing without even thinking about it, the way heroes and heroines were supposed to. Presumably I wasn't heroine material after all, because I was more or less certain that I wasn't going to do the right thing. I was going to keep an eye on Naomi, certainly. And I would grieve for Simon, to the extent that you can grieve for someone you barely know. But no, I wasn't going to go to the police. In fact, I was fairly certain I was going to use the murder as a way of ingratiating myself further into the vampire clique and specifically into Stefan's bed. Perhaps Simon would have approved.

Poor Simon. Poor Joanne. Poor Naomi, too, I supposed. These people seemed to be her closest friends, and none of them liked her. She must have been alone a lot. Alone with only her own thoughts for company, and given the kind of thoughts she seemed to have, that couldn't have been fun. Had she picked Simon because of his friendship with Stefan? Or did she just take the chance because it was there, because he turned up at the right time? Just a short guy she could take by surprise, there in that black alleyway round the corner where she must have been waiting. Waiting for Simon and his dead, dead leg. The Leg of Doom. A good title for a bad horror film. Perhaps I should go into filmmaking and direct a series of films, all about legs, and nobody would know why. Then, years later, on my deathbed I would reveal the Secret of Simon's Leg, which would be disappointingly mundane, really, I realised. Just the part of his body that I'd pulled out of the alley, no other significance, just the first bit of dead person I'd ever touched. The fact held no meaning for anyone but me. There was no mystery at all, no hidden arcane symbolism. Just a dead body and a murderess. A sleeping murderess. Let her lie.

"But what about his leg?" I said aloud. They all turned to stare at me, which made me giggle. "And the rest of him, of course, I mean," I added. "The body. You're just going to leave the body there? He'll get cold. And damp." I giggled and giggled. "She's all warm and asleep and he's out there in the cold and dark, all dressed up for the party, all covered with blood."

"We will call the police, certainly," said Justin reassuringly. "We don't want him to stay out there either. We'll call the police and they'll look after him, and we'll look after Naomi. And Stefan will look after you."

He and Stefan exchanged glances, and Stefan got up from the bed and came to sit beside me. He put an arm round me and I gratefully leant into it.

"Elinor," he said, holding me close, "I think you need to go home. Why don't I take you home? We can deal with this. Forget it ever happened. Tell you what, I'll drop you at home and I'll call you next week and we'll go out. We'll go and see a show together." His voice was low and soothing, so, so soothing. I snuggled against his slim velvet-clad shoulder. "I like you, Elinor. I'd like to see you again. Let me take you home and put you to bed, and I'll see you soon, and you can forget all about this. Doesn't that sound like a good idea?"

"Yes," I said sleepily, dreamily, snuggling against his warm body. "That sounds like a *wonderful* idea."

Chapter Ten
Sunday in the Park

Search term:
born again

Sunday October 5th— afternoon

It was almost October, but England takes no account of such arbitrary things as seasons, so it was almost sunny enough to be spring, though cold. St James' Park, which had been abandoned to squirrels and civil servants for the previous month or two, was blossoming with pram-wielding mothers, laughing groups of teenagers, and couples in hand-holding harmony, all wandering peacefully through the tidy brown-and-green landscape. There were no flowers, no ice-cream vans and few birds, but Londoners take their sun where they can get it and nobody was complaining.

Marianne and Carol sat on a park bench, looking at the ducks. Marianne hadn't been home yet. She and Carol had been talking all night in a bus shelter, then Carol had bought her breakfast and taken her to church. The church had involved a lot of crying on the part of both Marianne and the rest of the congregation, as Carol expounded on the theme of lost lambs brought back to the fold. The 'back' was dramatic licence, as this was Marianne's first ever attendance at a Resurrected Church.

"I found her," Carol had proclaimed dramatically, "in a den of sinners! I rescued her from blasphemers and idolaters! And now I claim her in the name of the Lord!" Applause sounded around the echoing stone walls, although it didn't quite manage to reach up into the rafters and disturb the bats. The congregation was used to Carol Cingin's style of rhetoric and had learned when to applaud and how much. They were saving their energies for the end of her speech, which they estimated was still some fifteen minutes away.

This was St John's Resurrected Church of Clapham, the venue for Carol's youth groups and hence the unwitting sponsor of CULT, though it was not an especially evangelical church by nature. The people who went there, in the main, were the people who had always gone there: the middle-aged and elderly, who had been attending Sunday services for their entire lives, and the children whose parents wanted them to be brought up 'properly'. When it had simply been a Church of England church, it had had a typical C of E atmosphere, dust, polite boredom tempered with the reassurance of routine, and vague undirected piety. Even when the C of E had been forced to rebrand itself by the CUS, it had managed to hold on to its traditions, as had most of the other English churches. But now it had been adopted by Carol and Himm, and the prevailing mood had changed dramatically.

There was singing — not the comforting monotone of nineteenth-century hymns, but enthusiastic singing, with guitars and recorders played by enthusiastic young people, and clapping, and sometimes cheering. There was a lot more praying, and these new people often prayed aloud, which was felt by the older congregation to be a sort of blasphemy. Everyone knew God preferred you to do these things quietly and unobtrusively, so he didn't have to notice if he didn't feel like it. Carol's devotees demanded Jesus' attention as their right.

At the end of every service, there was a perceptible air of disappointment that he had not materialised in person, or talked back at least. Carol addressed him with such fervour that you felt it would only have been polite to reply at least occasionally. You could see the young evangelists thought so. It wasn't hard to guess that what kept them coming back week after week was their hope that, eventually, Carol would succeed in summoning God to do her bidding. It was Carol who held their interest, and to a lesser extent, Himm, who hovered behind his wife and was allowed to take his turn speaking. Every now and then Carol would sing in church, and sometimes she sang 'Wind Beneath My Wings' in his direction, but it was quite clear that Carol made her own wind. There was a vicar too, Dr King, but he was elderly, traditional and visibly confused by the way in which the Cingins had managed to take over.

As a result of all this, the church's congregation had split in two. They all took part in the same service and repeated the same rituals, but the front three pews were filled with vibrant teenagers waving electronic tambourines, and the rest of the church, whose average

age was roughly thirty years older, watched them in bafflement. The children played up and down the aisles in blithe unawareness of the division, though they did like to have a go on the tambourines.

All of the CULT members except Ruth were in church today. Ruth went to a different church, she said, and had only found CULT in the first place through meeting Hannah somewhere and chatting to her. Hannah had been vague about this, but Hannah often was vague. Carol had tried to persuade her to attend St John's, but she had muttered something about commitments and family obligations and honouring one's father and mother by attending a church of their choosing, an attitude which Carol could hardly overrule. Anyway, the others were here and she was pleased that Marianne would have the chance to meet most of the group. She harboured high hopes for the girl. She was so eager, so malleable and yet so obviously and unshakeably committed to Jesus. A night of talking had revealed that Marianne had previously led a life of more or less total sin un-illuminated by even the faintest ray of Christian light. Carol genuinely felt that she had saved a lost lamb from the slaughter. As far as she was concerned, her protégé was now a warrior for the Lord.

Marianne had agreed wholeheartedly.

Fifteen minutes later Carol had finished her speech, which had taken in such topics as the evils of London, the evils of failing to go to church, the evils of being led astray by agents of Satan, and the evils of deviant sexual practices, as illustrated by the den of iniquity Marianne had been rescued from last night. This last theme united both the front and back halves of the congregation in horrified fascination, combined with extreme embarrassment. A lot of eyes turned to examine Marianne. She looked modestly at the floor, as befitted an innocent girl who had been rescued from a demonic web of sin.

Then there was singing and praying aloud, and then Carol allowed Dr King to take over and give communion. This was the more traditional part of the service, and there was little Carol and Himm could do to change it without attacking the whole basis of mainstream British Christianity, so they were quiet for a while. They had plans for mainstream British Christianity, naturally, but first things first. Then there was another song and the service ended.

And now, after some post-service chatting and tea drinking and various introductions, Marianne and her new mentor were sitting in St James' Park. Carol was initiating Marianne, carefully and cautiously, into CULT, while the ducks watched incuriously and tried to peck their feet.

"There is a lot of evil in the world, Marianne," she started. "More than people realise."

"I'm sure you're right, Carol," said her new recruit with enthusiasm. "There's this guy at work, he's *so* evil. Not that he's done anything, but the way he looks at me is just fucking creepy. Sorry, I mean, er, very creepy. And the managing director too, I'm sure she's stopping me getting promoted. And then all those creeps I went out with. They were all bast— they were all very nasty to me. And then," she added conscientiously, "there are serial killers and rapists and so on, as well." She paused. "God. The world really is evil, isn't it? I feel like I'd never thought about it properly before."

The sun had gone in. The ducks had started fighting each other for pieces of bread. Further down the park she could hear mothers snapping at their children and being snapped at by their husbands in turn. The trees above her were big and dark and old. Even the grass somehow managed to look sinister. Suddenly, Carol seemed like the only beacon of light in a black universe. Marianne could practically see a faint golden glow around her. Her eyes contained certainty, and compassion, and determination. This woman could save the world, Marianne thought.

"Most people don't see all that evil," said Carol quietly, taking her hand. "They can't afford to, because once you see the evil, you can't *stop* seeing it. Soon you see it everywhere. And then you want to do something about it, because otherwise life is not worth living. Everyone in their heart knows that they should be fighting evil, but most people are lazy and unobservant, or their own hearts are too evil to acknowledge the cry for good. Only a rare few are self-aware enough to rip their own wickedness from their souls, and only a few of those are brave enough to help others with the process. But the rewards are great. Once you have undergone this process, nothing you do can be wrong. Every action is blessed by the Lord Jesus, every thought is sanctioned by the Trinity, and" — her voice was rising in volume now — "I promise you this, Marianne, if you make this commitment, death will be the best thing that ever happened to you, because you will see Jesus afterwards.

"Are you afraid of death, Marianne?"

Marianne stared up at the trees. So old, so seemingly permanent, she thought. But they would die, and the flies landing on their branches would die, and the flowers and the ducks and the children who called to each other across the park. And she herself would die. She was overcome by one of those moments of realisation which combine utter banality with horrifying truth.

"Yes. Yes." Her body shook. She was only twenty-seven, but she knew now that she had been afraid of dying for years and years, that life had often seemed meaningless because of the fear, and that whatever else happened, she could no longer cope with a world which contained her own annihilation. She put her head in her hands and started to cry uncontrollably.

Carol stroked the girl's long, dark hair and patted her shoulder. It wasn't the first time she had seen this reaction. Crying was a good sign: she visualised the tears as pure clean water washing out the stain of Marianne's sins. Soon she would be good as new. Better.

A ten-minute interval elapsed while Marianne's tears turned to sniffles and were soaked up by Carol's pocket box of Kleenex.

"Are you feeling better, love?" Carol handed her another tissue.

"Yes... thanks." Marianne wiped her nose. "I don't know what came over me."

"I do," said Carol. "Salvation. The time is right for you. Turn to Jesus. Accept his love. Cleanse your heart of sin, and prepare to join the war against Satan. You can do it, I know you can. You want to achieve something in your life, don't you? Not to die forgotten?"

Marianne nodded hard. "Yes, oh yes. I want to be someone. I want to be remembered. How did you know?"

"Jesus told me." The woman took the girl's hand again and held it tightly. "I want you to get on your knees, right here in this park. Can you do that?"

Marianne gulped, nodded and slowly sank down in front of the bench, still holding Carol's hand. Carol rejoiced to see her face thrown back in ecstasy. They disregarded the nervous giggles of passers-by.

"Say after me, I accept Jesus into my heart."

"I accept Jesus into my heart." Marianne's voice was a firm whisper.

"I will fight the agents of Satan wherever they may be found, using whatever methods are necessary to defeat them. I will keep my heart and my body pure. I will resist evil in all its forms. I am one of God's children."

Marianne repeated it all faithfully, her brown eyes aflame with visionary fervour. Her right hand was clenched, clutching an imaginary sword. She did not pause to wonder whether Carol had any specific evil in mind — she was ready to go wherever she was told and fight whatever she found there. When she had finished her vow, Carol gently pulled her back up on the bench and they hugged for a long time.

"So, Marianne," said Carol finally, "are you ready to be told what the Lord requires of you?"

Marianne's eyes shone. "Yes, oh yes."

"There is a Project," began Carol. She spoke for several minutes, outlining the satanic Project Rupture which would make every Christian in the world believe the Rapture had taken place. Marianne had never heard of the Rapture in the first place, so Carol detoured to summarise the Book of Revelations for her, before climaxing with an impressive image of the post-false-Rapture world, with Christians everywhere denying God, abandoning their faith and effectively winning the war for Hell. Her listener's eyes grew wide.

"So you see," finished Carol, "something must be done to stop all this from happening. I know it sounds unlikely that a small group in a London suburb could have a chance of halting this worldwide conspiracy, but that is how God works. And we have some advantages. Firstly," she leant forward, "we know that the Project is due to be activated here, in London, later this year, so we are in an ideal position to prevent it. Secondly, we have an inside source — Ruth, you'll meet her on Friday — who knows the enemy's secrets. And thirdly," she paused dramatically, "we believe. Many people simply wouldn't have the strength to accept all this and to act on it. You remember what I was saying earlier about people ignoring evil because of laziness."

Marianne nodded.

"So we'll see you on Friday night then? For the next stage in the defeat of Satan's minions?"

Marianne nodded again, clutching Carol's hand as if it were the only certainty she knew. "Friday. I'll be there."

Chapter Eleven
Cat in a Hot Tin Hat

search terms:
psychicvampire.org, vampiresarereal.tripod.com

Saturday October 11th — evening

Stefan had rung me on the Wednesday after the party and proposed going out on the following Saturday. I was so pleased to be asked on a date that I didn't worry too much about his motivation. I was perfectly aware that he had been told to keep me happy so I wouldn't spread the news that Naomi was a murderer, of course. After some thought, I'd decided that I was OK with that, and had further decided that he already liked me, so he would have wanted to see me anyway. Never look a gift goth in the mouth, I told myself. You might find pointy teeth.

However, the extra leverage was useful, since it meant I got final say in what we were going to do on the date (and got Stefan to volunteer to pay for it). My initial proposal of going to see *Return to the Forbidden Plant,* the long-awaited — though badly-reviewed sequel — to *Little Shop of Horrors*, was met with such pointed silence that I took pity on him and asked what he would suggest. He mentioned that a triple bill of goth bands was playing in Camden that night: Bratkartoffelen, Existential Angst and Levi's 501 Button-Fly Corpses. I said "Really? How interesting," and just about managed to avoid informing him that as far as I was concerned, goth music sounded like a dead gerbil slowly falling over.

So in the end, I'd picked a new West End hit, the Dr Seuss/Tennessee Williams mash-up musical tragedy *Cat in a Hot Tin Hat*. I didn't think Stefan was enjoying it much, but I was. I sat enraptured as a spangly chorus tapped its way across the stage, spinning the man in the wheelchair with them.

"Would you, could you with your wife,
To give her kids and end her strife?
Or would you rather with a man,
All sweaty in his black sedan?"

The chorus wheeled Brick round to the front. He had one ankle bandaged, but he tapped with the other foot as he sang.

"I would not, could not with my wife,
Or with a man! You get a life!
I will not, cannot anywhere!
My leg it keeps me in this chair!"

It was all lost on Stefan. He winced perceptibly at every zany rhyme, although I didn't let that stop me from singing along with the choruses and occasionally, when required, dancing in the aisles. My date sat beside me looking tall and gothic, and occasionally raising a cynical eyebrow. Well, I hadn't been expecting our musical tastes to coincide.

However, Stefan cheered up as the play got more depressing, and he was positively upbeat by the end. "I liked the woman in the cat costume," he remarked as we headed along Charing Cross Road for a drink.

"Yeah, nice tail," I agreed.

We turned onto Greek Street and found a basement bar with a late licence, not far from where we'd first met. I ordered a cocktail comprised of butterscotch schnapps, crème de banane and Baileys: partly because I thought it sounded nice, in a diabetes-inducing way, partly because Stefan was paying, and partly because I enjoyed the expression on his face when he had to ask for a Wild Banana Orgasm.

"OK," I said when we'd found in a very small corner of the bar to stand in (this being a Saturday night in central London, we were lucky we weren't huddled under a table). "So, are we going to talk about it then?"

Stefan looked shifty. I'd thought people only did that in books. "It?"

"The murder," I said.

"Elinor!" he hissed agitatedly, shooting worried glances at the fifty or so people in our immediate vicinity.

"They can't hear us, as you know perfectly well. Even if they stopped talking about house prices for a couple of seconds, which they won't, they still couldn't hear us over this retro-techno version of the Bagpuss theme tune."

"Is *that* what that appalling sound is?" He looked pained. "Very well, we can discuss it. Briefly. If we must."

He looked gorgeous tonight. He was all in black as usual, but this time he'd added a dark purple silk shirt to the ensemble rather than the standard white lacy one. His pitch black hair tumbled about his shoulders in a way usually attributed only to Mills & Boon heroines, and his dark blue eyes seemed to contain worlds of pain and desire. But that was probably just me. Anyway, I was glad I was tall for a girl, so I could see the eyes close up. I wasn't nearly beautiful enough to match him, but I did all right, I thought. I'd dragged out one of my few dresses for the occasion, a long very dark green one which went with my red hair in an Anne of Green Gables kind of way, and which showed just the right amount of cleavage — i.e., lots. I like my cleavage. The rest of my body is unremarkable, but my breasts are very nice. I often find myself looking down at them appreciatively, though I try not to do it in company as it seems rude.

I thought I noticed Stefan sneaking glances down my top as well. I leaned forwards to make it easier and we shared a moment of mutual cleavage appreciation. I was almost too distracted to continue the conversation, but then I remembered there was something I wanted to know.

"How much was Joanne told?" I asked.

I hadn't contacted her since the party, and hadn't seen her before going home from it. Stefan had got a taxi for me, taken me home, put me to bed, stroked my hair briefly and left. (When I woke up the next morning there was a note on my bedside table, written in silver pen on black paper — neither of which I owned — saying: "Rest assured that you will hear from me." It had sounded rather threatening. However, I'd correctly surmised that he just meant, "I'll call you" but was constitutionally unable to write anything that concise.)

"Justin talked to her the next day, after Simon's, er, after Simon had been discovered." Stefan shrugged. "He is very persuasive. She has no reason to believe that any of us were involved, whatever she may suspect. As far as she knows, he was on his way to her party and he was stabbed by a mugger. He died from blood loss in the alleyway, unable to attract help."

"Doesn't she know there were bite marks on his neck?"

"There weren't."

"What?"

"Naomi does not have fangs, and biting human skin with normal teeth is hard to do, especially if you're trying to work quickly with an unwilling victim. Naomi used a knife and then drank some of his blood from the wound."

"I'd appreciate it," I said, "if you could sound a little more distressed when you're saying that. It would make me feel better."

"I apologise. Please believe me, I do find it disturbing, especially after last weekend. As Viola told you, Naomi rarely attacks people, and has never killed one before. Usually they recover and are compensated by her father. Simon was unlucky; Naomi must have hit an artery in the dark."

"So the police found him, then?"

"So I am told. Justin told the policeman who questioned him that Naomi was with us all evening. Various vampires are covering for her. Joanne can't contradict that. She was too drunk to have much idea who was where. There's no reason for Naomi to be suspected, and as you know, even if she is, no action will be taken."

I nodded.

"So am I to understand that you're covering for Naomi because you feel responsible for her?" He kind of shrugged and nodded at the same time. "So why are the others covering for her? Why am *I* covering for her?"

"They are doing it for several reasons. They are fond of me, and they know that getting Naomi into trouble would worry me and would probably also involve me. The ones who know about it are all members of Justin's church, and Justin is a friend of mine." There was a very slight pause before the word friend, and I took a guess that 'ex-boyfriend' might also be a perfectly accurate way of describing Justin. "And, of course, having any vampire tried for murder is going to undermine our image, even if they are clearly deranged. All our lives would be made public. There is a lot of motivation for all of us to keep quiet and try to deal with the situation ourselves."

"You didn't answer my second question."

"Why are you covering for Naomi? Well, surely you should be telling *me* that."

I looked up at him, letting my eyes meet his. "I think you know why," I said softly. "You and I have a secret to keep now. And secrets, especially dangerous secrets, can be very... erotic."

Corny, but it worked. "I think you may be right," he murmured, leaning into my ear. I could feel his breath on my neck. "Secrets can be very erotic. And I do like you," he added. "In case you were wondering. You're..."

"Please don't say I'm so different from the other girls and boys you've dated because I'm so forthright and upright and downright and generally right in all kinds of directions. I already know that."

"Oh." He seemed flummoxed, if goths can be flummoxed. "So... how did you know I have dated men as well as women?"

"Let's just call it a hunch." Which was, of course, exactly what it was, but I was trying to sound mysterious.

"Oh. Anyway. If you would rather I did not speak, perhaps I could replace it with..." He put his hand behind my head and kissed me.

The kiss passed my usual test, in that I didn't think of anything else while it was happening. It was a good kiss, in fact. Wholehearted, thorough, intense. I liked it. I let Stefan take me home.

There is a certain amount of etiquette involved in deciding whether you want to take someone back to your home or whether to go to theirs. The factors involved include distance, difficulty — some places in London are close together but complicated to move between — and the presence or absence of disapproving housemates.

There is also the issue of how tidy you think your flat is. Mine looked as though someone had thoroughly ignored it for several months whilst amassing second-hand books, forgetting to buy bathroom cleaner and failing to throw away the remains of a lot of takeaways. (Which was roughly what had happened.) So I accepted Stefan's invitation to go back to his.

It turned out that his flat was in Hammersmith. West London was still a bit of a mystery to me — in fact, so far, I'd only really mastered the Soho area and the bit of South London I lived in — but I'd been through Hammersmith on the bus and didn't think much of it: it seemed to be mainly concrete by-passes. However, it turned out that other parts of the area were next to the river and featured trees and gardens. This was where Stefan's flat was. Presumably sound engineering was wildly lucrative, or — more likely — he had rich and generous parents. I was impressed.

Moreover, the flat was both clean and tidy. And not as black as I'd expected. The walls weren't magnolia or anything, but they weren't dark; they were pale blue. The furniture was from Ikea. I hadn't thought all vampire-identified goths lived in rat-infested dungeons, but I'd been preparing myself for some degree of glamorous, decadent squalor. Instead there were wooden floors, and a tasteful red sofa, and Japanese prints on the walls.

"Was it you who decorated this place?" I asked. Stefan looked as if he'd heard that question before.

"Yes. People from work come here, and my parents when they visit. One can be a vampire anywhere, you know. The trappings are just that, trappings."

"So why do you wear the outfit?"

"I like it."

"Fair enough." I glanced covertly at the doors either side of the living room. One of them had to be the bedroom. Which?

"Would you like a drink?" Stefan opened one of the wooden doors to reveal a small but perfectly formed kitchen, inadvertently answering my query. "I have herbal tea and carrot juice, and vodka."

I remembered something I'd overheard from back before we'd technically met. "You're a vegan. I'd forgotten."

"I am, yes." He gestured towards a work surface which had jars on it with neat white stickers saying things like 'Brown Rice', 'Lentils' and 'Kidney Beans'. Suddenly I could have killed for a cheese-smothered steak. Wrapped in veal.

"I'll have a vodka on ice, please." Thank God he wasn't a teetotaller as well.

He reached down small glasses and started pouring what looked like quite expensive vodka.

Suddenly and horribly, I remembered something else he'd said in that café.

"Um, Stefan?"

He turned to hand me my drink and my hand brushed his. Smooth, pale skin. Dark eyes gazing into mine. I hoped my memory had been wrong.

"I... overheard you talking at the café that time, before I introduced myself. You were saying that you got pranic energy from lettuce —"

He looked faintly embarrassed. "I should not have tried to explain that to Joanne and Simon. I am not sure Joanne understood what I was trying to say."

"Oh, I think she did," I said, remembering Joanne's expression. "Anyway, after that you, er, you said that you were... celibate."

Pause.

"Yes."

"Oh."

He came closer and touched my shoulder lightly. "That is, I'm celibate in a metaphorical sense."

Oh, thank goodness. I was so relieved I didn't even care that what he'd said made absolutely no sense.

"Sex for me is food, you see. Sexual contact can produce intense pranic energy, and that nourishes me."

Whatever.

"I understand." I moved a little closer.

"Speaking of nourishment," he added, "I take it you do not wish to feed the Thirst in a more... direct manner? I do not have a regular blood donor at the moment and the Thirst is strong in me."

I tried to look sympathetic, rather than shouting, "Please God, stop trying to sound like a character from a bad vampire novel!" I thought I did rather well. My wince was brief and I managed to turn it into a cough before he picked up on it.

"No. Sorry."

"No problem."

"So, not celibate then," I said, getting back to the salient point.

A half-smile twitched at the corner of his mouth. "If you mean that you would like to share sexual energy with me, that is certainly my plan too. But in order for the energy to be successfully produced and stored, there are certain things that have to happen."

This was starting to sound like work. Did he have a small pranic energy factory in his bedroom or something?

This time, he did catch my expression. He smiled. "It is simply that I cannot allow any of my... essence... to leave me. I would lose too much power. Vampires are very wedded to bodily fluids and their loss weakens us."

"I think I understand," I said.

"I hope that will not be a problem?"

I shrugged. "Not at all, provided I'm not expected to show solidarity."

"No, no. The most intense energy for me will come from your pleasure. Your waves will flow through me and I shall be revived. Of course, you may feel a little drained afterwards..."

I smiled broadly, took his hand and dragged him towards the bedroom. "It's a risk I'm prepared to take."

* * *

Although I have a tendency to giggle during sex, while Stefan regarded it as a semi-divine process of spiritual renewal, we turned out to be surprisingly compatible. And that's as much detail as I'm going into about that particular three hours. Writing about sex is like dancing about economics. And anyway, it seems in bad taste, now, to reminisce about Stefan's sexual prowess.

The next morning was mildly awkward in the way that next mornings often are, but nothing I couldn't handle. Given that my previous sexual experiences had been conducted while living with my parents, I was just happy to have slept with someone I could actually stay the night with.

I was also looking forward to seeing what Stefan looked like without eyeliner and white foundation. However, it turned out that it didn't make much difference, since he had very dark eyelashes and very pale skin in any case.

"Just for show then, the make-up?" I said, stretching luxuriantly on my side of the wide, soft bed.

"It makes a statement," he admitted. "Trappings can be important."

"As a goth, or as a vampire?"

"Both. In most subcultures, what distinguishes you is partly to do with the appearance you project." He got out of bed, put on a dark red silk dressing gown and started making coffee. "Is soy milk acceptable?"

"Er, I'll just have orange juice, thanks. So is it true then, that London's teeming with alternative cultures?"

"Of course. They have nowhere else to go. You know what the rest of the country is like."

I did, unfortunately.

The American version of religion had taken hold of Britain like King Kong taking hold of Fay Wray — we had been overpowered and we simply hadn't had the strength to resist. Maybe we hadn't really wanted to. We'd been flattered by the interest, to be frank. Britain had long since lost its grip on the world, and we missed it. Here was a chance to find our identity again. Or at least to assume someone else's, which is always exciting. And so the Church of England, an institution going back more years than most Americans could even imagine, had been 'rejuvenated' and renamed as the Resurrected Church, and there was a law being debated which, if passed, would mean that anyone who refused to join would be prosecuted for heresy. As a result, the country was aflame with various forms of religious fervour and alternative cultures were being steadily squeezed out. London was practically the only place left where they survived at all. This life I'd discovered, of sexual exploration and illegal substances and weird, interesting, damaged people, was seriously endangered.

I felt it was time for some wildlife conservation. "Stefan?"

"Yes?"

"You know how I wanted to meet vampires and then I found you lot?"

"Mmm?"

"Well, I was thinking I'd like to find a few more subcultures. Go deeper into the woods. The... urban woods. Well, anyway, you know what I mean."

"What did you have in mind?"

I picked an example. "Werewolves, say?"

He nodded. "There are some of those around, yes. They overlap with us to some extent, in fact. It is possible to be a were-vampire."

"How does that work exactly?"

"Well, you have to get bitten by one, and then you turn into a vampire at the full moon."

I looked across at him, but he appeared to be perfectly serious. And after all, this was a man who believed that blood, sex and lettuce were all equally valid sources of spiritual and physical energy.

"So how did the first one happen, if you have to be bitten by them to become one?"

"I believe a lycanthrope and a vampire mated, and their baby contained the powers of both."

"OK," I said calmly. "Do you know of any other groups with, er, unconventional beliefs?"

"There are the various conspiracy theorists. The Christian-based ones —"

"No. No Christians. Nothing like that."

"How about aliens?"

"Aliens sound good. People who believe in fairies. People who believe they *are* fairies. Anyone with beliefs that aren't mainstream."

Stefan propped himself up on an elbow. "Why?"

"Why am I looking for these people? I told you when I met you. I moved to London recently, I want to meet people, and I want the people I meet to be interesting. Say what you like about someone who identifies as a werewolf, they're not going to be boring."

"You might be surprised."

"Anyway. Just because I personally don't believe in it, doesn't mean I'm not fascinated by it all."

"And there's no other reason?"

"No. No other reason." I untangled myself from the duvet, rolled out of bed with a distinct lack of gracefulness and said, "Do you mind if I have a bath?"

"Please go ahead." Stefan waved in the direction of the bathroom. I started gathering up the energy to get that far. Mornings are not my best thing.

"So, you'll take me to meet some of these people?"

"I will tell you when and where they meet, certainly, but I cannot guarantee that I will want to go with you. Some of those people are very strange."

I glanced at him one more time, but he was definitely serious. "OK, just tell me where to go. Maybe I can take Joanne with me."

"You might have to gag her." We grinned at each other. Stefan had made a joke. I made a note to remember this moment.

"Here." He reached under the bed, pulled out a magazine and handed it to me. "Read this in the bath."

I raised an eyebrow. "If you want me to get in the mood again, you just have to say so."

"No, nothing like that. It's an alternative culture magazine. It contains personal ads for lycanthropes, details of meetings, articles on problems vampires have, that kind of thing."

"You have a magazine? I didn't realise."

"There are a large number of us in London now. Ever since the Christian United States decided to take control of the internet, track down everyone it considered weird and throw them out."

"I knew about the expulsion of the Jews and the Hindus and the Muslims and the pagans and the queer people. I didn't realise they'd bothered with the smaller minority groups as well."

"They bothered with everyone." He sounded bitter. I knew how he felt.

The CUS was closed these days: closed, anyway, to everyone who wasn't prepared to undergo an exhaustive ten-hour interrogation about their religious beliefs, which was almost everyone. So hardly anyone got in. They still threw people out, but the rate had slowed since the initial waves. However, the initial waves had comprised millions of people being thrown out of one of the most spacious countries on earth and forced to seek shelter and jobs in some of the most crowded places on earth — the UK, Hong Kong, India.

The CUS seemed to have done fairly well out of the deal. Its population, now, was two-thirds what the US's had been. We saw pictures of said population on the TV and they looked very cheerful. Houses were getting bigger, it seemed, and food even more plentiful now that there was more space and fewer people. Of course, the people whose houses we were being shown were the ones who'd voted for and masterminded the whole plan in the first place — I had no doubt that the people who were cleaning those houses and providing that food were nowhere near as cheerful about their new nation. However, these days Americans only had one voice, and that was the official voice of the official government, which was under the control of the God'n'Guns party. I hoped they were happy.

Well, actually, they probably were, apart from the lack of people to castigate. But they'd probably find a new group soon and persecute them instead: people who wore hats, people who liked to take showers, something like that.

I was so angry thinking about all this that I almost forgot to enjoy my bath, which was large and full of satsuma-scented bubbles. In an effort to clear my mind, I opened Stefan's magazine, which was called simply *Below* — the mainstream presumably being Above.

It was something of a revelation. The crackdown on everything alternative had clearly caused the development of some very distinct underground cultures, all of which had to somehow coexist with each other with varying degrees of success. The magazine's editorial was a plea for all were-things to live peacefully together and specifically for the werewolves to stop trying to kill and eat the (steadily diminishing, apparently) were-rabbit warren. There were the articles entitled "How to Avoid Vampire Hunters' and "Why Faeries and Dragons Never Make Friends". (A question of size, I imagined?) And there were personal ads featuring, among others, a were-tortoise, a were-ferret and a were-shark. Their pleas to meet others of their kind sounded a bit desperate. Perhaps they could get classified as endangered species, I thought, and then the government would pay for their personal ads to help them reproduce...

I couldn't wait to dive in.

Chapter Twelve
Fighting the Forces of Darkness

"Weapons of War... A wooden stake. Although it is debated that it should be Ash, Hawthorne, or Rosewood to be effective. Any hardwood should do though. I would advise it be plunged straight to the heart, but I've heard that the vampire has a strange chemical reaction to wood, so if you need a second or two plunge it into the abdominal area or leg. It'll give you that second to catch your breath."
http://members.tripod.com/~ChrisLight7/destroy.htm

Search term:
vampyreverse

Up to October 17th

The Friday after Marianne's conversion in the park, Carol announced to the CULT meeting (their fifth) that they had a new recruit. They waited till 10pm to start the meeting, to give her time to find the church hall. Eventually Carol admitted defeat; though even after they had started, she kept glancing towards the door to see if Marianne was arriving.

She wasn't.

After a while, Carol stopped checking the door and her voice acquired an edge of betrayed bitterness. She was not used to being stood up. At the end of the meeting Carol gave a pointed speech about the folly of trusting people who turned out to be fly-by-night Christians without the spiritual strength to stay saved for more than a day or two. She then announced that seven was traditionally a holy number and that God clearly intended CULT to be composed of a holy number, so there would be no more recruiting. Everyone agreed that Marianne's defection was a sign from God and tactfully changed the subject.

In Marianne's life, a week was a long time. She had caught fire that Sunday in the light of Carol's fervour, but the flame was not really for Carol or for CULT, or even for Christ. What remained with her, in the next few days after Carol's influence had begun to fade, was her sudden, shocking awareness of evil.

The concepts of good and evil were not ones she had spent much time considering, previously. She worked in marketing. She was used to living in a world that consisted entirely of grey area. The people she worked with were presumably aware that some things might be better, morally speaking, than other things, but mentioning the fact would have been in very bad taste. This had always suited Marianne perfectly, as she was amoral by nature. Nobody with her ability for protective colouration could be otherwise. Before the fetish club adventure, she had been a post-punk raver; before that, she had hung around with a retro-1940s film noir crowd who talked in faux-Bogart accents, femme-fataled all over the place and pretended to betray each other to the police. Before that, she had almost given up her job to move to a Welsh commune with some anarcho-vegan lesbians who lived on acid and worshipped the Sister in the form of a small beetroot. Before *that* her memories got a bit hazy, but she remembered various periods of being an academic, radical feminist, couch potato, nihilist and right-wing poet, plus a brief flirtation with hallucinogens during which she believed she was a Weeble.

All in all, it had not been what anyone would call an integrated life. And none the worse for that, perhaps, but there had been side-effects. A lack of long-term friends and relationships, no sense of internal consistency, no feeling of achievement that lasted more than a day or two. Marianne was starting to wonder if she'd missed out somewhere. What had Carol offered that felt so right?

What was it she needed?

Sitting at her desk at work, she found that only half her attention was on the development of a campaign to promote a new brand of monster-themed biscuits. The other half was sifting through her psyche, separating the wheat from the chaff to discover the answer to her question. It wasn't the religious extremism that had resonated, she'd done that before — paganism, witchcraft, spiritualism and neo-Druidic rites had all formed part of her past, and had failed to provide more than a few weeks of fulfilment. A sense of being wanted and included, perhaps? But she'd had that before and could get it anywhere. She'd never had a problem being accepted into groups.

No. It was to do with identity. She'd had a glimpse of what it might be like to have a solid, consistent sense of self based on something real. Based on opposition to evil. Because evil was definitely incontrovertibly real, so opposing it — fighting it — that was the best kind of identity you could have. Look at superheroes. Look at the things they defeated.

Marianne stared thoughtfully at the images of cartoon monster-shaped biscuits on her PC.

At this point, her head of department wandered by.

"Everything going all right, is it, darling?" He liked Marianne. She made a point of not minding when he admired her cleavage or danced too close at the office Christmas party.

"Everything's great, thanks, Bill. Just looking at some ideas for these —" she gestured at her screen "— things. Are people really going to buy zombie-shaped, white chocolate cookies?"

"If we want them to, they will," he said, patting her on the shoulder. "You know that. Are the white chocolate chips supposed to be like bits of brain? That the zombies have eaten?"

"Eeew. Yes, I guess so. And the berries in the vampire cranberry shortbread pieces are supposed to be bits of blood, presumably. I'm surprised we're even allowed to market these. How are the CUS going to feel about edible demonic images?"

"They'll probably ban them eventually." He shrugged. "But the manufacturers are hoping it'll take them a while to get round to it, and after all, the Resurrected Church of America doesn't technically have any jurisdiction over the UK. Yet. Let's sell demonic cookies while we may and worry about excommunication tomorrow, shall we? Otherwise we'll never get anything done."

"True. OK, so what kind of market are we looking at here?"

"Er... Goths with children?"

"That seems a little specific, but I'm sure I can find an angle."

"Good girl. I'll catch up with you later, OK?"

"Cool."

Left alone, Marianne's thoughts began to drift back to her own problems, until she glanced round to find that Bill's PA was standing in line of sight of her PC, chatting to someone. She sighed and decided she'd better do a bit of research, at least for a few minutes. First step: seeing what the internet could throw up on the topic of vampires. Or vampires covered in cranberries. Shortbready vampires covered in cranberries. Probably best just to start with a search on vampires and see how that went.

The first page of hits was entirely composed of Biblical sites largely unrelated to the topic of the search. Which was standard these days. CUS-based search engines were legally obliged to show only Christian sites in their results. UK engines weren't, but a lot tended to come up anyway. The next three pages featured vampire movies, vampire books, vampire role-playing games and (almost certainly unenforceable) offers to buy vampires on various sponsored shopping sites. Marianne hit 'Next' and waited.

At the top of the third page was a site called '*Be A Vampire Exterminator!*'

The blurb read: *"Fight evil and Earn 'cash' in your spare time! Hunting vampires can make you over 2000% return on your outlay, and only takes a few 'hours' a week. Tap into this high-income opportunity! Own car essential."*

The phrase 'fight evil' caught Marianne's eye at once. She clicked.

There were pictures. There were weapons specifications. There were articles on safety while hunting. There was a drawing of an animalistic-looking male vampire, fangs bared and bloody, clearly ready to kill, with a terrified-looking girl swooning on the floor in front of him. It wasn't a great drawing and the way the vampire's teeth were drawn made him look a bit like a rabbit, but Marianne's imagination bypassed that easily. There were details of where to send the first £150 payment for the book on Vampire Killing in One Easy Step, but she ignored that —she was gullible in many ways, but that wasn't one of them — and read the blurb instead.

"I'm a vampire exterminator and you can be too!" wrote the slightly wild-eyed man whose badly-scanned photo adorned the top left-hand corner of the page. The words were dark red on a black background. Marianne squinted.

"I was unemployed and sitting at home wondering what to do with my 'life', when I received an 'email' from a friend telling me about Vampires! The more I read, the more I realised that 'Vampire Extermination' could provide me with a useful, fulfilling and lucrative 'career', working to my own hours and earning my own commission. You can do it too!"

At this point the text was interrupted with a cartoon of a stick figure stabbing another stick figure with — as it happened — a stick. Under the drawing it continued:

'Vampires are everywhere — just look around you 'on the street' and see how many people are dressed in black and how many look pale

and 'drained'. And you will notice that these people are mainly out when the sun has set! Sounding familiar? Look for the telltale signs of blood stained lips (some 'female vamps' wear dark red lipstick to try and conceal the stains, so be aware!). If one of these 'people' gives you a hungry or otherwise 'vampiric' type glance, then you know you've found you're vampire!"* (Marianne winced.) *"Please note we do not advocate killing real people, so its best to follow your 'quarry' until you actually see them attempting to drain a humans blood. For more tips on this, plus a full list of weapons to use, simply send a 'cheque' for..."* Marianne's glance slid off the page.

She already knew what killed vampires, anyway. Stakes. Sunlight. Garlic, unless that just slowed them down. Decapitation. And you could burn them with crosses, too. But mainly, stakes. This was, of course, assuming that vampires existed. Which most people seemed to think was unlikely. But the ranting man on the website had seemed so sure... Marianne gazed into her soul and found that she had added vampires to the list of things she believed in. She had put a lot of practice into believing unusual things, so it wasn't that much of a stretch.

And if they existed, they could be killed. By her. How was *that* for fighting evil? She would find a vampire and stalk it till it killed, or preferably almost killed, someone. Then she would attack it and stake it through the heart and it would disappear in a cloud of smoke and she was fairly sure that the feeling of achievement she got then would last for quite a long time. Especially if the person she rescued was incredibly grateful and saw her as their hero. That would be nice.

Yes. She would be a hero. She would save people. She would defeat the forces of darkness armed only with a pointy stick and a righteous expression. Eventually, there would be a statue put up of her: 'Marianne Swift, Saviour of the People of London'. Or something — she could work on the wording later, and decide between marble and bronze. And best of all, the whole thing was all her own idea, so nobody would start telling her what to do or correcting her, nobody would tell her she was wrong because everyone knew it was good to fight evil, and she was sure that this was a cause she could believe in for a long time.

She spent the afternoon looking up vampires online — occasionally pulling up some information about vampiric food products in case anyone was watching — and quickly came to the conclusion that not only did they exist, there were *lots* of them.

And lots lived in the UK. She read a press release from the God'n'Guns Party on the subject of vampires. Apparently drinking blood was forbidden by the Bible, so they'd exiled anyone who admitted to being a vampire, which included virtually everyone they could track down who'd ever posted on a vampire-related newsgroup, mailing list or online community of any kind. Most of them were guilty of other unchristian behaviour as well, anyway, they said.

She also read a BBC news story from a year or two previously which reported that a large proportion of alternative communities had fled to London after being thrown out of America. Some vampires had tried the more-traditional Eastern Europe, but apparently they'd found it too cold.

A further search for 'London vampires' brought up some stuff about the vampire bats in London Zoo and a promotional website for something called the iTem, which Marianne had vaguely heard of during a brief phase of being a retro-geek, and which sounded promising. She skipped through the small print (which, incidentally, contained dire warnings about the long prison sentences involved in using an iTem to commit a crime) and found an address on Tottenham Court Road where iTems were to be obtained.

Tottenham Court Road was just round the corner. It was a slow Friday afternoon and the office was quiet. Marianne left a note on her desk saying, 'Gone to do research for promotion' — the standard company excuse for skiving, which was usually seen through but rarely challenged — and set off to acquire her new toy. Or rather, weapon.

Chapter Thirteen
Some Were

*"WereCreatures are mostly a pretty nice bunch of creatures (unlike most
vampyres) and they are rarely mentally ill or anything like that. The best
way to picture Werewolves are closer to something like your cats, (dogs
are tame animals, hardly any wild left in them, cats are wild still and
fairly Wolflike) things that are harmless and friendly, yet wild with a
nightlife all their own, and a few 'disgusting' but harmless habits like
constantly dragging dead rabbits into the house as loving gifts to win
your approval."*
http://www.geocities.com/Area51/Lair/6918/handbook.html

*"Weres do seem to be able to 'shift'. There are a few different kinds of
'shifting' which include astral shifting, mental shifting, and the elusive
physical shifting. Were phenotypes do tend to be predators, but there
have been some non-predatorial animals such as ducks, mice, and
other such types observed as phenotypes... Weres tend to be loners in the
outside world and seem to instinctively seek out others like them or who
understand their uniqueness."*
http://www.geocities.com/lady_shadowmyst/TWSP/what.html

Search terms:
otherkin, astral shifting, therianthropes, otakin, hollow earth

Thursday October 16th — evening

Joanne was waiting for me when I arrived at Tottenham Court Road
tube station, dressed in what I now thought of as her usual black
and red — perhaps a little more black and less red than the previous
times I'd seen her. She looked more subdued than usual, too. Of
course, I hadn't known her for long enough to be confident about
what she was usually like. On the other hand, I did know that one

of her best friends had been killed less than two weeks earlier, so it was a fair guess that she wasn't in her most upbeat mood.

I hadn't seen her since the party, but I'd sent an email of condolence and we'd been chatting intermittently online. I hadn't been sure that she would agree to come out with me tonight. I didn't really know how long you were supposed to wait after the death of a close friend before you starting socialising again. But in fact she'd admitted by email that she was starting to get cabin fever from all the staying in and moping, and that she felt she could do with an evening out, particularly one that involved meeting new people and making fun of them. Everyone has their own ways of dealing with grief.

Simon's funeral had been held the previous week. Joanne didn't volunteer any details about it and I didn't ask for any. I don't like funerals. They make it difficult to keep up the ironic detached amusement that I prefer to cultivate when possible. I wondered how Joanne had managed. We didn't discuss the circumstances of his death either. I assumed that Joanne wanted to avoid the subject because it was painful, and I knew I wanted to avoid it because I didn't want to lie to her unnecessarily.

Anyway, the evening ahead was going to be a conversation starter all on its own.

"Did you set this up then?" she asked. "Tonight, I mean."

The iTem flashed to indicate a right turn off Oxford Street. I guided us down the badly-lit street towards the backstreet pub that was hosting the monthly 'For the Others' meetup, which was where we were headed.

"No, no." I flourished the magazine I'd borrowed from Stefan. "I found the details in here. It's for all kinds of alternative people, not specifically for weres or vampires or anything, so there should be a good range of, you know, weirdness. Plus, I emailed a few people from the personals section and told them they'd probably find their soulmates if they turned up tonight. I thought we could try and set a were-cat up with a were-mouse, what do you think?"

Joanne raised an eyebrow. "Might work if they're both into cartoon violence. So, what's our excuse for being here? I mean, if we just turn up and go 'hi, we'd like to mock you, please,' I don't see us getting much of a reception."

"I thought we could be lesbian were-lizards."

Joanne raised the other eyebrow.

I grinned. "Well, vampires just seem so... standard now."

"Yeah, I know what you mean." We both took a moment to admire our jaded attitude towards the undead.

The iTem flashed green to indicate that we'd arrived. I led Joanne down a small, dark side street, where a dingy sign proclaimed 'The King's Arms'.

"This looks like it," I said confidently, hoping I was right. I thought I probably was: the pub was black and forbidding with a tiny oak door, like the Stephen King version of a hobbit hole. Joanne pushed at the door gingerly and it opened with a slow ominous creak, just as both of us were expecting. There was a narrow flight of stairs down to the right with a handwritten sign saying 'To The Others'. We glanced at each other and started making our way gingerly down the steps.

"Fine, lesbian were-lizards it is," Joanne whispered.

"OK, so just remember, at the full moon our tongues get longer and we get scaly and start craving flies." I hoped it wasn't a full moon tonight, or people might start asking awkward questions.

"And why the lesbianism?"

"It'll stop us being chatted up."

"What if I want to be chatted up?"

"Well, if you see anyone you like, tell him you're getting tired of being a lesbian reptile."

"Fair enough."

We'd reached the bottom of the stairs by now and were outside another door, which was just as small and sinister as the first. Beyond it was the muffled hum of conversation, some strange dragging sounds and what sounded like growling, yapping and purring. Joanne made a sudden backwards motion, so I grabbed her arm and whispered, "They're just people! Well, sort of." She nodded faintly, and I opened the door.

Not entirely unexpectedly, the room beyond was low and dark. It was quite large, though, and full of people. Some of them looked completely normal. Others looked completely normal except for a detail or two (pointy ears, cat's eyes). And some were more dramatic — naked except for a furry loincloth, or dressed in white with wings and halos, or with all-over body tattoos in a tiger-stripe pattern. Some people were milling about, some were huddled in small groups in corners and others were crawling on the floor, making the animal noises we'd heard outside.

Joanne took a firm grip of my hand. "I don't know whether to laugh hysterically or run away screaming," she hissed.

"I suggest neither. Let's get a drink." I made my way towards the small bar along the left-hand wall, Joanne clutching my hand as if it were her only chance of getting out alive. I was rather enjoying the fact that I was calmer than she was.

I reached the bar to find a man in a cat costume was rubbing himself against my leg. "Purr?" he said hopefully when I looked down. I thought for a second, flicked my tongue out at him and hissed aggressively. He scooted backwards very quickly, and I smiled at the barmaid, who was dressed in black and looked bored. I guessed she had seen enough of their meetings to have lost all interest.

"Hi," I said. "Gin and tonic, please. And —"

I turned enquiringly to Joanne. A tall man wearing large white wings, a robe and a fluffy pink halo was leaning over her shoulder, murmuring in her ear. I had an extremely horrible feeling that he'd just asked her if she'd hurt herself when she fell from heaven. I said, "What do you want to drink?" but she just stared blankly at me. I shrugged in the direction of the barmaid. "Oh well, make it two G and Ts."

It occurred to me that Joanne had lost some of her previous poise. Perhaps it was only vampires she could deal with. Or maybe Simon's death had changed her. I could sympathise, though I didn't have anything similar to help me empathise. Nobody close to me had ever died, and my life so far had been relatively unexciting. I hoped to change that soon, though.

Waiting to be served drinks always makes me pensive. I leant on the bar and stared thoughtfully at the row of pumps in front of me. It was OK for Christians. They didn't have to worry about achieving anything during their lifetimes. They had heaven to look forward to, or so they believed. Even Naomi had hell, and though I doubted she was looking forward to it exactly, at least she felt God was showing an interest. I, on the other hand, had never managed to convince myself that there was anything after death at all. The resulting sense of impending annihilation had filled me with an intense and somewhat annoying need to make my life meaningful in some way.

"Eight pounds, please," said the barmaid, waving a hand in front of my face to attract my attention.

I glanced round the roomful of oddly dressed people and smiled at her. "This is all a bit strange, isn't it?"

She gave an impassive shrug. "You should know — you're one of them, aren't you?"

"It's my first time," I said. "I'm feeling a bit overwhelmed." I glanced back at Joanne, who seemed to have regained some of her cool and was chatting to a stocky, dark, fairly normal-looking man with the words "Were Am I?" on his T-shirt.

"Oh well, they're mostly harmless," said the barmaid dismissively. "Let me give you a quick tour. The people who talk to animals usually hang around that corner." She pointed. "The people who believe they *are* animals tend to stand next to them — you can see why those two groups would get on well."

"When you say talk to animals..."

"Oh, they believe the animals talk back. So the were thingies are a godsend to them, because they actually *do* talk back, of course. Well, sometimes."

"OK, what about that lot?" I pointed at another corner which featured small clusters of people who didn't seem to have any immediately animal-related theme going on.

"Elves, fairies, angels, djinns, dryads..."

"They believe in them?"

"They think they are them."

"Right."

"Then there are the ones who believe in aliens, though as far as I know none of them believe they *are* aliens. Could be wrong though. Over there." This was a largish group of men and women, most with tee-shirts featuring traditional alien faces.

In the fourth corner were two men standing close together but pointedly ignoring each other, each clutching his pint and staring straight ahead. "Who on earth are they?" I asked.

The barmaid sighed with an air of resignation. "The one on the left is the only surviving member of the Flat Earth society. The one on the right is the only surviving member of the Hollow Earth society. They don't socialise with the others much, but they seem to enjoy coming to the meetings and standing in the corner next to each other. Sometimes they have screaming matches, but that usually just means they shout 'Flat!', 'Hollow!', 'Flat!', 'Hollow!' at each other for a while."

"You seem to know a lot about them."

She shrugged again. "I've worked here for five years. The meetings happen every month, and at some point most of the people here have got drunk and started telling me about their lives. I found it all fascinating at first but the novelty's worn off now, to be honest."

"I can see it would, if you don't share their beliefs."

"Well, it's not like they even share each others', is it? This is the closest they can get to being in a roomful of people who don't think they're weird, and in fact, practically everyone here thinks everyone else is weird anyway. Have a chat to them and you'll see what I mean."

"Thanks." I finally turned to give Joanne her drink. She smiled thanks at me and nodded to the guy she was chatting to. "Elinor, this is James. He's a vampire."

"Really? I thought from your T-shirt..." I remembered what Stefan had said. "Oh, I see. You're a were-vampire? You turn into one at the full moon?"

"God, no," he said in a broad Yorkshire accent. "Those people are insane. Spend their lives telling people how unusual and interesting they are because once a month they decide to start craving blood. Anyone can crave blood once a month. It's hardly an effort."

"So...?" I said enquiringly, dipping my eyes to his "Were Am I?" shirt.

"I'm a vampire who takes animal form. It's a rare talent these days, I can tell you."

"Oh. Oh, I see. You can take *bat* form? Wow."

Joanne looked mildly embarrassed — clearly she'd just had this conversation. "Not actually a bat as such, Elinor, no," she said. Her lips twitched.

"A wolf? A fox?" I tried to think what other animals might fit in with the vampire canon.

"No, no," James said impatiently, "it's got to be a bloodsucker, hasn't it? That's the whole point."

"Oh, right. Of course."

There was a pause. I wondered if I was supposed to be guessing or if James was just trying to put off telling me the answer. I could only think of one other blood-sucking animal, and I really didn't want to suggest it or find out I was right. But as the silence lengthened, the word "...mosquito?..." came shyly out of my mouth, and immediately wished it hadn't.

"Absolutely right!" said James with determined cheerfulness. "It makes me quite unique among vampires, you know."

"I'm sure it does. So, you actually, you actually, you actually..." I seemed to have got stuck. I looked at him imploringly.

"Change?"

"Er, yes. You, er, do that, then?"

"More or less, yes. I shut myself away to make sure I don't hurt anyone — I mean, a mosquito my size could cause serious problems for people."

I nodded in agreement, picturing the damage that a 190-pound mosquito could cause if it wanted to. (Mainly because of the chaos caused by people running away extremely fast screaming 'Giant mosquito! Giant mosquito! Waah!')

"Isn't this a problem for your work?" I asked.

"Oh, it only happens at night. I may behave a little oddly during the day, but I'm a clairvoyant and Tarot reader by profession, so nobody notices." He smiled engagingly. "Here, have a card." He produced an extremely normal-looking business card which listed him as 'James Gray, Freelance Psychic' with an address in Brixton. Must be successful, I thought. Brixton was intensely trendy these days. I put the card away carefully in my wallet.

"...So I don't know exactly what happens or what I look like," he was saying. "I go into a trance during which I experience life as a large bloodsucking insect. Then, when the full moon goes down, I'm normal again. Well, you know, normal for a vampire."

"But surely traditional vampiric animal forms aren't tied to the full moon?" I asked innocently.

"Well, my girlfriend's a were-rat, so I adjusted to suit her," he said, with the air of one who feels his explanation is perfectly satisfactory and rational.

"Right. Yes." A rat and a mosquito. God, I thought, their cleaning bills must be huge.

"Shall we mingle?" said Joanne brightly, grabbing my arm. We both smiled our goodbyes at James and moved away. When we were out of earshot she hissed, "He's got a girlfriend!"

I looked at her. "*That* was your problem with him?"

"Well, OK, he was also a part-time insect. But a good man is hard to find."

"Yes, fair enough, but he wasn't even claiming to be a man, let alone good. Or, indeed, hard."

"Look who's talking." Joanne shot me a sharp glance. "You shagged Stefan, didn't you?"

"Er, maybe," I said guiltily. "OK, you have a point, but Stefan's a lot less mad than most of these people."

"Is he, or do you just fancy him more?"

"I refuse to answer that question on the grounds that it may incriminate me."

She grinned. "So, who do you want to talk to next?"

"I think those two." I flicked a finger to indicate the Flat Earth and Hollow Earth men, who hadn't moved since we'd arrived.

"And they would be...?"

"One of them thinks the world is —" I made a 'flat' motion with my hand, "and the other thinks it's —" I made a 'round' shape with the same hand.

"One of them thinks the earth is round? How unusual."

"Hollow. You try making a 'hollow' shape with one hand."

"Oh, OK. Right."

We reached the corner. The two men looked surprised to see us. I guessed they didn't get a lot of visitors. I put my drink down firmly on the small brown table between them.

"Hi," I said, putting my hand out. "I'm Elinor, this is Joanne, we're lesbian were-lizards, we just thought we'd come and say hello. Hello!"

The man on the left, the one the barmaid had said was the flat earth guy, stared at me and said nothing. He was quite flat himself — fine pale brown hair, thin, expressionless. The one on the right smiled broadly and shook my hand. He was dark-haired with an eager, friendly expression and a damp handshake.

"Hi, Elinor and Joanne! I'm Paul McManus, nice to meet you. So, lesbian lizards, eh? That must be interesting."

"It passes the time," I said briskly. "So, I hear you have a whole hollow-earth thing going? That sounds like it must be fascinating."

Suddenly his face lit up with the authentic flame of obsession. "Very much so. Whatever some people may think." Paul glanced at the flat earth man, who was still ignoring all of us. "Did you know that as you get closer to the North Pole, it actually gets hotter?"

There was a brief pause.

"No," Joanne said, "we weren't aware of that."

"Oh yes. There are warm winds and open sea at the centre of both poles, too. Little known fact. And that's because of the openings, you see."

"The openings?" I said, as that seemed to be expected.

"The openings that lead to the centre of the earth. Where the little people live."

"The little people?" Joanne came in on cue.

"The little people. They're from Venus originally, of course —" ("Of course," we both said simultaneously,) "— but they moved here a few million years ago. Their civilisation is much more advanced than ours. Some day we may be worthy of their notice, but currently they regard us with justified contempt."

"I regard *you* with justified contempt," said the flat earth man suddenly, scowling at Paul. "You have absolutely no idea how the world really works. Where does the Bible mention little people living in the Earth's core? Where does it mention the Earth's core at all? The Bible says the Earth is flat, so it's flat."

"Completely?" I asked, turning my attention to him. Paul looked a bit put out.

"No, of course not completely. There are hills and valleys. It's bumpy. But it's not *round*. The idea of it being a globe is self-evidently false."

"Self-evidently?" asked Joanne.

"Well, it's evident to me," he said, with an air of finality that really didn't brook any argument. Certainly none I could be bothered to make, anyway.

"And you would be...?" I asked, taking the opportunity to ask a non-geography related question.

He pulled out a card. Everyone seemed to have cards. "Ranjit Dhesi. Here, have this." The card contained the words 'Ranjit Dhesi, Last Remnant of Rationality on The (Flat, Even if a Bit Bumpy) Earth' and a website address. No details of what he did for a living.

"So what do you do for a living, Ranjit?" I asked.

"Why?" he riposted. Touché, I thought.

"Well, I just wondered if you were, you know, in a position to do anything about your beliefs —"

"They're not beliefs! Beliefs are what you have when you don't have facts! These are *facts*!" I had rarely heard so many exclamation marks in one outburst. Of course, I had mainly been hanging round with vampire goths recently, all of whom were far too cool to use exclamatory punctuation of any kind. They probably saw question marks as dangerously vulgar.

"Sorry," I said in a placatory fashion. "Facts. I mean, can you use your work to spread the, er, good news?"

"Good news? Hah." This was from Paul the hollow-earth guy.

"As if you knew anything about it, you alien-obsessed freak."

"Freak? Look who's talking, you geographically retarded lunatic."

"Lunatic? Hah."

"You wouldn't recognise the truth if it kidnapped you, took you up to its spaceship and anally probed you."

I was starting to wonder if I should be asking whether one of them always told the truth and the other always lied.

"Don't pretend to know the truth," snapped Ranjit. "Anyone capable of saying that there are little people living in the centre of the earth has no right to even discuss the concept of truth." An interesting point, I thought, though something of a pot-kettle situation. But then their entire lives seemed to embody the pot-kettle concept.

"Anyone who thinks the earth is flat has a lack of knowledge about the world that could only have been gained from living in a ditch for the past thirty years."

"Anyone who thinks the earth is hollow *should* have been living in a ditch for the past thirty years."

"I'll happily pay for you to go and live in a ditch on the other side of the world if that will help your delusion. It'll certainly make me happier."

"I'll happily fund your trip to the Arctic to look for small green aliens or whatever it is you expect to find there. With any luck you'll fall into an iceberg."

"They're not green, you moron! They're just like us, only more intelligent. Which in your case is hardly difficult."

"Imbecile."

"Moron."

"You already said that."

"Well, it's still true."

"You can't even come up with new insults, how can you believe you know anything about the earth's geography?"

"At least I know it has some! If the earth's flat, what's underneath? Tell me that!"

"I'm not telling you anything! If the earth's hollow, why hasn't it collapsed?"

"I refuse to discuss these matters with someone who is incapable of understanding basic shapes, like 'sphere'."

"I refuse to discuss anything at all with someone so blatantly self-deceiving and self-righteous."

"Fine," snapped Paul.

"Fine," snapped Ranjit.

They relapsed into silence and glared in front of them, refusing to catch each other's eye.

I glanced round and realised that most of the room had broken off their own conversations to listen to the row. I began edging over to the opposite corner where the elf-dryad-angel lot were standing, as I felt I'd had enough geography for one evening. Joanne followed me.

"Next time I'll bring score cards," she said quietly, grinning. "That really cheered me up! Thanks."

"No problem. They were sweet, weren't they?" By this time we were standing near the faery-type people, one of whom overheard us.

"They're very cute, aren't they?" she agreed. "You must have been good for them, they never normally argue that loudly. Or coherently."

"Oh, I'm sorry," I said.

"No, I'm sure they enjoyed it. And it's more interesting for the rest of us than having them standing around silently glaring."

"I suppose so."

She was very, very thin and young, and she had pointy ears. I could just about see the join where she'd glued them on, and I knew where you could buy them (Ferret and Sons, Covent Garden) but still, they were impressive and they suited her. Her long blonde hair covered her slim shoulders, which was just as well because her dress didn't cover anything much. It was wispy and pale, like her.

She smiled faintly at us and said, "My name's Ethereal Starshadow," reaching out a hand to touch Joanne and then myself lightly on the arm.

Of course it was, I thought. She'd obviously spent her entire life having people tell her she looked ethereal, and had decided to take the initiative. Or possibly her parents, having been burdened with the surname Starshadow, had decided to be cruel.

"They live together, you know." Ethereal nodded at the Earthmen.

I stared at her in disbelief. "What, those two? Ranjit and Paul?"

"Oh yes. They've been together for a couple for years. Weird, isn't it?"

"Even by my standards of weirdness." I turned to look at Ranjit and Paul again. They were still fixed in Position A, where they stared straight ahead, drank their pints and ignored each other. "And as a lesbian were-lizard, my standards are pretty high, I can tell you."

"Oh, you're a reptile? Better stay out of his way." She pointed at a tall, gangly man nearby who appeared to be haranguing a group of pixies. "He thinks alien reptiles control the world. He might try and get you thrown out."

"Thanks for the tip. Oh — I'm Elinor, this is Joanne." We all shook hands. Ethereal's handshake was so insipid that it was barely there.

"I'm an elf."

We both nodded gravely. It wasn't exactly a surprise.

"I thought as much," said Joanne. "That or a fairy."

"I find fairies a little... vulgar." Ethereal wrinkled her small, pale nose. "The elf folk are more truly *spiritual*."

"Yes, I agree," said Joanne solemnly. "It's something to do with the ears."

"So, Ethereal," I said quickly. "How long have you been Otherkin?" (I'd done some brief research on the iTem the previous night to find out the correct terms to use.)

"Well, my whole life in one sense, of course. Elves are born, not made."

"Oh, so your parents were elves too?" Joanne definitely seemed to be getting back to her old self.

Ethereal took the question at face value. "No, that's not how it works. We are not bound by our bodies, nor by the material world, and we are not limited to a single lifetime. We are spirit and we are eternal, we elven folk." She looked down at herself. "Otherworldly. Strangely compelling, semi-invisible when we choose to be, hauntingly beautiful, vividly sensitive, sometimes dangerous... Elven." She gazed into the middle distance with a hand pressed to her heart.

I took Joanne's hand and pushed a sharp fingernail into her palm. She shot me a grateful glance and stopped choking.

"So, Joanne," said Ethereal, "tell me about yourself. Where are you from?"

Joanne sighed imperceptibly. "London."

"No, I mean... *originally*."

Joanne sighed less imperceptibly. "London."

"But your people?" For someone claiming to be vividly sensitive, Ethereal was proving somewhat impervious to Joanne's body language. Which was impressive, as I could actually see her fist clenching.

"We'd better go," I said edging away. "Nice talking to you."

"Some people do find me a little overwhelming," said Ethereal understandingly. Joanne muttered something indecipherable (although I caught the phrase "overwhelmingly racist, maybe...") and moved away.

I was about to do the same when a thought occurred to me. "You don't happen to know what Ranjit and Paul do for a living, do you?"

"Well, they try to keep it quiet, but it's generally known around here that they work in the government," said Ethereal in a barely audible whisper.

"You have to be kidding."

"No, really. Not that high up, of course. They're both too — alternative for that. But minor civil service, yes."

I filed away that information to process later, and gave Ethereal a brief goodbye wave. She smiled distantly and turned back to her group of almost-identical pixies, elves and for all I knew leprechauns. They seemed to be discussing mortgages.

It occurred to me that Joanne and I hadn't had any trouble posing as part of this group. Nobody had asked us a single question about our cover story, in fact. They were all too caught up in their own private realities. Was this the price for leaving the mainstream — that you became defined by your weirdness?

The vampires hadn't been too bad, now that I had people to compare them with. They were helped by having a fairly large community, of course. These people had to bear the weight of their worlds on their own shoulders alone, and no wonder it made them a little self-obsessed. I felt a bit sorry for them all, suddenly. Still, I thought optimistically, if Ranjit and Paul could stay together — not to mention hold down government jobs — there was hope for anyone. (Except possibly the government.)

We chatted to the alien people for a while, and got lectured on the evil reptilian race from Venus that was slowly taking over the earth; we didn't mention the were-lizard thing by tacit agreement. After that and a brief conversation with the people in the animal corner — brief because we didn't want to blow our cover by showing ignorance of the latest flame war on the were forums — it was past ten o'clock.

"We could talk to that guy who thinks he's an angel?" suggested Joanne.

"Thanks, but no. Too Christian."

"You really don't like religion much, do you?"

"The short answer is 'no, not really'. Do you want to hear the long answer?"

"Oh, go on then." Joanne ostentatiously settled herself against a pillar to listen.

"Religion's like a disease," I said. "A virus. It creeps in and suddenly people are screaming about sodomites and sin and having sex before marriage, and you can't get a job unless you go to church, and you're supposed to stay in your allotted social space because that's where God wants you. And if you don't love him of your *own free will*, you go to hell. That's a mockery of the idea of free will." My voice had got loud. People turned to look at me but I ignored them. I'd meant to give the sardonic, laidback version of my rant but I seemed to have ended up with the emotional, angry one. "Christianity is the *enemy* of freedom. It doesn't leave you any space to be yourself. Everyone's fitted into the same small box and if you don't fit, you're supposed to cut your own limbs off to make sure you do. No self-determination. No freedom to choose. And all of this in worship of a God who quite obviously doesn't even *exist*, so there's no reward, because there's no heaven."

"Wow. Cool." Joanne looked impressed and a little taken aback.

"Thanks." I shrugged. "Everyone has something they're irrationally passionate about, don't they? I do apologise."

"Not at all." There was a moment of silence.

"Time to go, do you think?" I said. "We seem to have covered everyone."

Joanne nodded emphatically. "Oh yes. Otherwise we might have to talk to Ephemeral again."

"Ethereal."

"I stand by my choice of word."

"OK, let's go," I said. "Let me just do one thing first, though."

I rummaged through my bag and found a lipstick case. I walked over to Ranjit and Paul and held it up to them. "Flat," I said, indicating the top of the case. "Hollow," I said, opening the case and showing them the inside. "Objects can be both flat and hollow. See?"

They stared at me. Both said, "Don't be ridiculous," in perfect unison. As I turned away I saw them exchange an identical glance of pure contempt.

In a way, it was rather sweet.

We passed James as we left.

"I don't suppose you're free for a drink on Saturday?" he asked Joanne hopefully.

She barely broke stride. "Sorry, I'm having my ears waxed."

"Good answer," I said at the door.

"I've had it saved up for years."

On our way out, incidentally, I was entertained to overhear a snatch of conversation between a largish middle-aged man and a largish middle-aged woman standing by the bar.

"...So you're my natural predator?" he was saying enthusiastically.

"Well, one of them, yes. I understand turtles get eaten by a large variety of animals, but certainly sharks are a threat."

"Wow. Cool."

"Why, would you like me to eat you?"

The were-turtle man choked on his drink.

Looked like I could chalk up 'brought two lonely souls together' on my spiritual balance sheet. I decided to assume it worked out and they lived happily ever after. Why not?

Chapter Fourteen
This is the Blood

*"I find it quite interesting that many can believe in a heaven and a hell,
Lucifer and God, extraterrestrial beings from outer space, and visits
from loved ones who have crossed over, but they will view you as a
mentally unstable individual if you give the slightest indication that
immortal vampires may be out there somewhere. Why is that?"*
http://letum.dhs.org/ImmortalVampire.html

*"I'm not surprised that a lot of vampires convince themselves that they
are immortal, or pretend to be immortal so that they can feed off the
adulation and trust and admiration of others. It's quite a temptation."*
Sarah Dorrance
http://www.darksites.com/souls/vampires/vampdonor/essays/
immortality2.html

Search terms:
immortalis-animus, drinkdeeplyanddream

Friday October 17th — about midnight

"Very nice," I said, speaking in a rather higher pitch than usual
in order to be heard over the music. The dark basement club held
about three hundred black-clad goths, all of whom appeared at
this moment to be dancing languidly in front of me. Stefan and I
were sitting with Justin and Viola at a small, low table by the main
dance floor, drinking Snake's Blood (otherwise known as cider and
cranberry juice). Viola had just asked me what I thought of the song
being played.

"Nice?" Viola stared at me, incredulous. "Knoblauch-Huhn!
Nice!" (Obviously I'd been wrong about goths being too cool to use
exclamation points.) "They're the best post-neo-proto-goth band in

the UK! They're the symbolic manifestation of the darkness residing within every human soul! People have been known to commit suicide after hearing one of their songs!"

"Which one?"

"Any one."

"I can understand that."

Viola sighed. "You're just not one of us, are you?"

"I think I'm one of me," I said. "Sorry."

"Oh, we strongly believe in being yourself and not conforming to the crowd," said Justin reassuringly.

"Having said that," added Viola, "it's probably wise not to insult goth music too loudly in a goth club or you might get in trouble with some of the clubbers. Though of course, that probably just means they'll bitch about your make-up."

"But I said I *liked* the music."

"No, you said it was nice. That's a mortal insult round here." She smiled a fanged smile at me.

I glanced wryly at Stefan, who put his hand on my shoulder. "It's my fault. I had hoped that if she was exposed to the music, she might come to appreciate it more."

"He's getting his revenge on me for taking him to a folk-metal concert on Wednesday," I explained to Viola.

Stefan gave a delicate shudder. "I believe we agreed never to mention that occasion again."

"Well, I think we're even now. Though I like this club, actually. Very, er, redolent of the black despair that forms the undercurrent of all sentient life."

All three goths looked approving.

We were in Necrophidius, which I gathered was a regular haunt of the Jesus' Blood church. It was just a brief visit. Apparently we were stopping off on our way to a graveyard somewhere. I hadn't been fully informed as to the evening's events. But I'd given in to Stefan's pleas and dressed all in black for the club. I'd even put some inefficiently applied eyeliner on.

I fitted in reasonably well, I thought, provided I didn't actually say anything.

We were quiet for a moment. Viola was singing along to the music. I caught the words 'razor blade', 'crucify' and 'desiccated corpse'. I didn't ask who the band was. For all I knew, just saying their name aloud inside Necrophidius might summon a demon from the rancid depths of hell. It felt like that kind of place.

Or at least, it felt like the people who came here wanted it to be that kind of place. But I wasn't going to quibble.

"So, did your Adult Lego idea work out, Elinor?" asked Justin with a polite inclination of the head.

"Oh, that. Didn't really get going in the end. I tend to get these ideas and then they fizzle out. It's just part of my need to be famous and save the world in some way."

"Adult Lego would save the world?"

"Well, no, not as such. But, you know, once you get the fame, you can work on the saviour stuff afterwards, or something. I don't really mind which way round it happens, I just want to make a difference and be remembered." I winced. Why is it so difficult not to sound clichéd when you're being sincere?

"I believe having a child is the usual way to ensure that. Or you could write a book, or become a rock star, or make films?"

"Yeah, but everyone has children. It's not exactly groundbreakingly original, is it? And I can't sing, my acting skills are minimal and you've got more chance of winning the lottery than having a non-Christian novel published."

"But the lottery went bankrupt two years ago."

"My point exactly."

"So, what else have you tried to get famous and make a difference?" The phrase sounded much better in Justin's gentle American accent.

"Er, actually tried? Not a lot, to be honest. I'm more in the planning stage. Like I said, I want to save the world really, but that does mean waiting till the world needs saving."

"Of course," said Justin after a pause, "there are... other ways to ensure that you are remembered." He and Stefan exchanged a glance.

"Yes?" I actually didn't know what he meant. I'd forgotten our very first conversation.

"Yes. The best way to be remembered after you're gone," he said, leaning in across the table and looking intently into my eyes, "is not to go in the first place."

I stared at him. "Oh. I see."

Justin and Stefan exchanged another glance. Stefan, who was sitting next to me, leaned close and spoke into my ear.

"Try not to be too judgemental, Elinor. I am not asking you to believe, not yet, but try to be at least open-minded, please? This is important to me."

"I think I'd find it easier to be open-minded if you told me what was going on in the first place," I said levelly.

A third glance was exchanged, this time between Justin, Stefan and Viola.

"Shall we go?" said Justin, getting up and wrapping his long black cloak around his shoulders. The others stood up too. I took a quick last gulp of my cider and cranberry, then collected my coat and followed the others through the dancing black-clad throng, past the bar with the huge metallic angel hung behind it, down the stairs with the alcove where teenagers swapped drugs and gossip, and out the door to a cold dimly-lit passageway that smelled of sewage and dogs. Justin's car was round the corner, parked in a handy alleyway.

We drove for about half an hour through the chilly autumnal darkness, beyond London and out through the suburbs to... What? Middlesex? Hertfordshire? Norfolk? Being a South London girl, and only recently a London girl at all, I had absolutely no idea where we were. Stefan and I sat quietly in the back of the car. I gazed out of the window at endless rows of terraced houses, and noticed out of the corner of my eye that Stefan was putting his fangs in. I would have liked to know what was happening, but clearly I wasn't going to be enlightened until we got to wherever we were going.

The car pulled up on a small side-road in what appeared, geographically speaking, to be the middle of nowhere. When I got out, I saw that it wasn't exactly nowhere, because there was a graveyard next to the road. There were some people in the graveyard. I couldn't see much in the almost-blackness, but I thought I recognised a few of them from Joanne's party and the previous munch. There seemed to be about ten of them, and they were all wearing black and standing in a circle. I wondered briefly why nobody ever used, say, triangles, for ritual purposes. Or rhomboids. If I ever had a church of my very own, I'd get dozens of people and make them stand in really complex shapes.

Justin swept towards the circle, his cloak billowing out behind him in authentic vampire style. I have to admit that my heart caught in my throat for a moment. Viola was behind him, less impressive because she was shorter and couldn't stride quite as effectively, but still looking really quite vampiric. Stefan took my hand. His fingers were long and cool.

"I asked for you to be here," he told me, leaning in to speak quietly in my ear, his silver fangs unsettlingly close to my neck. "You are not involved in the ceremony, do not worry."

"Oh good — I was starting to wonder if you'd decided to turn me," I said, frowning in the darkness as we picked our way between the gravestones and grassy hillocks. I *had* had a moment of worry, to be honest. Not that I believed in it, obviously, but I was against people draining blood from me as a matter of principle.

"No, no. I would never turn anybody against their will," Stefan said, perhaps having forgotten our conversation two weeks earlier.

I coughed gently.

"Oh. Apart from what happened with Naomi. I would never turn *you* against your will."

I coughed again. "Actually, you told me you couldn't turn people at all."

"Oh. Did I?" He sighed. "Why do I tell you all my secrets?"

"I'm a good listener."

We reached the centre of the graveyard, where Justin was standing in the middle of the vampire circle. Viola was standing just behind and to the right of him, like a magician's assistant. There was something on the ground behind her, but I couldn't see anything but a pale shape. It was a cloudy night with no moon and few stars, and we seemed to be nowhere near any street lights, so the darkness was almost overwhelming. There were a couple of lanterns perched on gravestones, though, giving off just enough light for me to see a lot of fangs glinting. It wasn't reassuring as such. As we came closer, a ring of just-visible faces turned to look at us, and I saw Justin raise his arms in welcome.

"Greetings, Stefan the Tormented," he said in a deeper tone than usual.

I shot Stefan a glance, but he avoided looking in my direction. Couldn't blame him, really.

"Come to us," intoned Justin. Stefan briefly put his hand on my shoulder, then walked forward to the circle without looking back at me. I found a handy tomb to climb onto just outside the vampire ring, which gave me a reasonably good view of what was happening inside the circle. Stefan was standing next to Justin, looking, I must admit, quite tormented. Not to mention gorgeous, as usual. Viola was behind them, pulling something up off the ground.

No, not something. Someone. The pale shape was Naomi.

Shit.

She looked scared. And cold. Which wasn't surprising, because she was naked. She had her arms over her breasts and was trying to stay curled up to avoid exposing herself. Viola pulled her hair backwards and she jerked upright, whimpering. They had blindfolded her with a length of black velvety material and her brown hair hung loose over her shoulders.

"You may sit down." Justin was talking to the vampire ring, not Naomi. They obeyed: some of them knelt and some sat on the grass. It made my view a lot better. Only the four in the middle were left standing: Viola, holding Naomi by the wrist (and twisting it, from what I could see); Justin turning to face the two women, fangs showing; and Stefan, standing a few feet away from the other three, looking down, perhaps frowning, I couldn't quite tell. He didn't catch my eye and he was definitely trying to avoid looking at Naomi, I thought.

"You can't kill her!" My voice sounded louder than I'd meant it to, but also thinner and higher-pitched. Justin looked up at me perched on the tomb, and grinned. His fangs flashed at me and I shuddered. For the first time, I found him genuinely frightening.

"We would not dream of doing so," he said, mock-shocked. "And certainly not with this many witnesses." The grin flashed a little wider for a moment. "She is merely a necessary part of the ritual, and we will let her go free once it is completed, I promise you."

I looked past him at Naomi's shivering body and said seriously, "Justin, I promise *you* that if you hurt her, I will tell the authorities."

"She will be alive and unharmed when we are finished. Perhaps not unscathed, but she deserves a little... scathing, after her recent actions."

I couldn't really argue with that. I sat back on the chilly tomb, wrapped my arms around myself and watched, glad I'd brought my long wool coat with me.

There was a moment of silence. I had a sudden impulse to break it by telling a joke about chickens, but resisted as I didn't want to get myself thrown out of the meeting, or ceremony, or whatever it was. Ritual? Church service?

Justin was taking his black cloak off and replacing it with a dark red one. He tossed the black cloak towards Naomi.

"Put that around her," he instructed Viola. "We need her blood warm." I thought it might already be too late for that, but Viola took the large heavy garment and wrapped it around the naked girl. Naomi clutched it like a lifeline. All I could see of her now was the part of her face that wasn't hidden by the blindfold or her long, lank hair. It was hard to tell what she was thinking.

"Welcome to the consecrated ground, honoured and chosen representatives of the Jesus' Blood Church." Justin turned slowly to face everyone in the circle. "I wear the cloak of the Blood. I am the leader of the Church. I am the mouthpiece of the Son and in His name I can grant immortality, as I have granted it to all of you. We worship the Cross and we worship the sacred Blood that falls from it. We worship the First Vampire, who gave us eternal life through His power and grace. We honour the Twelve who drank His Blood and ate His Body and were granted immortality." The ring of people bowed their heads briefly in acknowledgement. I remembered that according to Justin's story, the disciples had in fact been killed before they could enjoy much of their immortality, but it didn't seem like a good time to quibble.

"We are here tonight for a special ceremony," resumed Justin after the pause. "A two-fold ritual: a Cleansing and Purification, and an Initiation. Stefan the Tormented, please kneel."

Stefan did so.

Justin looked round at the assembled church members. "Some of you have wondered why Stefan has not yet been initiated into our Church. The reason is this girl."

He reached behind him as Viola pushed Naomi forward. She stumbled and almost tripped over the long cloak. Justin gripped her shoulder.

"This woman, Naomi, believes that she is a vampire. Stefan allowed her to believe that he had Turned her, though he knows he cannot Turn humans until he has become part of our church. She is insane. She has killed, she has drunk unwilling blood, she has defiled our community. Because of this, I felt that I could not allow Stefan the Eternal Gift."

He pushed Naomi forwards and she fell awkwardly onto the ground, next to Stefan. He put out a hand to help her up and she knelt beside him, huddled inside Justin's cloak.

"However," he resumed, "I brought you here tonight to announce that I have reconsidered. There is a way that we can accept Stefan as one of us. This woman, Naomi, must be cleansed of her insanity. Stefan must be purified of her taint. Then we can initiate him."

The vampires bowed their heads in acceptance. They all seemed to have non-speaking roles, or possibly they'd already been informed of what was going on. Justin moved aside to leave a space in the centre of the circle.

Viola came forward, removed the cloak from Naomi's shoulders, laid it out on the grass and pushed her forwards fairly gently, so that she fell spread out and face down on the cloak. "Turn over," she whispered audibly, and Naomi turned over to lie on her back. Her small pallid breasts looked pretty in the faint golden light of the lanterns. Her face was nearly invisible from this distance. She didn't seem to have said anything at all yet. Had they told her what they were going to do? Did she just do as she was told? Perhaps they had threatened her.

Justin knelt at her head and spoke to her, quietly, but loudly enough for all of us to hear.

"Naomi? Do you wish to be healed?"

She nodded, or tried to. It's difficult to do when lying down.

"We can help you, Naomi." Justin's voice was low and perhaps he meant it to be kindly but given the context, there was no chance of that. "You can be released of your curse. We do not worship exactly the same God, but I understand and sympathise with the fact that your religion does not accept vampirism, and that you believe it is a demonic affliction. But what demons gave you, demons can take away again. Nod if you wish this to happen."

Nod.

"Very good. Give verbal consent of some kind, and then we will begin."

"I consent." Naomi's voice was barely audible, and she spoke very slowly. The words sounded slurred. I realised that they had probably given her something — magic mushrooms perhaps?

Justin nodded at Viola, who handed him a small sharp knife. Well, I couldn't actually tell if it was sharp from where I was, but I deduced it when he bent over Naomi and made a quick shallow cut over her left breast. A long dark line formed on her skin. She didn't move or cry out — definitely on some kind of drug. Justin leant forward and sank his fangs into the cut.

To say he drank from her would be overstating it, I suppose. He didn't take much. But when he got up, his mouth was darker and his fangs didn't gleam any more.

"Viola." He motioned towards Naomi. Viola took the knife from him, knelt down and made another cut in the skin, this time on the left arm. She put her mouth down to it and when she stood up, her fangs were dark too.

One by one, all the vampires except Stefan came forward, took the knife, made a cut, and took some of Naomi's blood. Stefan, kneeling beside the girl, never took his eyes off her damaged body. His expression was unreadable.

When they were finished and everyone had gone back to their places, Viola started cleaning the cuts with antiseptic wipes. Even then, Naomi didn't speak, though I thought I saw her wince a couple of times. When Viola was finished, she sat Naomi up and put the cloak back round her. She didn't take the blindfold off.

"Naomi," said Justin in the same low tone as before, "you are cleansed. We have taken from you your vampiric nature and left you with your humanity. We have done this so that Stefan will be released of the sin he committed by Turning one who was unwilling. Now that he is purified, you may go."

Naomi stared at him blankly. I don't think she'd understood a word he'd said. He seemed to realise the fact, and nodded at Viola. "Take her home."

As Viola and Naomi left the circle and walked towards the car, Justin took Stefan's hand and helped him to stand. I suddenly remembered that all this was actually to do with Stefan. Poor Naomi, I thought. A supporting actor even during her own torture.

"We shall now initiate our new member into the Church, and into the Gift. We will drink from him and he will drink from us. We will make him truly a vampire, and truly immortal." Justin looked up at me. "Elinor, you do not have to stay for this. It will take a long time, and it is essentially a private ceremony. Viola is taking Naomi home. You can go with her."

I hesitated for a moment. But it was cold, and I felt I'd seen enough of people's blood for one night. Anyway, though Justin had phrased it politely, he clearly wanted me to leave. Fair enough. I thought about wishing Stefan good luck or congratulating him, but the atmosphere seemed wrong. We exchanged a brief glance instead. We were meeting on Sunday anyway, so I looked forward to finding out then how the rest of the night had gone.

I scrambled off the tomb and went after Viola, who was moving slowly since she had to lead the blindfolded Naomi through the graveyard. Once we'd made it to the car, she took off the blindfold and Naomi curled up sleepily in the back seat.

The ride back was quiet. Viola was obviously making it as quick as possible so she could get back and grab some of Stefan's blood before it was all gone, and Naomi seemed virtually comatose. We dropped her off outside a largish house in Hampstead somewhere. On being informed that I lived in Morden, Viola groaned in a not incredibly subtle way, and offered to let me stay the night at the flat she and Justin shared in the much nearer Walthamstow. I agreed.

Lying in Viola's bed, in an unfamiliar bedroom full of CDs from bands whose names sounded like German pharmaceuticals, I stared out of the window into the orange-lit street and was unable to sleep. I thought about the fact that Stefan was currently lying in a graveyard just outside London, having some of his blood removed by a group of Christian(ish) vampires who believed they were conferring eternal life on him. Did he really believe he was becoming immortal?

On balance, I thought he probably did.

Chapter Fifteen
CULT — Who to Kill

"The biggest lie in all of history is set to wash over you in a very Earth-bound holographic light-show in the very near future. You are already witnessing it in the current light-holograph called a comet. Get ready, get set, and I suggest you carefully consider where and how you GO."
http://members.aol.com/phmikas/infos/blue_.htm

Saturday October 18th — evening

It was the penultimate meeting, although they didn't know it, of Christians Under the Lord's Thrall. The meeting was taking place on a Saturday this week, because Ruth had said she couldn't make it on the Friday. Normally Carol liked to stick to routine regardless of the convenience of others, but this particular meeting required the presence of Ruth specifically.

This week, there were custard cream biscuits. Mabel had tentatively proffered a tin of chocolate fingers, but they were vetoed by Carol on the grounds that their shape was inherently sinful.

There were no discussions about church matters this week. Hannah and Mabel had already made their report the previous week. They had told the meeting that the general congregation, while in principle supportive of Carol and her acolytes, did not react well to more detailed hints relating to worldwide conspiracies, the prospective rule of Satan and the need for occasional extreme violence. Carol had already imagined as much, though she did not tell them so. It had been worth a try, anyway. Luckily, as she later commented to Himm, nobody was likely to take the two elderly ladies seriously, so there was no danger of anyone talking to the authorities. CULT needed two more weeks of undisturbed planning; then it would be time to act. And after *that*, everyone would know anyway, and the authorities — so-called authorities, for of course nobody but God could really claim that title — could do what they liked.

In the meantime, Carol and Himm knew, there was a lot to arrange.

The Bible was brought out and the familiar sentence read: not peace, but a sword. Tonight it had an extra-special meaning and Carol read it with extra-special emphasis. Afterwards, they got down to business.

"Pete, shall we start with you? I see you have something for us!" Himm smiled at the nervous man and at the long dark bag under his chair.

Pete nodded and pulled out the bag. "Took a while, but here you go. I'm starting to get a bit worried about all this, though. I mean..."

"We'll talk about it fully in a moment, I promise," said Carol, breaking off her conversation with David and Ruth about the technicalities of broadcasting satellite imagery. "For the moment, let's just have a look at the swords, shall we?"

Out they came from the black bag, five of them. (It was decided last week that Hannah and Mabel should be excused from any direct swordplay on account of their arthritis.) Pete removed one of the scabbards and the room was silent as the blade emerged, slim and shining. Mabel and Hannah looked scared; David stared, fascinated. Ruth just stared. Carol and Himm exchanged satisfied glances. Carol ran a finger along one edge of the blade and inspected the long razor-thin line of blood on her skin with a pleased smile. "Very nice."

"You don't think guns...?" said Pete hesitantly. "I probably could have got you guns."

"No, no. Guns aren't mentioned in the Bible," sad Carol. "The line is not 'I bring not peace, but a revolver', now, is it? God only approves of deaths that are up close and personal, as it were. In Biblical times they fought hand to hand and each death was earned. Each man who killed risked his own life to do so. We shall be doing the same."

"Risking our lives?" said David apprehensively.

"Risking our freedom, at least, yes. Of course. We are obeying Christ's laws, but we will be breaking the laws of our secular government. There may be a price. People may not understand why we have done what we have done. You must all be prepared for that."

"We are martyrs," Ruth said earnestly to David. "We are placing the good of humanity above our own selfish, petty desire not to spend a lifetime in prison. We talked about this last week, didn't we? God demands sacrifice, and we must provide. Sacrifice is holy."

Carol held up her bloody finger. "Look at this," she said to the group, "and remember. We are going to spill blood. With our own hands we are going to commit what the world calls murder. I want you all to understand this fully. The people we are going to kill are evil, and if we do not destroy them, Christianity itself may be destroyed. Nevertheless, we should not expect other people to appreciate what we have done — not even other Christians. We look only for God's approval. And I promise you, we have that." Carol's voice was low and passionate. She was perfectly sincere. She believed in the cause with all her heart. She was not in this for the money (there wasn't any), or the fame (which would be infamy if anything). She believed she was God's instrument. Possibly a trumpet.

She was convincing, too. Himm pressed her hand, David's eyes lit up, and Hannah and Mabel put their hands to their hearts in admiration. (Carol had told them that although they weren't able to stab anyone, they could be in charge of the burning of the bodies.)

Pete reverently sheathed the sword, put it back in the bag with the others and slid the bag back under the chair. Carol's words had affected him, too. He looked less nervous now and more resolute.

"So," said Himm in a businesslike fashion, "we have the weapons, we have the determination. What we need now are more details of the targets. Ruth?"

Ruth's white eyes made her pale skin look darker than it was, and her long black hair was unkempt. She rummaged in her bag and handed Carol a crumpled piece of paper with a list of names. Carol scanned them slowly, nodding.

"I'm very proud of you, Ruth. Very good work, excellent. Why don't you tell us all who these people are and how you found them?"

Ruth looked round the room. All eyes were on her. She clutched her bag in her arms.

"One of them is a psychic. Two are members of the Civil Service. Two work in the computer industry. And one is a sound engineer. I don't have all their details yet, but I have the names. You can see how these six people are ideally placed to operate Project Rupture — three of them work the technical side, the two in government have the contacts and are probably very highly placed in the New World

117

Order, and the psychic will control the telepathy angle, broadcasting thoughts right into our heads. Of course," she added, "they are only the active arm of a much larger organisation, but if we get rid of them, we'll destroy the immediate threat, and the Project will be made public. Which means the New World Order won't dare try it again — or if they do, it won't work, because everyone will be aware it's a fake. After all, the only way that Rupture can be dangerous is if the public believes that the images are real, are from God."

David put his hand up. "Um... so can't we just tell people about it? I mean, do we actually *have* to kill anyone? Surely if we make it all public, we'll remove the threat anyway?"

"I'm afraid not, David dear," said Carol kindly. "We wouldn't be believed. People have tried before — there are websites and magazines with lots of details about Rupture and other conspiracies, and nobody pays any attention. These days, if you want people to listen to you, you have to make the news. And in this callous world which is so blasé about crime and unnatural passions and such things, there aren't many ways to make the news. So you see, executing these six people will have a twofold effect. It will remove the threat, and it will make our cause public. With any luck, or rather with God's help, we will be heroes. Even if we are vilified, our mission will have been accomplished, and we will have changed the world for the better. Isn't that what you want?"

She spoke to David, but it was Ruth who answered, her pale eyes blazing. "All I've ever wanted to do," she said, "is to change the world for the better. If I can manage that, I'll die happy."

"You are an inspiration to us, my dear," said Carol. She glanced at the paper in her hand. "Do you know who's the leader of the Rupture group?"

Ruth nodded eagerly. "It's the male IT worker — the programmer. His deputies are the female IT worker and the sound engineer. They're all members of the same underground cult, which thrives on blood and death, and they've sworn to rid the world of traditional Christianity."

Carol took out a red pen, circled the top name on the list Ruth had given her, and underlined it. "Wonderful. Can we have a round of applause for Ruth, everyone? Our new recruit has really proved herself to be invaluable, hasn't she?" The bare room echoed with understated British claps. "Well done for finding this one, Hannah."

"Oh, thank you, Carol dear," flustered Hannah. "Not that I found you exactly, did I, Ruth? You found me, really."

"I suppose so," said Ruth, smiling. "I overheard you talking and I was so impressed with your Biblical fervour that I followed you — I meant to ask you what church you went to. And then you came here... and I found all of you. Thank the Lord for that. You've helped to give a meaning to my life, all of you. But especially you, of course, Carol." Carol, who was sitting next to her, stroked Ruth's shoulder affectionately.

"Anyway," said Himm, "we're doing very well. Practically all set. Next week we can work out exactly who's doing what — yes, Hannah, I know you want to be in charge of the burning, and that shouldn't be a problem — and then it'll be D-Day."

He waited for a nod of affirmation from his wife before continuing. "I think I can tell you all now that we have another piece of information. We know the date. Ruth calculated it from a study of the numerical symbolism in the Book of Revelations. Project Rupture is scheduled to go live on the night after Halloween, the night of All Saints Day. Carefully chosen for its symbolic value, of course. And it's equally symbolic that our own pre-emptive action will take place on the night of Halloween itself. That's in two weeks' time. In fact," he added cheerfully, "it'll fall on a Friday, so it'll be just like our usual weekly meeting, in a way, only with violence!"

"We thought we'd call it Operation Trick or Treat!" said Carol brightly. "Isn't that cute? And the best part is, we can all dress up as pirates, and then it won't look odd that we're wearing swords!"

"I've got a pirate costume," said Pete, who had been listening attentively but hadn't had much chance to contribute to the discussion since his production of the swords. "I think I've got my son's one too, somewhere. You'd fit into that, David."

"Well, isn't that handy?" Himm said enthusiastically. "That proves we're on the right track, if God is providing for us like that."

There was an appreciative pause. Carol said, "I think Himm has made a valuable point here, and a good one to end the meeting on, too. You know, they say God moves in mysterious ways, but as far as I'm concerned, they're only mysterious if you don't try hard enough to make sense of them, or you just don't want to understand. Personally," she finished, looking round the room to make her point, seeing all the heads nodding in agreement, "I've always found the ways of God quite easy to understand, myself."

Chapter Sixteen
Not Exactly Buffy

*"**Alex Whitington:** What would you do if a vampire asked you to kill him?*
*"**Sean Manchester:** Vampires cannot be killed. But they can be released from the torment of that condition called undead. It is a blessed hand which strikes the blow."*
Transcript of BBC interview with Sean Manchester
http://www.bbc.co.uk/wales/talkwales/vampiretranscript.shtml

"Haters hate because they do not understand the meaning of what it is to be a vampire, and if they do, maybe they are really screwed up or suffer some type of mental illness...
http://www.geocities.com/Area51/Hollow/6416/vampirehaters.htm

Sunday October 19th — midday

"Cut yourself shaving, then?" I said, grinning. Stefan's previously smooth, flawless skin looked as if someone had splattered it with thin lines of faded red paint. I saw bite marks on his neck, too.

Stefan smiled wearily. I think the weariness was less to do with my joke and more to do with the lack of sleep. He'd got to bed at 6am on Saturday morning — the bed in question being the one I was in, since Justin and Viola had brought him back with them. It was nice to sleep next to him, but it had been a bit of a shock to wake up and see the pillow flecked with blood. Still, he'd seemed cheerful, if tired.

Somewhat to my relief, Justin and Viola hadn't emerged before we'd left. I hadn't really felt like making small talk with them. I'd said goodbye to Stefan and headed home. He'd done the same, claiming he needed to meditate on what had happened the previous night. I'd interpreted that as meaning that he intended to spend the next 24 hours fast asleep, but apparently I'd been wrong judging by how tired he still looked.

And now it was Sunday afternoon and we were both drinking very strong coffee in a small café off Old Compton Street. It occurred to me that it had only been about a month ago that I'd met Stefan, in that bar not far from where we were.

Weird.

How much did I really know about him anyway? He was a goth with very strange ideas about himself. He had a nice flat. He was good in bed, though he took it a bit too seriously for my liking. He was very pretentious in a way I found cute, although I wasn't going to tell him that. He was an accessory to murder, but then, so was I. He liked music I hated. He was bisexual. Not very much to know about someone, but on the other hand, not bad for only a month. It was certainly more than he knew about me.

I still found him gorgeous. And charming in a weird kind of way, and interesting to be around. And sometimes when he looked at me, there was a kind of hiccupping/thumping thing in my chest that I found mildly painful. Could've been angina, of course.

We'd fallen silent, like you do in cafés when one of you hasn't slept a lot and the other one is trying to work out what to say.

"Hang on a second," I said, seeing him yawn again, "aren't you supposed to be nocturnal? Why the sleepiness?"

"I would be if I had the choice, but very few jobs allow you to work at night. It does not matter. I may be physically tired, but my soul is feeling energised and alive."

"I'm sorry, you have a *soul?*"

"As you are aware, I am now a follower of the Vampire Jesus. I have a vampire soul. An immortal vampire soul."

So much for my hope that he was just going along with it for Justin's sake. I kept my expression extremely neutral. Didn't help, of course. He looked deeply into my eyes and sighed.

"I can see what you are thinking."

I took a sip of coffee. "Yes, you probably can. I'm sorry. I like you a lot, Stefan, but I've never believed in adopting a boyfriend's hobbies wholesale. I mean, if it was football or gay porn or something I might consider making an effort. But this whole immortal vampire thing, er... it's not really me."

I paused, a little surprised — I hadn't intended to be having this conversation. Still, it would have happened sometime soon, if not now.

Stefan looked hurt. "You knew I was a vampire when you met me."

"I knew you believed you were one," I corrected him. "That's as far as I'm willing to go. And you knew I didn't believe in it."

"Yes, I suppose so. But Elinor, you must realise that I cannot possibly hope to sustain a relationship with someone who is unwilling to accept me as I am. Especially now."

I looked over at him. "You really do believe you're going to live forever, don't you?"

Large, dark eyes stared back at me. "Not necessarily. I can be staked or decapitated, for example. Other than that, though — yes, I do. I believe I will not die. You cannot understand... Friday night was like nothing I have ever felt before."

"Yes," I said, "I can understand that. I saw what it was like for Naomi." I knew my tone was sharp, but I didn't try to soften it.

He looked down. "For there to be ecstasy, there must be sacrifice."

"Your ecstasy. Her sacrifice."

"She was not seriously hurt." He still hadn't met my eyes. "I doubt she will even remember much of what happened."

"No, she probably won't. Because Justin and Viola fed something to her. They gave hallucinogenic drugs to an insane murderer without her knowledge, and then tortured her."

"I suppose you could put it that way."

"And," I was getting off-topic, but it was something I'd been wondering about, "why all the rigmarole, anyway? They don't believe she's a vampire, and neither do you. Was all that 'we remove your vampirism' stuff just for her benefit?"

"Partly, yes. Surely you can see that it would be beneficial for our community if we could convince Naomi she is human. She might stop attacking people, for one thing."

"OK," I said, "that's a nice sane explanation for what you did last night. By your standards, anyway. Is that the only reason?"

"No. Justin believes that because I drank Naomi's blood, I was tainted by her insanity. In order for me to become part of his Church I had to be freed of that taint. The ritual last night performed the function of cleansing Naomi of insanity by allowing a selection of Church members to drink from her."

"But you don't know she's free of insanity. In fact, I wouldn't be surprised if she was actually a little less sane now than she was before. I would be." I took another sip of coffee. Remembering where we were, I glanced round the café, but the room we were in was empty apart from us. We were on the second floor. Most of the customers were downstairs, and not even the waitress bothered coming up that often.

"That does not affect the ritual. She is sane as far as the Church is concerned."

"I see." I paused for a moment and went back over the last few sentences. "Stefan? Did you just break up with me?"

Stefan cradled his cup of coffee and stared into its depths as if about to tell me my fortune. Well, I suppose in a way he was.

"I said that I could not sustain a relationship with someone who does not believe in me."

"I believe in you in a lot of ways. I just also believe that in twenty years' time you're probably going to get grey hair" — he looked outraged at the very thought — "and in sixty or so years you're going to die. Or quite possibly sooner than that, if you keep hanging around people like Justin."

"I see."

I looked straight at him. "I also believe that you're seeing me partly or mainly to keep me quiet about Naomi."

There was a pause.

"I like you," he said carefully.

"I like you too," I said, and I did. "But there's no point pretending this is going to go anywhere. You won't date someone who doesn't believe in vampires, and I — I won't date someone who believes in God."

He looked startled. "Why not?"

I took a deep breath. "I came to London to get away from having religion pushed into my face at every opportunity. The Resurrected Church ruined my previous life. I wanted to find a new one. Something different, something cool and non-mainstream. But when I do, it turns out it's already contaminated. Apparently even vampires go around worshipping Jesus." My voice had risen. A woman had come upstairs and was sat at the table next to ours. I stopped talking. Stefan was staring at me.

"Elinor, tell me something. Do you have an agenda?"

"No," I said flippantly. "Why, do you have a copy of the minutes?"

"You know what I mean. Is there another reason for your interest in me, in us? I hardly know you. What are you really like? What are you thinking?"

"Me? I hardly ever think. It's easier to just get on with stuff and see what happens. Sorry, I don't know what to tell you."

I held out my hands in an apologetic gesture, and to avoid looking at Stefan's face, I looked over his shoulder at the woman who'd come in. She was short, pretty in an understated way. The black jeans and green shirt she wore emphasised her curves; her dark ponytailed hair curled round her left shoulder like a thin cat. She was a little older than me, and her handbag was a bit too large, but then I knew nothing about handbags. We hadn't had fashion in Somerset, just clothes. She looked nervous, or possibly determined, or possibly both.

Stefan said, "I agree. We are not compatible and you refuse to let me find out anything important about yourself. I do not see this relationship — if that is what it is — going any further."

My voice rose again. "I told you the most important thing about me a moment ago. You just don't listen to anything that isn't about you or your insane, violent, blood-drinking cult, you vain, deluded, pretentious freak."

The good thing about flinging lots of insults at someone all at the same time is that they don't know which one to attack first. Stefan settled on "I am not deluded." He then added, "and the church is not insane."

I shrugged. "Whatever."

"I am not deluded!"

He was starting to get angry, and I could see he didn't like it. The immortal vampire does not allow himself to be baited by mortals. He stopped, took a deep breath and when he looked up at me again, his eyes were calm.

"Elinor..."

"Patronising bastard," I snapped.

He leaned towards me and stretched out a slim hand. I think he was going to try and calm me down by patting my shoulder or something, but he stopped when he saw I was looking behind him, past him.

The attractive woman from the next table had got up and was coming over to us, holding a strangely familiar object in her hand. I had a moment of déjà vu from the opposite angle, as it were, as I watched her come towards our table towards Stefan, holding an iTem.

Stefan turned round, and he and the woman stared at each other for a long moment. As I looked at them, I felt something crawling inside me — perhaps apprehension, perhaps something else. I stared at the woman, but I don't think she had any idea I was even in the room. She and my ex-semi-boyfriend were gazing at each other. They continued doing it for longer than I felt was strictly necessary.

"Are you Stefan Drayton?" said the woman at last, holding up the iTem in her hand.

"Yes. Yes, I am." Stefan and the strange woman were still looking at each other. I coughed pointedly. Stefan started — I think he'd forgotten I was there, as well — and turned back towards me.

I looked up, about to say something like, "So who are you and what are you doing here?" when I saw the woman lean down, put the iTem away and take something out of her bag. She was shaking.

"I am Marianne the Vampire Killer!" she hissed (thereby answering my question). "Taste my stake!"

I felt shock and an overwhelming impulse to giggle in precisely equal quantities, and therefore froze. The girl took a deep breath, lunged forwards and plunged something into Stefan's chest. He fell forwards onto the table, making a sound as if all the air had been pushed out of him at once. I stood up unsteadily.

"What did you do?" I said to her. The wooden stake dropped out of her hand and clattered on the polished floor. She looked stunned.

I leaned over and shook Stefan's shoulder. "For God's sake, get up! You're not dead, you idiot!"

Slowly he sat up, groaning. "She staked me," he said, wonderingly.

"I know she did, but you can't actually kill people with a wooden stick, you know. You'll have a nasty bruise tomorrow, but that's all. She doesn't have the strength to get past your rib cage, you stupid man." I took a breath. I'd been shaken. I'd thought for a moment that she had a knife, or a gun.

"I'm alive," he said, putting a hand to his back and touching it gingerly. "Ow."

"You're alive," said the woman at about the same time and sounding equally astonished. I looked at her angrily.

"And you're fucking stupid. What were you expecting to accomplish? God, you're as moronic as... as he is." I glared at both of them and thought about striding out of the room. But I didn't want to miss anything, so instead I sat down on the window-sill and glared some more.

Stefan bent down, with a grimace of pain, and handed Marianne her stake. It was a fairly pathetic specimen. She'd clearly spent too much time on the internet, or something, and had expected to be able to kill a vampire simply by waving a pointy stick vaguely in its direction. She took the stake and put it back in her bag (aha, I thought, that's why she needed a big handbag). Then opened her mouth, but nothing came out. I could see why she would have trouble working out what to say.

"I'm a vampire exterminator," she said finally, with a combination of shyness and pride. "I found you." She pointed to the iTem in the bag at her feet.

Stefan shot a glance at me.

I shrugged. "If you will go around listing your name and location on these things, what can you expect?"

"Very funny," he said dourly.

Marianne looked at us. "I was going to kill you," she said to Stefan.

"So I saw."

"I was fighting evil."

"I see," I said, wanting to join in. And I did, of course. In a world where Naomi could exist, Marianne's delusions were practically mundane. It should have occurred to me before that if people could believe they were vampires, other people could believe they were vampire hunters. Actually, since Stefan seemed to be the only representative of London vampirism who was easily findable, I was surprised he didn't get people trying to stake him on a daily basis. Or maybe he did, for all I knew.

"You thought I was evil?" he said.

I would have said it in an annoyed, possibly even angry, tone. Stefan said it as if he was flattered.

Of course he was, I realised. Why else would he have signed up to the iTem in the first place?

For a narcissistic vampire, nothing could be better for one's self-belief than a pretty slayer turning up, armed only with her virtue and a phallic symbol. The whole thing was so riddled with sexual symbolism that I started wondering if I should leave and let them get on with it. The feeling was intensified when I leaned forwards and noticed that Stefan had an erection. (His black jeans were very tight.)

"Well, you are a vampire, aren't you?" said Marianne, crossing her arms and trying to look righteous. It was adorable.

"I am, yes." His dark blue eyes looked at her slowly and enigmatically, long black eyelashes sweeping down and up, his cheekbones jutting out at her. She looked flustered.

"I — I..." She trailed off.

"Are you going to try and kill me again?" he asked, smiling. She shook her head. "Then you may sit down." He indicated the chair I'd recently vacated. I shifted up on my windowsill to allow her to get past me. She picked up her bag and sat down next to Stefan, looking up at him with wide eyes.

"This isn't turning out like I expected." She was still trembling slightly. "You were supposed to be evil. I thought I was risking my life trying to kill you. It was an adventure."

"It still is." Stefan reached for her hand; she let go of the bag and allowed him to put his pale hand over hers. "You have met a vampire. Is that not an adventure in itself?"

She looked up at him. "Meeting you feels like the most adventurous thing I've ever done." Her voice was breathy.

Oh, he'll like that, I thought.

He did. His eyes flashed at her. "Would you like to know about what it means to be a vampire? To be immortal?"

"Yes. I want to know everything about you," she said. I noticed she'd assimilated the word 'immortal' without so much as an eyebrow lift. I had a feeling she and Stefan were going to get on well together.

She said: "I'm so sorry... I'm so sorry I tried to stake you."

"You are forgiven," he said, smiling again.

They looked at each other. There was something in their mutual gaze that I couldn't quite cope with. I got off the windowsill and said flatly, "I think I'd better go."

Stefan and I glanced at each other. He nodded. "Very well."

I remembered something I'd meant to ask earlier. "Oh — can you give me Naomi's address? I want to check up on her."

"Certainly." He scribbled *Naomi Reed, 15 Branch Hill, Hampstead* on a piece of paper, while I stood by the table trying to look as if I had millions of important things I needed to go and do urgently. "I will email you, Elinor. I would like to finish the discussion we were having about... about us."

I stopped at the door to look back at Marianne one more time. She was really very pretty, I thought. You could lose yourself in the oceans of belief shimmering in her eyes. "I think it's already finished," I said, and left.

Chapter Seventeen
Cast Out

"Because of the universal taboos and biblical commands against blood drinking, many newly saved Christians, whose past included vampirism, now struggle with serious issues. 'Can I be a Born Again vampire?' 'Can God forgive me?' 'Will the church ever accept such a monster as I?'"
http://www.christiangoth.com/vampires.html

Sunday October 19th — afternoon

It was warm under the duvet. She liked that. And it was quiet. That was nice too. But things hurt, bits of her skin hurt, and her head felt weird and swimmy. She was in her own bed. She knew that. But she didn't know how or why, or what had been happening. All she knew was her body, lumpy and familiar under a lumpy and familiar duvet, warm but hurting.

"Are you OK?" said a voice.

Was she OK? Slowly, reluctantly, she swam up to consciousness. Her head was under the duvet (which was blue-and-white striped and old and comforting), so she couldn't tell who the voice belonged to, but it sounded familiar.

"Naomi?" said the voice. Someone was sitting down on the bed. Someone was pulling the duvet back. She squinted into the dim light of her bedroom, and the person started to come into focus. Red hair. Tall.

Yes.

"You're the girl from the party," she said. In her head the words were all clear and coherent, and she had no way of telling that they came out slurred and slow. The girl stroked her hair.

"I'm Elinor. Yes, I'm the girl from the party."

The party. There was something about the party that was bad. Something to do with her, with this girl. She didn't want to think about it. She pushed the memory away, but of course, as soon as she did that, it came back, jolting her head and forcing out a brief cry.

That boy. That had been the party where she'd done the thing. The thing she did to the black-clad boy. The bad thing.

Every morning she woke up feeling blank and empty and OK, and she liked that moment of forgetfulness. But after that, with a nauseous jerk, it would come back to her. Every morning. The thick taste of his blood, and the surprised look on his face.

She wished she could say sorry properly to the boy. She had said sorry lots of times already, but she didn't think he could hear, not now, because he was in the ground. And his soul was in hell. He hadn't even been a Christian, probably, and he'd hung around with the undead, so he probably had gone to hell. And she had sent him there. She deserved to die. She wished she was dead. She should be dead, not stuck here in this life, a life that seemed composed solely of guilt, and shame, and anger, and hatred.

She curled up back into the bed and put her head down, away from the girl's stroking hand. The girl was probably here to punish her. It wasn't fair. She'd already been punished, and she would be punished again later when she was dead. Couldn't she just have this moment of peace under the duvet, for once, without being reminded of her sins?

"Leave me alone," she said, voice muffled by her pillow.

"I just want to see how you are. Naomi, I want to help you. I'm not here to hurt you. I think I can help."

We can help you, Naomi.

She remembered that Justin had said that to her. Not long ago, but she couldn't remember where or when. Had she believed him? She wasn't sure. She had been scared of him — yes, she knew she had been scared of him and scared of the others, the members of his so-called church. The ones who had kept her there in a circle.

Memories jolted back. Yes. Two nights ago. (Had she been in bed ever since? Yes, she thought so.) There had been a graveyard. There had been a ring of pale fanged faces, staring at her with impersonal hunger. One of them had blindfolded her and given her some bitter chewy stuff to swallow, and she'd swallowed it, and then after that she didn't remember very much.

There had been blood and pain and a sense of evil. But that was true of most of her nights.

She peered cautiously over the edge of the duvet at Elinor, who didn't seem to be about to do anything bad to her. But you could never be sure. Naomi moved a little further up the bed and sat up against the wall, holding a pillow in front of her like a shield.

"Do you... do you know anything about what's been happening to me? About Friday night? Only I can't really remember much." Her words sounded faint in her own ears, and frightened.

Elinor looked across at her. "What do you remember about it?" Her voice was kind. Naomi lowered the pillow.

"I remember that two of the vampires came to my house and told my dad they were my friends and we were going out for the evening. He was pleased I had friends. He worries about me. I knew they weren't my friends but it didn't matter, I went with them anyway. They said we were going out somewhere fun. I asked them what I should wear and they said it didn't matter."

"Did you think you were going somewhere fun?"

"No. Of course not. I told you before, I don't have fun. It's best that I'm not allowed to have fun." She curled up against the headboard.

"Weren't you suspicious? Weren't you afraid that they'd hurt you?"

"I knew they would. I didn't mind."

"You felt you deserved it?"

"Of course. I always deserve it."

"Right. So, you went with them."

"Yes. And they took me to that graveyard." She paused for a moment, as the memories slowly came back. "And they made me take my clothes off, but they said I could have them back later. They made me sit in the circle. I ate something they gave me."

"And then Justin and Viola and Stefan arrived. I was with them."

"Did they? Yes. Were you? I remember... I remember Justin saying he could help me."

"Do you know what they did to you?"

Naomi ran her hand over her sore arms and her sore breasts, wincing. "I don't really know. But they cut me, I think. I mean, I can see they did."

"Yes, they did. They drank from you."

"They... drank? From me? But I'm one of them. In a way. I mean, I'm a vampire, like them."

Elinor was silent for a moment. Then she looked up at her and leaned forwards.

"Not any more," she said quietly.

Naomi stared blankly at her. "What?"

"Listen to me." Elinor took her hand. "They cured you. They performed a ritual, they drank your blood, and they drained out the corruption. You're not damned any more."

She stammered, "But — but they're demons. How can demons have cured me?"

"*Only* demons could cure you." Elinor's voice was low and persuasive, and she felt herself starting to shake. "It was a demon who infected you in the first place, after all. Only they can draw out their own taint. I was there, I saw it. I saw your face and body change after the ritual was finished. You looked so different, so much... lighter, so free. Trust me, Naomi. You're not a vampire any more."

"Then. Then — what am I?" Naomi hugged the pillow.

"You're human again. One of God's children again."

Naomi's grip on the pillow grew tighter. She was shaken to her depths. She barely remembered what life had been like before she'd become damned. Well, of course it had been better, because she'd been one of God's chosen and destined for heaven, but somehow when she thought back, it all seemed colourless and uninteresting, compared with the dark allure of the vampires.

She shook her head. No. It was wrong, it was evil, to think that. That had been the demon vampire talking, trying to drag her down and make her lose sight of her goal. She knew that all she wanted was her life back the way it was, and to be back in God's good graces.

Was she normal again? Was she really free of the taint of evil? She stayed very still and cleared her mind, as far as possible given that it was humming with fear and memories and guilt and what felt a bit like a hangover. She dug underneath all that — and it suddenly occurred to her that the fact she *could* dig under all that meant she was a lot more together than she had been for a while. Her brain felt clearer, more coherent. She was an empty vessel, shining, new, ready to be filled again with the love of Jesus. Jesus had rescued her from her life. He had chosen to use demonic vampires to work His will, but who was she to question His methods?

It was over.

She was saved.

Wide-eyed, she looked up at Elinor. "I'm normal again," she said, putting a hand to her mouth. "I cast out the demons!"

"Well, technically, they cast *you* out. But the effect's much the same."

She rocked back and forth in a sudden access of joy. "I'm cured! I don't have to want to hurt people any more! I can go back to church and I don't have to wear black all the time. And I don't have to feel guilty about that — thing." She bounced a little.

"Naomi?" Elinor had stood up and was leaning against the window beside the bed.

"Oh Jesus, thank you for letting me survive this test. Oh Jesus, fold me back into your heart. Oh Jesus —"

"Naomi?"

She stopped bouncing for a moment. "What?"

"Well, there is one thing."

Her heart sank. "No. No, you can't take it back. I believed you. Tell me it was true — tell me they did release me. Please. Please."

"It is true. Carry on bouncing. Don't worry, your soul is saved. In principle."

"In principle?" She wasn't sure she felt like bouncing now.

"Well, there is the question, or rather the issue, of... Simon."

"Oh." She deflated, almost with an audible pop. "But I was possessed by *demons*. Surely that doesn't count?"

Elinor sighed and ran a hand through her long hair. "I'm afraid it will count. Legally, for one thing —"

"Oh, but that's OK," she said cheerfully. "Dad won't let them prosecute."

"— and also morally. You know the rules, Naomi. Murder is a sin, and unrepentant sinners go to hell. You don't want to miss out on heaven because of a technicality."

The pillow crept back into her clutching arms. "Oh no. I have to go to heaven. I have to. Please, tell me what I have to do."

"Simple. You repent of your sin —"

"I do! I have, ever since that night!"

" — Good. And then you pay the price for it."

"Oh."

"I'm sorry, but I think it's your only choice. You have to suffer a little more for what you did. But," she added quickly, "this is only bodily suffering. Spiritually you'll be happy every single day from now on, now you've been reunited with God. A prison cell isn't going to take that away from you."

"A... a prison cell? Do I have to?" She squeezed her eyes tight. Was that to be the price? It was a high one. But she knew she deserved it. I am saved, she told herself. I can cope with anything now that I'm saved.

"I think you know you do. Your dad may protect you, but he won't be able to stop you going to prison if you confess. Don't worry about it. A few short years in prison will give you a chance for reflection. You can commune with Jesus much more effectively than you'd be able to if you were out here, with all these worldly distractions."

She sighed. "I know you're right. I... I can do it. Yes. It will make me closer to God. I have to pay for my crime. God will approve." She paused. "Do I have to do it right away?"

"No, no, not at all. I think you should wait a couple of weeks, just to see what happens. You want to be sure that you're clear of the vampiric taint before you give yourself up."

"Yes. Yes, that would be a good idea."

"Leave it to me. I'll check up on you in a few days and we'll see how we go, shall we?" Elinor had taken on some of the briskness of a teacher instructing a pupil, or a general giving orders to a soldier, but Naomi didn't care. She knew that she had some guilt to expiate, and if it wasn't going to be burnt away in hell, it would have to be worked off in prison. She was already becoming reconciled to the idea. Maybe some of the other prisoners would form a prayer group with her, and she could impress them with her experiences of demonic possession.

"OK," she said docilely. "I won't do anything right now. I'll wait for you to tell me when's the best time and what to do."

"Good girl." Elinor bent down and patted her head. "Congratulations again on being saved."

"Thank you!" She looked up gratefully at her saviour — or at least the person who'd delivered the news of her salvation — and, for a moment, she almost thought she could see a slim, translucent halo hovering behind Elinor's head.

Chapter Eighteen
The Foiling of Project Rupture

Friday October 24th — evening

The seventh and last meeting of CULT was brief, and did not include biscuits. The youth group were ushered out at eight-thirty sharp, Carol smiling distractedly at them as she patted them on the shoulders and sent them on their way. One girl made a tentative effort to stay and talk about her problems with her boyfriend, but Carol fobbed her off with a leaflet on the evils of drinking — not entirely relevant, but she was in a hurry. As the youth group left, some of them looked curiously at the seven people in the kitchen, picking up on their air of suppressed excitement. The CULT members barely noticed them. Each was sunk deep in fantasies of glory, world-saving, blood and fire. Some of them were focused on the world saving; others were more oriented towards the blood and the fire. Each to their own.

The flimsy wooden chairs were drawn forwards into a circle. Hands were nervously rubbed together, tea was sipped, glances were exchanged, and there were some high-pitched giggles from, unexpectedly, Pete and David. The usual Bible passage was read, but this time Carol added another verse:

> *"For the Lord himself shall descend from heaven with a shout, with the voice of the archangel, and with the trump of God: and the dead in Christ shall rise first. Then we which were alive and remain shall be caught up together with them in the clouds, to meet the Lord in the air: and so shall we ever be with the Lord."*

She looked up, eyes gleaming. "Now that's the genuine article. That's the Rapture we want. The select few who have kept the faith rewarded for their loyalty. Swept up to be with our Lord."

Noticing that Pete looked confused, Carol nodded encouragingly at him.

"Just wondering," he proffered tentatively, "about the select few thing. I mean, because all of America is saved, isn't it? And a lot of the rest of the world is getting there because of, you know, America invading them in order to spread the word. And quite a lot of Britain must be saved by now, now it's almost illegal not to be. So... won't the real Rapture capture, like, most of the world?"

"Not if the false Rapture happens," said Carol, adroitly deflecting the subject. It was wonderful that so much of the world was now Christian, she knew, but it did make the rhetoric a little difficult sometimes. It was much easier to preach as a persecuted minority. "If Project Rapture succeeds, millions will lose faith and when the real Rapture happens Heaven will be empty. Perhaps we in this room will be the only ones saved. Imagine that." She paused for emphasis.

David's imagination told him that this scenario would mean they had a lot more space, not to mention personal attention from God, but he decided to keep quiet.

"When you see a sinner in the street, you want to stop them, don't you?" Carol continued. "And tell them about the love of Jesus? That's what evangelising is all about, isn't it? Well, what we're doing is something like that, only on a bigger scale and in a more... preventative way. We're stopping the spread of lies, thus freeing the world to hear the Truth. I want to make sure you all understand that," she ended, rather severely.

There was a murmur of largely sincere agreement.

"Very well. Let us pray quickly, before we start the meeting proper."

Heads bowed. Pete started muttering *"Eu quero Jesus pat meu cabelo e chamar-me Bernard..."* (*I want Jesus to pat my hair and call me Bernard...*), but Carol wanted to get on with things, and cut him off in mid-babble.

"OK, everyone. I'm very proud of you all. You will be rewarded, have no doubt about that. Right, let's get on to the details. Ruth?"

Ruth's eyes gleamed palely in the bare yellow light of the church hall. She leaned forwards. She had made no notes this time. She knew her facts by heart.

"All the members of the Project Rupture conspiracy will be having a secret meeting in a pub next Friday night, the night of Halloween, prior to carrying out their Satanic plan on Saturday.

My research indicates that they will be meeting in the Cornish Arms, near Bank station, at ten-thirty that evening. That part of London is relatively quiet on Saturday nights, which is probably why they chose it. I suggest that as they leave, which will probably be closing time, we intercept and... collect them. We use the swords to incapacitate them, then pile them in the van — Pete, you did say you had a van?"

Pete nodded.

"— And bring them back here for the burning. Hannah and Mabel will be waiting here with wood and matches."

The two elderly ladies fluttered with anticipation.

"Excellent work, Ruth," said Carol approvingly. "Has everyone got that?"

"What if someone sees us with them?" asked David, a little nervous.

"We tell them our friends were drunk and we're taking them home," said Ruth. "Or if they're visibly bleeding, we say we're taking them to a hospital. It'll be easier than you think — in big cities, people don't see what they don't want to see."

"It's a sign of our moral decadence and lack of Christian spirit," said Himm. "Though of course, very useful to our purposes right now," he added hurriedly, having noticed that he'd momentarily come down on the wrong side.

"Remember, we only have to get away with it for that night. After that, it won't matter who knows." Ruth pushed her black hair back from her face. Her eyes were almost other-worldly in their intensity. "And remember that God is on our side. We will succeed. And we will announce the next day that we have executed the leaders of a Satanic conspiracy. We'll have the CUS on our side too," she added more prosaically, "so we may well be exempted from the human laws on murder. If not, we will become martyrs for the cause, a glorious fate in itself."

"Indeed." said Carol. "OK, so the five of us will meet here at seven, prepare and pray, and then drive to Bank in Pete's van. Pete will bring the swords. And we'll divert suspicion best by being noticeable, so as discussed, all of us will be dressed in pirate costumes."

There was a brief pause, but nobody felt up to arguing with Carol on this point.

"Will five of us be enough to manage the six of them?" asked David.

Carol sent him a sharp glance; he was being far too negative. "They won't be expecting us. And angels will be fighting at our back."

David nodded uncertainly.

"Does anyone else have any questions?"

There was silence.

"Fantastic. I'll see you all next Friday — Hannah and Mabel, you're sure you don't mind running the youth group next week while we're off picking up the people for burning?"

"Not at all," said Mabel. "I thought I could teach them how to crochet. The world needs more crochet."

"Excellent," said Carol enthusiastically.

"I thought I could tell them about varicose veins," said Hannah.

"Excellent," said Carol again, a touch less enthusiastically. "I'm sure they'll appreciate your expertise. And you'll make sure they've all gone before we bring the Rupture sinners back here? And you'll guard the woodpile in the cemetery?"

"Oh yes, Carol," they chorused, if two people can chorus.

"Wonderful." She smiled. They basked in her approval.

Carol and Himmler nodded at each other. "Great," he said, "see you all next week! Don't forget your costumes! And please, make sure they're dark-coloured. You know," he added cheerfully, "for the blood."

"And remember," Carol said in conclusion, as the group got up to leave, "if we wake up on Sunday morning and there's a giant fake Jesus outside our bedroom windows — it'll be nobody's fault but our own!"

Chapter Nineteen
Twelve Days

"Are vampires immortal? ... If you mean, 'Are vampires capable of living for periods of time extending well past the average human lifespan?' then the answer is that I do not know. Many believe so, and I have met and talked to other vampires who claim to have lived for an extended time. I cannot personally vouch for the validity of this claim... If you mean, 'Are vampires capable of withstanding extreme and usually fatal injuries, such as being hit by a train or being shot in the head?' then the answer is 'No.'"
http://www.sanguinarius.org/faqs/immortal.shtml

Search terms:
haemavore.com, are vampires immortal?

Up to October 31ˢᵗ

The first conversation between Stefan and Marianne lasted for eight hours (concluding only when they reached Stefan's bed that evening and found less conversational activities they also wanted to explore). Amongst other topics, it included their childhoods (suburban), their adolescences (lonely, misunderstood), their previous relationships (unsatisfactory, meaningless) and their hopes and dreams (suddenly bright, now that they had encountered each other).

The next day, they both called in sick to work and stayed in bed, eating vegan pizza and finding that despite the previous day they still had an endless number of things to talk about. Marianne, of course, instantly accepted that Stefan was an immortal vampire. Indeed, much of the conversation on the second day revolved around discussions of when she herself could be Turned and accepted into the Jesus' Blood Church. Stefan assured her that he had no doubt she would be welcomed. They agreed, though, that Marianne's vampirification would be a private ceremony between the two of them. Marianne tentatively suggested the night of Halloween for the ritual. She was worried that he would think it too gimmicky and obvious, but he was enthusiastic.

On the third day of their love, they spent most of the day in Stefan's bed in a state of mute, blissful communion.

On the fourth day of their love, a Wednesday, they finally went to work — sidling in, late and unwashed and bleary, and avoiding their colleagues' cheerful questions about what they'd been up to. Most of Marianne's colleagues had in any case given up asking what she'd been up to, in case she told them. After work, Marianne went home long enough to pack a bag, and returned to Hammersmith.

Halfway through Friday afternoon, on the sixth day of their love, they gave up trying to stay at work, pleaded headaches, and met each other in Regent's Park, where they spent the afternoon holding hands at the zoo. Stefan spent a long time in the nocturnal section, looking thoughtfully at the bats.

That night he took her to a vampire club in Camden called Schadenfreude. It was officially just a goth club, but there was one large corner where his kind congregated. They'd spent the late afternoon shopping. Marianne had bought a long dark purple dress in velvet and silk, low-cut and strapless. She'd bought shoes too, short black boots with high heels. In normal shoes, she and Stefan had trouble holding hands when they walked. She also bought fresh mascara and eyeliner and dark, dark lipstick. She would have dyed her hair, but it was already black.

They walked into the club hand in hand. Marianne chatted to the vampires as if she had been part of the community all her life, and danced to the music as if she had been a goth forever.

The seventh day of their love was Saturday. They did not rest. They came home at 6am, slept, and got up in the afternoon to see a film, a CUS-funded production about a homosexual who visited Hell, was horrified by the pain and suffering he saw there, repented of his soulless existence and asked God to forgive him his sins. But God wouldn't listen and so the man was sent to Hell for all eternity.

They agreed that movies had really gone downhill since the CUS took over.

On Sunday they visited a small shop in a back street near King's Cross and Marianne had a pair of fangs fitted.

On Monday they did not even bother to discuss whether or not they were going to work. There were more important things to do, namely planning Friday's ritual.

On Tuesday, the tenth day, they talked about what they would do in eternity together — the house they would live in, the travels to India and Thailand and Prague and Vienna, whether or not they would be able to have children. Could immortal vampires reproduce? Would the children be vampires? Stefan said he would ask Justin. Surely there would be some Church members who were old enough to know.

(Later — much later — when repeating the conversation to me, Marianne noted that neither of them had questioned or doubted the Church, even though there were so many questions needing to be asked and doubts that could have surfaced. They were caught up entirely, hurtling towards their finale on an unstoppable wave, believing and passionate and blind.)

On the evening of the eleventh day, they had dinner with Justin in Camden and he gave his permission for Marianne to be Turned. He gave them some magic mushrooms for the ceremony.

On Thursday, the twelfth day, they bought candles and champagne and black silk bed-sheets. By now, both of them had a series of polite and increasingly anxious messages from their workplaces, wondering where they were and if they could possibly get a doctor's note. They ignored them.

Thursday night and Friday were spent apart, in preparation for the ritual. Marianne went shopping for something appropriate for the occasion and ended up with a long black silk dress with dark red lace, and a black velvet cloak. It was only after the shopping trip that she realised she would almost certainly be naked for the ceremony anyway, but she didn't take the dress back. She had an eternity to wear it in, after all.

That Friday, October 31st, was the thirteenth day of their love.

Chapter Twenty
Operation Trick or Treat

"The uninformed Christian has no idea that there truly are demonic spirits which are contacted and activated as people call out to them in jest or in seriousness. Every act around Halloween is in honor of false gods, which are spirits in the realm of the Satanic. Those who have been deeply involved in witchcraft and who are now free, declare that even those who say they worship spirits of nature are in actuality contacting the Satanic realm without knowing it."
http://www.webzonecom.com/ccn/cults/issu37.txt

Search term:
Jack Chick Halloween

Friday, October 31st — evening

In the busy darkness of Halloween night, Clapham High Street could almost have been Soho: restaurants bustling and bright, pubs packed and screamingly loud, queues stretching round corner after corner, even in the cold, for big clubs staffed by stolid unsmiling bouncers. Up and down the streets people hurried and argued and giggled and drunkenly weaved around each other as fireworks squealed and popped in the distance.

That was in the main streets, though. Off on the side roads the noise decreased sharply. Going further down along the curving rows of big, quiet terraced houses, the babble of Friday night fun became as faint as the noise of the aeroplanes passing above. There was little similarity to Soho here.

A few more roads away from the centre and the houses were smaller, the roads narrower, the pubs quieter. There was noise tonight, though. Although Clapham Common was holding a big firework display, some households had opted to do their own, and 'whee!' sounds arose from several back gardens as rockets were released by parents squinting against torches in the dark, accompanied by small children oohing or crying according to temperament. A couple even had bonfires, though they had fallen out of favour in recent years.

There was a bonfire, too, that nobody saw. In the cemetery of the local Resurrected Church, earlier that evening, the youth group had been encouraged to pile up wood and burn an effigy of Satan. They had been pleased to be allowed to do anything at all on Halloween night — usually Carol just sat them down and read them tracts about devil-worshipping witches who mixed broken glass into trick-or-treat sweets — so they amassed piles and piles of wood. It was more than they had time to burn, but Hannah and Mabel said that was fine. The two elderly ladies seemed unusually nervous and excited, thought some of the teenagers, but they put it down to the nearby fireworks. Or perhaps to the allure of the flames. When the teenagers left, both women were gazing entranced into the heart of the bonfire, as if waiting for something.

Meanwhile, a few miles north of Clapham, the City contingent of CULT had arrived at their destination. The pub to which Ruth had directed them was a large and ancient two-storied affair by the river. Conveniently, there was a tiny dark cul-de-sac opposite the road leading to the entrance to the main bar, so they reversed Pete's van as far down it as they could and felt satisfyingly hidden. Carol, Himm and Pete stayed in the van, with David loitering at the cul-de-sac's entrance in what he believed was a convincingly casual manner in order to monitor arrivals and departures. Ruth, they hoped, would soon arrive at the pub to meet the conspirators — the *other* conspirators, the evil ones — but none of them had spotted anything yet. In accordance with the plan, they were all dressed as pirates, with plastic scabbards hiding real swords.

At ten past ten, things began to happen. A familiar shape appeared, scurrying along in the dark, then turning down the road toward the river, and David texted to let the others know that Ruth had arrived. By half past ten, five of the six members of the Rupture conspiracy had entered the pub. Ruth had given David detailed descriptions and he easily recognised them all. The two IT people, Justin and Viola, arrived together and David heard them say "... better not take too long..." and "...starts playing at midnight...", presumably intending to go clubbing after the meeting. They were dressed up in lacy black and heavy make-up, and he found them scary. Ranjit and Paul, the government conspirators, also turned up together, but did not speak to each other on the way in. James, the psychic, came alone.

"I wonder where the other one is?" Himm worried. He liked things to be neat and complete.

"Stefan?" said Carol, consulting her notes. "Well, maybe he's just late. Punctuality probably doesn't mean much to that type."

"I'm sure you're right," said her husband loyally.

They waited. It would be untrue to say that an air of suppressed excitement pervaded the van: it wasn't suppressed at all. Every now and then one of them burst into giggles. The pirate costumes didn't help, of course. Their hats kept falling off, which made them all giggle more. Innocent of all recreational drug or alcohol use, the members of CULT were nevertheless vulnerable to the heady intoxication of adrenaline, a feeling they rarely experienced to this extent and which made them, not to put too fine a point on it, high.

Outside, seventeen-year-old David crouched in the alleyway opposite the pub, cold but excited. David's dreams had recently been of guns and blood. Tonight, he thought, his dreams would come true. Well, apart from the guns. But he was quite happy with swords instead. He had been practicing.

Poised and hidden, pretending with concentrated intensity that he was a Vietnam soldier in the jungle – not an easy thing to do in a British autumn – David was so lost in fantasies that he nearly missed it when two of the conspirators left the pub. But Justin was too conspicuous a figure not to spot, and a frantic text reached the van just as the goths paused under a streetlamp to light cigarettes.

Thirty seconds later, Himm stepped out from the alleyway, resplendent in knee-high boots, tricorn hat and an inflatable red parrot attached precariously to one shoulder. "Excuse me?" he called across the road. Justin and Viola looked over. "Um... do you want to buy some drugs?"

They glanced at each other and shrugged. "Sure, if you stop shouting like that," Justin said, "although I have to tell you, most dealers dress a little more conservatively than you. But who are we to criticise?" They walked across the empty road towards the alleyway.

"It's a new policy," said Himm, desperately wishing they'd practised this bit more thoroughly. "We find we sell more drugs if we wear pirate costumes. Just one of those bits of market research, nobody knows why it works but it does." He beckoned them into the alleyway. "Here, my assistant Dav... er, Daniel, has all the drugs laid out for you. LSE, magic toadstools, you name it, we've got it!" The patter was difficult for him, but he'd got them into the passageway's entrance and that was what mattered. He nodded at David, who had drawn his sword.

"Cool," said Justin. "Is that for sale, too?"

"Er... no." Himm drew his, too, glanced briefly up and down the street — it was completely deserted — and stabbed Justin in the leg.

"Fuck!" Justin staggered against the alley wall. David lunged forward and stabbed Viola in the arm. "Fuck!" she echoed, falling against Justin. But there wasn't anyone around to hear.

"Oh no, I'm so sorry," Himm said quickly and apologetically. "We've only just bought them, you see. We haven't practised using them much, we didn't mean to get you... here, let us take you to hospital and get those cuts looked at."

"Fuck off," Justin and Viola groaned in near-unison. But they were hurt, and confused by Himm's inoffensive demeanour. It seemed incredible that someone like him could have attacked them. Maybe, they thought, the stabbing had been accidental, somehow. And Justin couldn't run, anyway.

"Come on," said Himm persuasively. "We'll take you to hospital. Trust me, I'm a church warden." (He was.) He nodded to David and they gently pushed Justin and Viola down the alleyway towards the van, where Carol was ready to welcome them with a cheerful smile. They acquiesced — they were out of their depth, and that wasn't somewhere they were used to being. Carol opened the back of the van and said firmly, "Come on now, there's a good boy and girl. We need to get those nasty cuts seen to."

Obeying some atavistic instinct, the goths got in the van. Carol's primary-school-headmistress persona both terrorised and appealed to the inner five-year-old in almost everyone. You just knew that if you didn't do what she said, you'd get a smacked bottom.

"OK," said Carol, patting Viola cheerfully on her damaged arm, "now just wait in there a sec, I think there may be some more wounded people along in a minute. Dangerous places, pubs, you know." She slammed the back door, leaving Pete in the driver's seat and the goths curled up, confused and in pain, in the back of the van. As Carol, Himm and David scurried back up the alleyway, they could hear Justin asking Pete if he had any drugs.

Ranjit, Paul and James emerged from the pub a few moments later, looking mildly annoyed.

"...thought she said she had some important information that she needed to tell us..."

"...complete waste of time..."

"Hey!" called Himm, emboldened by the success of his first trap. "There's something weird going on over there." He pointed to the alleyway. "It almost looks like... aliens!" (Ruth had given them a few notes on roughly what to say.)

Paul's eyes lit up at once. "Aliens? Really?"

Ranjit groaned. "For God's sake, Paul..."

James looked enthusiastic. "Oh come on, let's have a peek. My instincts tell me that no harm will come to us — and if it does I can always take my animal form and the aliens will appreciate that I'm a higher form of being." Ranjit and Paul groaned in unison. But all three crossed the road.

"Hey, why have you got an inflatable parrot on your shoulder?" Ranjit asked.

"It's not inflatable," said Himm, improvising, "it's just quiet. It brings me messages from other dimensions."

"*Which* other dimensions?" said Ranjit.

"The, er, seventh one. And, er, the one with the tiny red goblins, I'm sure you know it. Look, just stand here, will you?" Himm positioned them firmly in front of the alleyway and the three men peered down, hoping for flickering lights or the sound of high inhuman voices asking to be taken to someone's leader. Instead they got stabbed by David, who was really getting into it now and managed to poke all three in quick succession through a variety of legs.

"Aliens!" shouted Himm, pushing them through the alleyway. "Aliens stabbed you! Come this way!"

A few minutes later, the van contained five stab victims, all a bit stunned and in quite a lot of pain. They were all gagged now, with hoods over their heads, and handcuffed to a large wooden plank. That had taken quite a bit of struggling, but CULT had the advantage of weaponry, determination, and having the full, uninjured use of all their limbs.

"Right," said Carol, standing outside the van with the others. "We've got five, but we need the sixth, Stefan Drayton. He's probably completely untrustworthy, even doing Satan's work. Himm and I will take our car and go and get him." It was parked a few streets away in case of just this kind of emergency, and luckily, Ruth had given them Stefan's home address. "David, you and Pete take this lot back to the church, OK? Don't burn anyone till we arrive."

As instructed, the van docilely headed south towards Clapham and the church, where two old ladies with a large box of matches were eagerly awaiting their arrival. And off the Cingins drove to Hammersmith, to kidnap their sixth victim.

In the excitement, everyone forgot to wonder where Ruth had got to.

Chapter Twenty-one
Love and death

Friday, October 31st — evening

Later, when Marianne would look back and remember the twelve brief days of her vampiric romance, it was perhaps inevitable that all of it seemed to be merely prelude, foreshadowing. The time felt like an inappropriately cheerful accompaniment to its sudden, faintly ludicrous end. She seldom dwelt on it, because she had thrust that memory down into a mental oubliette from whence it rarely escaped. That Halloween, with its ritual and blood, became a night that cast a very long shadow behind it, a shadow that greyed out Marianne's memories of the love affair like a blurred photocopy.

But that was later. At the time — although she did begin the evening believing that a climactic point in her life was about to be reached — she completely failed to foresee what that climax would be. In fact she got it backwards. She believed that the evening would culminate in life eternal. That she and her beloved would never grow old, never die, and live together in bliss and bloodlust forever. (Did she believe, *really* believe that she would live on the blood of others for always? Did she really think about it?)

At first, when she let her mind run back to the events of that evening, she remembered nothing until the end. And then, the aftermath.

But eventually I did make her tell me how it happened.

* * *

"So you don't think it being Halloween is too gimmicky?" she asked, dipping an exploratory finger into the magic mushroom herbal tea and licking. It tasted hot and fungal and slightly bitter.

"Perhaps a little. But it taps into a powerful tradition, after all. Besides, I couldn't have waited any longer." Stefan smiled at her and carefully poured out the tea into two delicate china cups. He and Marianne were both naked (Stefan had put the heating on to make this viable) and freshly bathed. Dim red light from stained glass bulbs faintly illuminated the flat and made the wooden floors and pale walls look almost exotic. Outside, orange street lights shone and flickered on the river Thames, but they weren't looking outside, and anyway, the blinds were closed.

The flat was quiet, just some classical music playing unobtrusively in the bedroom. Marianne didn't recognise it, but it fitted her mood, which was calm, solemn and anticipatory. In the bedroom there was a small glass table on which lay two sterilised scalpels, a bottle of antiseptic, and tissues. They were visible from the kitchen, and she couldn't stop herself from continually glancing towards them. Stefan caught her shiver of excitement and smiled at her, his fangs exposed. She shivered again.

"Are we ready?"

"I think so." He picked up the cups. "Let us adjourn."

They crossed the living room floor, cool wood against their bare feet, and shut the bedroom door behind them. Here the dim red was replaced by the shifting yellow of seven candles, placed around the room so as to give just enough light. The black-sheeted bed looked sinister in that glow, especially with the ropes tied round the bedposts and the two gleaming scalpels lying on the table.

Now it was real. Marianne was afraid, but in a way she found nervously enjoyable. She hugged herself, damp hands sliding over smooth silky hips and smooth silky breasts, her body pale in the candlelight, her eager dark eyes fixed on Stefan with absolute trust. He handed her the tea and they sipped it, standing up and side by side, facing the bed.

They finished. They put the cups down on the table.

"We should complete the ritual in the next twenty minutes or so," he said, "before the drug kicks in." She nodded. He held her tightly for a moment, then said, "I love you. Lie down, face up." She spread herself out on the bed, slithery sheets against her skin, pushing her hair up out of the way. He tied her wrists to the bedposts. It wasn't a necessary part of the ritual; she had suggested it. Some of her previous experiences had had an influence.

Stefan stroked her shoulders and breasts and stomach and thighs and ankles, and she felt herself relax. She stole a glance down at her body and thought how nice it looked, warm and golden in the candlelight. She thought about it being like that always, never wrinkling or fading. As the thought occurred, Stefan picked up one of the scalpels and slashed her.

"Ow!" she said involuntarily, head back and wrists pulling against the ropes. He licked her stomach, and that hurt more than the cutting had, but she had begun to find a kind of exhilaration in the pain. She watched with fascination as each drop of blood appeared on her skin and was absorbed into his mouth. He cut her again, over the left breast, and that was too far up for her to see the blood, but she could almost touch Stefan's dark hair with her tongue as he lapped.

She began to feel as though the pain and the blood and the licking were taking her somewhere, taking her away, fusing her mind and body and soul into the single entity they should always have been but never were. An entity that was wholly given over to rosy, formless ecstasy.

He sat up, keeping a hand on her left breast. She felt the nipple crinkling under his palm. "Jesus, first of the vampires, this offering is to you. This woman is dedicating herself to you. Drink her in and drink her deep." He bent to lap at her again. Marianne hadn't felt so peaceful in a long time.

Finally, he sat up again and smiled dizzily in her direction. "That was wonderful." She tried to nod but only managed to incline her head slightly and smile back, feeling so happy she thought she would die. He untied her wrists and kissed the ridges where the ropes had marked them, kissed her cuts, and kissed her face. He helped her sit up and she clung to him. When she opened her eyes again, the flickering-yellow dark of the bedroom had taken on a new vibrancy. All the colours were brighter, almost fluorescent, almost alive. If the colour yellow could talk, what would it say? She giggled, suddenly and explosively.

"Are you all right?" Stefan's voice was crimson and purple and it wound round his head in a meandering wavy line. "Marianne?"

"Oh, I'm fine." She giggled again. "I'm wonderful. Are you wonderful?"

"I am very happy." He moved her to the end of the bed and lay down. "Now you must drink from me."

"Hurray," she said, watching the word 'hurray' spiral across the bed and drift towards the ceiling in a luminescent pink haze. "But I have to tie you up first."

"If you wish." She pushed his wrists against the bedposts and knotted the ropes, chatting. "Last time I did this was with a guy called Martin. He made me a domina, domina, dominininatrix. It was fun. I tied him up and beat him and he loved it. Did I ever tell you about that?"

"Yes, you did." In the preceding twelve days they'd told each other virtually everything there was to know about their lives.

"Good. I want you to know everything about me."

"I want to know everything about you."

"You've got an erection," she said informatively. "Shall I cut it?" "Er, no. Just stick to the neck and chest, darling. Are you you sure up to this?"

"Oh, yes!" She picked up the clean scalpel. "Looking forward to it. I want to drink from you. Do I have to say the stuff you said, to Jesus?"

"No, just drink from me, and then it is finished. And then we can make love all night and live forever."

She smiled down at him, although he seemed to be quite a long way away. And yet his eyes were very close to her. She vaguely noticed that they looked a little worried. The colour of worried was brownish-purple-gold.

"Marianne?"

"Yes?"

"I think the mushrooms have kicked in for you."

"That would explain the colours," she said, dreamily waving the scalpel in the air to see its trail sparkle like diamonds.

"Perhaps we should — listen, would it be best if we waited — aaah!"

She sliced at his chest. He breathed in sharply.

Blood welled up on his skin and she hummed to herself with satisfaction. She bent in and sucked, tasting the copper, and felt the blood sigh with pleasure as it dissolved on her tongue. She could feel it dissipating through her veins, mating with her own blood as her blood was mating with Stefan's in his veins. "It's done," she said aloud, not realising she was saying it aloud.

"It's done," said her lover. His body was gleaming at her, dazzlingly bright. They were immortal.

"We'll never die," she said. The words "*We'll never die*" danced across his stomach in a rainbow swirl. The words were beautiful.

"We are bonded forever," he said. They looked at each other and both saw tiny lightning flashes sparking between them.

There is a reason why magic mushrooms are often used in rituals.

She sliced him again, laughing at the rush of it. Lines of red traced across the white. Then they began to spill into each other.

"I can hardly see your skin any more," she said.

His breathing became shallower. He made small, panting noises.

She cut and cut. The blood was baptising her hands, running down over the bed, trickling across the wood of the floor. Stefan's wrists sagged against the bedposts.

Lost in the drug, she didn't even notice when he stopped breathing.

Chapter Twenty-two
Find Me a Grave Man

Friday, October 31st — midnight

Carol drove the car, while Himm removed his Jolly Roger hat, eye patch and the parrot on his shoulder. He unfastened Carol's parrot, too. She'd already taken the eye patch and hat off to drive. It took them just under an hour to get to Hammersmith, including finding Stefan's flat. Himm accidentally directed them towards Wimbledon, but they found their way back eventually. When they arrived, it was just after midnight. They quickly removed their pantaloons and doublets, so that they were now wearing respectable dark suits.

They buzzed the entry phone.

A pause, then a woman's voice. "Hello?"

Carol frowned, wondering why her voice sounded familiar, but she stuck to the script she'd chosen.

"Hello, we found something in the street and we think it may belong to the owner of this flat. Can we come up?"

There was silence from the other end of the phone. Carol tried again. "It looked quite expensive, this, er, thing. I'm sure the owner would like it back. Can we speak to him?"

The crackly phone gave out a faint, strangled laugh. "No. No, I don't think you can." There was a pause. "I know your voice," said the phone. "Who are you?"

"My name's Carol."

Another pause. Then the voice said, "Carol, I think you'd better come up," and the buzzer sounded.

The flat was on the third floor. They knocked gently on the door and when it opened, Carol knew why the voice sounded familiar.

"Marianne!" she exclaimed, astonished. Marianne cast a quick look around the hallway and shushed them. She drew back and the Cingins entered.

"Sit down," she said. Temporarily feeling out of control of the situation, they sat on the Ikea sofa while Marianne paced up and down the living room. Carol thought she looked terrible. Her face was white and strained, her hair looked wild and her eyes were black-ringed. Her dark red silk dressing gown covered the rest of her body, but Carol thought she could see a bloody mark on her neck.

"What's going on, Marianne dear?" she asked carefully. The girl had betrayed her, but now didn't seem like a good time to mention it.

"Nothing. Nothing's going on." She stopped for a moment and looked at Carol and Himm. "Wait a moment. Why are you here? You didn't really find something in the street, did you?"

Carol looked at the girl for a moment and decided to tell the truth.

"No. We came for Stefan Drayton. This is his flat, isn't it?"

She resumed pacing. "Oh yes, yes, it is. I'm his... I was his girlfriend."

"I see. Well, there's a coincidence. Anyway, the thing is, Mr Drayton is, well, he's involved in a conspiracy. I told you about Project Rupture, didn't I?"

"False Rapture. Demonic telepathy. I remember." Marianne gave a short almost-laugh. "Though it all seems a really long time ago."

"Good. Well, I'm afraid we discovered that Mr Drayton was one of the Rupture ringleaders. We came here to... confront him, and take whatever measures were necessary to stop him."

This took Marianne aback. She stopped pacing and stared wide-eyed at the couple.

"You were planning to — to kill him? Stefan?"

"Well," Himm equivocated, "if necessary. Yes. A bit."

"I see."

She stood absolutely still for a moment, looking desperate and thoughtful, arms wrapped tightly around her body. Eventually she appeared to come to a decision.

"Carol."

"Yes?"

"I said I'd come to your meeting, didn't I?

"You did, yes." A very slight tinge of frostiness crept into the woman's tones.

"I'm sorry I didn't come. The truth is..." she paused, then took a deep breath, "the truth is, I was overwhelmed. By the things you told me. The idea of a false Rapture, it was so evil, I couldn't even bear to think about it, you see. And then I met Stefan. Through a – a mutual friend. We fell in love. And I told him about Project Rapture. And, and he confessed to me that he was in charge of it. Tonight. He confessed tonight that he was in charge, and I was... aghast. Appalled. It was terrible." She paused again.

They nodded eagerly and sympathetically. Marianne was back on their side.

"Anyway, so I was very angry. And I knew I had to stop him. So, I, so I, so I..."

"You killed him!" Carol exclaimed, surprised and joyful.

"Yes. I killed him. Yes. He's in the bedroom. He's all yours. Take him away. Please." She gestured towards the bedroom door with a weak little flourish of the wrist.

The Cingin couple exchanged triumphant glances. This was better than they could have hoped for. Himm got up and disappeared into the bedroom, and Carol smiled at her newly redeemed protégé.

"Well, thank you very much, Marianne dear. We'll certainly take him. There's a ceremonial bonfire all ready for him, right behind our church. And we've got a nice car all ready downstairs. He's, um, easily transportable, is he? You didn't cut him up into little bits or anything?"

"No, I just... sort of stabbed him."

She curled up in a corner of the sofa. It's obviously been a strain on her, Carol thought kindly. Well, no wonder.

"Would you like to come with us, dear, and see him burnt? Might help to cheer you up a bit?"

"No, thank you. You go ahead. I'll just stay here and think about what I've done. I mean, about how wonderful and Christian it was. If that's OK."

"Oh, certainly, no problem."

"There was one thing."

"Yes, dear?"

"If the plan should fail... I mean, if the police become involved at some stage..."

"You'd rather your name wasn't mentioned?"

"Please."

Carol patted her hand. "No problem at all, dear. If you don't want to share the glory of our mission, that's entirely up to you. You've certainly done your bit."

She curled up even tighter. "Thank you."

"We'll just say we took him alive. It looked a bit better for us, anyway, to be honest — it's neater if we officially kill them all together."

"You sound as if you're expecting the police to catch you."

"Well, you have to take these things into account, don't you, dear? We're all prepared to be martyred for the glory of God." It was fairly obvious at this point that Carol wasn't just prepared, she was eager. She wanted to be caught. She wanted the martyrdom. Her face was lit up with it.

Himm emerged, looking rather sick and dragging a tall crumpled shape with some degree of effort. To Marianne's relief, the body was wrapped in a large sheet. "He wasn't, er, he wasn't wearing very much, so I —" he gestured to the sheet. "We just need to get downstairs without anyone noticing and we should be fine. But we need to be fast, the blood's going to soak through in a minute." Carol and Marianne both simultaneously realised that the dark sheet was darker in some areas than others, and looked away. Himm shifted position and grunted. "Carol dear, I think I might need your help."

"Of course." Between them, they got Stefan's body off the ground. Marianne opened the door for them with a blank expression that Carol interpreted as pleased relief.

"Nice to see you again, dear." Carol tried to shake hands, but couldn't let go of the body and ended up gesturing with one of Stefan's arms instead. Marianne shuddered. "I'll be in touch."

"That would be nice." Slowly, gently, Marianne closed the door behind the two of them, or rather the three of them.

Stefan fitted on the back seat of the car, if they pushed him together a little and put the pirate costumes in the boot. They glanced back at him occasionally as they drove cheerfully back to Clapham, visions of fire in their heads, glowing with achievement.

Chapter Twenty-three
A Cult Hit

"...how can a true Christian even imagine to have anything whatsoever to do with this hideous, horrible, and macabre eve of pagan glorification of Satan, witchcraft, demons, ghouls, sorcery, and diabolical Satanic deception?"
http://www.hope-of-israel.org/hallowen.htm

October 31st — late

The fact that the bonfire behind the church was still burning at 1am was unusual, but nobody came round to complain. Very few windows overlooked the churchyard, and after all, it was Halloween. Church members were perhaps the most likely to wonder what was going on, but in anticipation of this, Carol had taken the precaution of reading out a notice at the previous week's service, announcing that her country dancing group would be having a late practice on Friday night and would be learning a new version of Morris dancing which involved setting the sticks on fire. The younger half of the church applauded Carol's innovation; the elderly half listened bemused, but didn't dare question her. The vicar was appeased by a promise that all funds raised by the fire-assisted Morris dancing would be put towards replacing the church tower.

Carol's only aim was to get through the night undetected. She hoped the vicar and the church would support her when they found out the truth, but she didn't really care. She could feel Jesus standing behind her, laying an approving hand on her shoulder and telling her that she was His representative on earth. She would turn England into a genuinely Christian country like America, not this secular irreligious place where atheists, Catholics and homosexuals were free to walk the streets as if they belonged. In the light of the flames her eyes flashed wide and bright and clear. Her conscience was untroubled.

"Over here, bring them over," Himm instructed, and David and Pete obediently dragged each of the limp figures out of the van and across the yard until five of them sat lined up along the back wall, like tired children waiting for their turn at rounders. Four of them were upright. One kept slumping sideways, and had to be propped up a lot. This was Viola. Due to the jiggling about in the van, and a few over-enthusiastically inflicted stab wounds — David, sitting in the back of the van with the prisoners, had discovered he had a taste, not to mention a talent, for stabbing people — Viola had died by the time the van arrived at the church hall.

"Not fair," complained Mabel, poking the corpse. "You promised you wouldn't start without us."

"Sorry." David shrugged. "I didn't think she'd be that fragile."

"You need to learn not to judge by appearances," said Carol, spotting the opportunity for a moral lesson. "Just because someone wears black and paints her face like a whore, that doesn't mean she's hard inside. Someone like that can still be delicate and weak and die from a mere handful of stab wounds."

"Yes, Carol. Sorry."

"That's fine, David. I'm sure you won't make that mistake next time."

"No, Carol."

"Great. Now, let's take a look at how the fire's going."

The fire was going well. The flames flickered high like a medieval vision of hell, if hell contained two elderly ladies standing next to the fire and giggling. Hannah and Mabel looked younger and more energetic than they had for years, even though it was several hours past their normal bedtime. They even had pitchforks — or at least sticks — which they were using to poke the figure tied to the pole in the centre of the flames. When they weren't busy with the burning corpse, they were chatting about knitting patterns, rival brands of chocolate bars and the speed at which skin burns. With every poke they visualised the rule of Satan retreating further back into the shadows, and they glowed with achievement. Everyone needs to feel that they've made a difference in life.

The figure on the bonfire was the late Stefan Drayton. His body provided a centrepiece to the macabre scene, his face covered by his crackling hair. The smell of burning flesh was off-putting, but nevertheless the atmosphere was high-spirited and celebratory.

David guarded the prisoners. Himm and Pete circled the graveyard, keeping an eye out for intruders. Carol oversaw.

Everybody had now noticed that Ruth was missing, but the mood was too buoyant for anyone to mind much. She'd served her purpose.

They hadn't bothered talking to the prisoners. There was no point. They already knew about the conspiracy, and they were already committed to the course of action they'd chosen. Anyway, communicating with the conspirators would be communing with the Devil, and thus practically dabbling with the occult. No — gag them and burn them, that was the plan.

They could be taunted, of course, nothing wrong with that, provided they didn't answer back. David had been firmly warned that he wasn't allowed to kill any more of them before they got to the bonfire, but he still couldn't stop himself poking bits of bodies with his sword, the bits he thought wouldn't be fatal. (Feet. Hands. An occasional face. Doing the Lord's work felt *good*.)

The prisoners moaned. David told them about Hell, with reference to the bonfire in front of them. Hannah and Mabel joined in, with no apparent sense that in the scenario they described, they had cast themselves as demons. Himm and Pete discussed the cricket scores, with the air of adult men who felt that the business of stabbing and burning was best left to the women and teenagers.

Carol worried. The fire wasn't hot enough; it was taking ages to burn Stefan's body, and then there were five more to go. Still, she considered, two out of six were already dead, and that wasn't bad. Should they kill the other four now and just burn the bodies? But then it would all be over far too quickly. Perhaps they could stretch out the killing for a little longer. But on the other hand, what if the police came and not everyone was dead? That would be a catastrophe.

She was in the process of trying to make the decision when Ruth appeared.

Chapter Twenty-four
The Sound of Sirens

Friday, October 31st — late

I couldn't resist.

There was no need for me to be there. I hadn't planned to be there. I had very specific plans revolving around me *not* being there. But when it came to it, I realised that I'd underestimated my own desire to be on the spot, to see for myself how it was going. So I put on the wig and the contact lenses for the last time, and I went to church.

"Ruth!" Everyone turned round. But Carol didn't sound angry that I was so late to the party. "Ruth, thank you so much." She clasped my hands. "You've delivered the evildoers into our hands. I'm so glad you're here to witness their punishment."

And at that, I had to look at what I'd been avoiding looking at — Stefan, ablaze on a pole, no longer recognisable really, except that I knew it was him. I glanced at him, then glanced at the hunched victims waiting to be burnt, then looked away. I could have avoided this bit, I thought. Stupid me. But if you're going to sacrifice people to your ideals, you owe it to them to watch it happen. Or maybe I'd just been curious. I'd lost the ability to tell which of my impulses were altruistic and which were selfish.

"You got them all, then?" I said, remembering my lines. "I had to rush off from the pub, sorry. But I knew you'd manage."

"No problem at all." Himm beamed at me. "Like lambs to the slaughter. Evil lambs," he added hurriedly. "Not the innocent kind. Sheep of evil. Criminal... mutton." Carol gave him a look and he stopped talking.

"Listen, Carol." I leant in to her. "I need to talk to you privately, OK? I have something very important to explain."

"Anything for you, my dear. Himm? I'll be five minutes."

We went indoors, to the church hall where I'd spent those long meetings with her and the others. It smelt of cheap wood and tea, as always. In a way I'd miss those Friday evenings, I thought. It had been fun, dressing up, being someone else, moulding those naïve, bigoted people to my will. Leading them to murder. I still couldn't believe it had actually worked.

Anyway.

We leaned on the kitchen counter and I looked into the eyes of my enemy. Accomplice. Victim. "Carol."

"Yes?"

I took a deep breath. "The police are coming."

She stared at me. "What?"

"You've been discovered. The police are coming. One of the Project Rupture people must have managed to text them while they were in the van. They're on their way. I saw them."

There were mile-wide holes in my story, but I counted on Carol focusing on the salient point, and she did. She gave a quick indrawn breath. "Police? Here?"

"In about two minutes. Listen. I have a plan."

I outlined it very quickly. She didn't have much time to think and I didn't want to give her any extra. She took it all in, blinking.

I held my hands out. "So. Yes? Are you in?" There was urgency in my voice. I thought I could just hear the sounds of sirens, and the entire basis of my plan depended on me getting out of the way before they got much closer.

Carol stared into my face. I think she was looking to see if she could trust me. I held my breath.

She sighed out.

"Yes. OK. Yes. Hurry."

I hugged her briefly. It felt right. "Thank you. I'll be in touch. God loves you."

"I know," she said.

I left without looking back at the fire. I knew what I'd done. I didn't need to see it again.

* * *

This is what happened after I left.

At first, it sounded as though the sirens were a long way away and going somewhere else. Then, quickly, it was apparent that they were coming to the church. Carol hurried back outside. The sound reached the ears of the prisoners and Justin looked up, groggy but awake. He managed to stand up. Fixated by the increasingly louder sirens, nobody stopped him, and he lurched forwards, making incoherent noises behind his gag. He almost reached the bonfire before he collapsed.

Onto the fire.

In the process, he knocked over Mabel, who fell into Hannah. He was tall, and they were short and elderly. They both fell forward, automatically reached out to stop themselves, and found that their hands were in the fire. Justin and the two women screamed. The sirens were very close now.

"Himm!" Carol cried, distraught. Himm and Pete were already hurrying towards the fire. David had his sword out again. He was at the fire too, thrusting his sword into Justin's screaming body and shouting something that sounded like "Die, die, die!" Hannah and Mabel were on fire, their pastel dresses blazing like huge birthday candles. There was no water around, no rugs to smother the flames in. The screams and the sirens were the loudest sound, but underneath them was the noise of Carol, Himm and Pete shouting instructions to each other, and David yelling at Justin's body. Justin was no longer making any noise. David, still stabbing at the body, lost his footing. Then he, too, was amongst the flames. Pete left the two women, who were beyond help, and rushed to pull David from the fire, but it was too late.

By the time the sirens arrived, only seconds later, all the screaming had stopped. The police arrived to find Carol, Himm and Pete standing, shaking, between the four burnt bodies by the fire and the three gagged men seated by the wall. Ranjit, Paul and James hadn't moved during all this, seeming to have reached a tacit agreement between themselves to stay still and avoid being noticed.

The police handcuffed the conspirators first, then untied the live victims, who were very quiet. In therapy later, all three of them would describe themselves as "numb". Ranjit and Paul held hands.

The police put the bonfire out, gagged at the smell of roast flesh. They collected the bodies of Stefan, Justin, Viola, Hannah, Mabel and David. So many people, dead so quickly.

The remaining members of CULT looked blank and shocked. They didn't resist arrest. And yet, in spite of everything, there was a glow of triumph in Carol's eyes.

Chapter Twenty-five
The Kindness of Almost-Strangers

"...thoughts of hydrogen and aqua coloured pastel planets touch my soul as I gaze out through the clear atmosphere and at the universe beyond, pink, purple and white dots are flying at me from the sky, the beyond is touching the depths of my being and a wave of pleasure rolls over me, goosebumps cover my skin and tears fill my eyes..."
"I could draw on the ceiling with my fingers, leaving a trail of transparent rainbows behind them. I could see my hands move. I could actually see movement behind my hands. Out of the corner of my eye the door slid away from me and fell backwards."
"For some reason I kept thinking I was in Sweden. I've never been to Sweden, but everything around me seemed to be saying 'Sweden, Sweden, Sweden.'"
Descriptions of mushroom trips from http://www.shroomery.org.

Friday October 31st — late

Left alone, Marianne stared at the door for a while. Then she wandered back into the living room and stared at the sofa for a while. Then she walked into the bedroom and stared at the bed for a very long while. The sheet had gone, but there were blood marks on the mattress. She touched them all lingeringly, one by one. There was no way of telling which were hers and which were his. She sat down on the bed and curled into a foetal-shaped ball and rocked, and rocked, and rocked. Around her, the flat was achingly silent.

Some time later, minutes or hours, she uncurled a little, wiped her eyes and nose, and knew that she couldn't be alone. She couldn't spend the night here in this flat, on this bed, on her own, without something breaking.

But she couldn't call anyone. She didn't have anyone to call. Her father was dead. Her mother lived in New Zealand with a sheep farmer. She was an only child. Her work colleagues were just work colleagues; her friends were... varied, and variable, in the sense that she kept acquiring new ones and losing touch with the old ones. She'd only just started acquiring the current set, which in any case all consisted of people who would be very angry with her over Stefan's death.

But then, she thought, how many people *did* have someone they could ring at one in the morning after committing murder? That was the kind of thing even husbands and wives turned each other in for, let alone close friends.

Maybe she should have gone with Carol and Himm, but she didn't think she could have watched them burn her boyfriend without screaming. No, this was one of those things you were expected to get through on your own. Possibly with a large jar of sleeping pills and a bottle of whisky.

At that point, her phone rang.

She didn't recognise the sound at first. She had a mobile phone, but that wasn't what was ringing. She hadn't explored all the features of her new iTem yet, and hadn't realised that it too had a phone, or that it had automatically registered her in the directory of iTem users. But after a few seconds, she identified where the beeping sound was coming from and blearily managed to find her bag. The iTem's screen announced that Elinor was calling. For a moment she couldn't remember who that was.

She pressed a big red button. A small tinny voice came out of the iTem's speaker.

"Marianne? Are you there?"

"Yes," she stammered. She coughed, wiped her nose again and said weakly, "Elinor? Stef... Stefan's Elinor?"

"If you like," said the voice, sounding mildly amused. "How are you?"

"I..."

"Never mind. *Where* are you?"

"I'm in... in Stefan's flat." She gulped.

"Can I come over?"

"Come over?"

"Come over. I need to talk to you."

"Oh. Yes. Yes. Please do, please do come over."

"Good. I'll be there as soon as I can get a taxi."

The iTem hung up. She stared at it and felt a tiny, dark flicker of hope.

* * *

By the time Elinor arrived — or rather I arrived, but I'll stick to Marianne's perspective for the moment — Marianne was very drunk. Stefan's flat was short on comfort food but big on organic vodka and tomato juice, though thankfully he hadn't had any sleeping pills. The thick taste of the tomato juice seemed more rich and tangy than usual, but she was able to recognise that as a side-effect of the mushroom trip. When the entry phone buzzed, she answered it with a slurry welcome that contained far too many vowels for its own good, but she did manage to press the buzzer. As Elinor entered the flat, the two women hugged instinctively. Marianne clung to the almost-stranger with absolute need and absolute desperation.

"It's OK," murmured Elinor. "It's going to be all right, don't worry."

"But you don't even know what the matter is," slurred Marianne. "Stefan is dead?"

She looked up, blurrily surprised. "Oh. You knew. How did you know?"

"I was just in Clapham — that's where I called you from. I was just coming back from a night out but I got caught up on my way home. The police were all over the place. Something about a fire in the local church, but it looked as if someone had set it deliberately. There were bodies. And I caught a glimpse of one of them — it was burnt, but I thought it looked familiar. So I thought I'd call you, and when I heard your voice I knew something was wrong. So I assume that *was* Stefan's corpse I just saw. What happened?"

Elinor sounded strangely calm, or maybe Marianne was just so drunk and distraught that everyone sounded calm compared to her. Either way, her calmness was reassuring. Elinor felt like someone she could lean on. Who would look after her.

Someone she could trust.

They sat down on the sofa, and she told her everything. The immortality. The blood drinking. The drug-induced death. The arrival of the Cingins. Her panicked decision to get rid of the body any way she could. Her betrayal.

"I think 'betrayal' is a bit strong," Elinor interjected during the last part. "I'd have done the same. In fact, I'm very impressed by your quick thinking."

"You are?" By this time, Marianne had expected Elinor to be standing on the other side of the room shouting at her, or on the phone to the police. The fact that she was still sitting on the sofa hugging her was difficult to assimilate.

"God, yes. You were tripping and you'd just accidentally killed someone — most people would have been curled up somewhere with a sharp knife and a couple of handy arteries. But no, you pull yourself together, lie convincingly and manage to get someone else to dispose of the body for you and take the blame. I mean, wow." Elinor took an absent-minded swill of vodka and tomato juice and added, "And currently you're drunk *and* coming down from mushrooms, and dealing with what's happened. And you're still coherent. You must have the metabolism of an elephant."

Marianne smiled faintly. "I hadn't thought of it like that."

"Well, you should. I'm seriously fucking impressed."

"I was lucky that Carol already knew me," said Marianne, wiping her eyes and feeling a little better for the first time. "And when I was talking to them, somehow I almost started believing that I really was on their side. It was weird."

"One of the side-effects of mushrooms is that they make you suggestible."

"Oh. That makes sense." Marianne paused. "Do you mean... does that mean that when I felt so amazing earlier, when I thought I was being made immortal..."

"I'm afraid it was largely you tripping, yes."

"Oh."

"But still a valid experience," added Elinor reassuringly.

"Do you think so?"

"All experiences are valid. The important thing is to appreciate them and learn from them, and that's what you're doing."

"But aren't you angry with me? Aren't you going to call the police?"

"Oh, darling." Elinor hugged her tightly. "You didn't mean to kill him. Don't worry about it. The fact is, Stefan was mad. I mean, literally, clinically insane, the way Justin is. Well, the way Justin was."

"Was?" asked Marianne, temporarily diverted.

Elinor paused. "I think I recognised a couple of the other bodies in Clapham. They looked like Justin and Viola."

"Oh." Marianne was blank. There wasn't anything left inside her with which to process that information, so she just accepted it. "Were they part of Project Rupture too?"

"Well, from what you told me about that woman Carol, I'd guess Project Rupture exists only in her mind. But yes, I expect she thought they were part of it."

"I suppose so." Marianne paused, and went back to her main concern. "So you don't think I'm evil?"

"No." Elinor kissed her hair, still holding her tightly. Marianne was mildly surprised, but found herself snuggling against her. "I think you're very brave. If maybe a bit too influenced by other people."

"Oh God." Marianne sat upright. "You don't know the half of it."

"Then tell me."

Briefly, Marianne outlined her recent adventures.

Elinor raised her eyebrows. "And that's just in the last couple of months?"

"I know. I'm so stupid. So suggestible."

"No, no, I wasn't going to say that. You're trusting, you have a need to belong, and there's nothing wrong with that. We just need to get you to believe in yourself a bit more and believe what other people say a bit less."

"Do you think so?"

"You've always believed what the people around you believed, haven't you? The fact that Stefan managed to convince you he was immortal the day you met him... that shows a level of, er, acceptance I've rarely come across."

"You mean gullibility, don't you?"

"Well, maybe a little bit. But anyway, you know what I think you should do? Learn to stand up for yourself. Be independent. You're an interesting and worthwhile person under all those borrowed opinions. I can feel it."

"You're right," said Marianne sleepily, leaning against her new friend. "I should stand on my own two feet, have my own ideas."

"Exactly. For instance, have you thought how you feel about those people, the Cingins?"

"Um... well, they seemed quite... deluded," Marianne ventured cautiously. Elinor nodded. "And obviously they've been going round killing people, which is bad."

Elinor nodded again, encouragingly. "And why have they been killing people?"

"Er, because they think God wants them to... "

"Exactly. So whose fault is it really?"

"God's?"

"Well, in a way, but we don't know if he really exists, do we?" Marianne, who for the past month or so had firmly believed in God, shook her head. "So whose fault would you say it was?"

"Er... Christianity's?"

"Excellent!"

Marianne felt herself glow a little in the familiar warmth of approval. The hot despair of the last couple of hours had begun to cool. She smoothed over the recurring memories of what had happened, and focused on Elinor's face. It felt so wonderful to be held and looked after. So wonderful. The feel of Elinor's skin against her skin was so comforting.

"Elinor?"

"Yes?"

"Why are you being so nice to me? I mean, if you look at it one way, I stole your boyfriend and then killed him."

"Yeah, well. He wasn't really my boyfriend, and he was a very silly man. I'm sorry he's dead, but to be honest it's not the end of the world. And I told you, you have to stop thinking that you killed him. Those Christians killed him. I mean, they meant to, and they would have done even if you hadn't... accidentally done it first. So the best thing would be if you just kept remembering: they killed him. *They* killed him."

"They killed him."

"Yes."

There was a pause.

"There is a specific reason," Elinor said quietly, "why I'm not angry with you."

"Is there? What?"

They shifted position slightly, Marianne lying with her head on Elinor's lap. She looked up at her, feeling a little more sober now, and smiled. It felt wrong to smile so soon after... after the thing, after Stefan. But she so badly wanted to put that behind her, to forget about it. She hated being this unhappy. She wanted to be happy again, as soon as possible.

The hair was stroked back from her forehead. A thumb smoothed the skin above her eyebrows. She closed her eyes.

"When I saw you in that café," Elinor said, taking her hand, "I thought you were gorgeous."

"Me? I assumed — I mean, I saw you looking at me but I thought..."

"That I was jealous? I was. But not the way you thought."

"Oh." Marianne sat up, and immediately clutched her head. She'd forgotten she was still a bit drunk. "Oh." She paused to assimilate the information. "Oh."

"Stefan and I were never that compatible. We knew that all along, really. With you I feel... I don't know, I just wanted to say that I — like you. And I shouldn't be saying that to you now, because you're all vulnerable and I don't want to accidentally manipulate you, but I seem to be saying it anyway. Sorry. All I mean is, I like you, a lot, and in a way you possibly didn't expect. I hope that's not too much to cope with right now."

The words were apologetic, but the tone was assured, confident. Marianne found the effect of that combination oddly captivating. She searched through the bewildering variety of responses thrown up by her brain and found nothing that she could put into words. "I —"

"It's OK." Elinor patted her leg. "You don't have to say anything."

They fell silent.

"No," Marianne said suddenly.

"Sorry?"

"No. I can't. I'm sorry." She got off the sofa and crossed to the window, staring across at the closed bedroom door. "Thank you for being so nice to me and I'm flattered, but I... I just can't. Not now. I need at least some time to recover from all this, and even then I'm not sure... I'm sorry." She hugged herself, starting to shake.

"Don't apologise, it's my fault. I should never have brought it up, not tonight anyway. My timing is appalling, I'm sorry. I didn't mean to." Elinor stood up too. "Should I go? I can call you tomorrow and see how you're doing, maybe meet up for a coffee. Or not. Sorry. I feel like I'm pressuring you and I don't mean to." She stood up. "I'd better go."

"It might be best," Marianne said, trying to be rational. The though of being alone was bleakly terrifying, but she seemed to have got herself trapped in politeness. And it would be embarrassing to spend the night with Elinor here, now she knew how she felt.

Elinor moved towards the door. Marianne thought of something. "How are you going to get home? It's —" she glanced at the big silver clock on the wall "— almost three o'clock. You'll need to call a taxi."

"I suppose you're right." Elinor turned away from the front door, reaching for her iTem phone.

"Don't go."

The words fell out flatly into the blank room. They both watched them fall.

"I mean..." Marianne paused. "I mean, please don't go. I can't be alone tonight. I can't. I'll die." The way to escape from a web of politeness, she thought to herself, was with the scissors of honesty. For a moment she saw the web and the scissors floating clearly in the air in front of her, sharp silver blades snapping in front of her eyes. "Please don't leave me," she said helplessly. "Please."

"Oh, darling. Of course I won't leave you." Elinor crossed to the window and put her arms round Marianne again. "I'll stay as long as you want. And don't worry about what I said, just ignore it. All you need to know is that I'm here to look after you."

"Thank you." Four years older and more experienced in almost every way, Marianne nevertheless felt very small and dependent as she clung to her friend. Her face was against Elinor's breasts, and the sensation was warm and wonderful.

* * *

It has often been noted that people frequently react to grief by suddenly, desperately needing to have sex with someone. It will also be clear by now that Marianne and I were destined to be together — or at least it was clear to me, and Marianne soon came to agree. Furthermore, both of us were spending the night on the sofa, since neither of us felt like cleaning up the bed. (Luckily, the sofa folded out into a double mattress.) What happened during the night was more or less inevitable. But details will not be forthcoming. If you don't know by now what women do in bed together, you haven't been reading enough websites, and if you think I'm going to reveal prurient details of one of the most significant nights of my life, you don't know me. But then, I guess, you don't know me, do you?

All you need to understand, anyway, is that I had been waiting a long time to find someone like Marianne. And now that my immediate mission was completed, I could focus all my attention on making sure she knew it.

Chapter Twenty-six
Ruth and Naomi

"Paisley print is something you see on ties, shirts, blouses, dresses, curtains, rugs, furniture, etc. If you wear it, you may be carrying around some demons, which could be the cause of some of your "problems"... In the PAISLEY PRINT PATTERN, you have a connection with CATHOLICS, THE COUNTRY OF INDIA (WITH ALL THEIR GODS), GOAT HAIR (GOAT IS THE SYMBOL FOR THE DEVIL), MUSLIMS, PRAYER RUGS, JESUITS, CULTS, SEERS, MAGICIANS, OCCULT."
http://www.demonbuster.com/paisley.html

Some months later

"God, that woman is weird," said Marianne to me after the trial, when we were in my flat packing for the flight. She hadn't met Naomi before, of course. "And why disguise herself anyway? I mean, Ruth/Naomi, yes, I get it, very Biblical. But I don't see the point." She looked critically at a small black dress, then shoved it into a corner of her suitcase. I made a mental note to buy an iron as soon as we arrived.

I shrugged. "Like she said, she was worried that someone would track her down and tell her father. He's fairly well-known around London. But yes, she is weird. And *extremely* Biblical."

"So you've known her for ages?" Marianne had been impressed at my connection with the celebrity murderess. Or conspiracy-to-murderess, anyway. "You could have been a character witness."

I smiled, and reached up to the top of my wardrobe to get down my spare pair of boots. "I don't think it would have helped. The stuff I know about Naomi would hardly have reduced her sentence. I could have testified that she was dangerously insane, but they knew that already."

Marianne was quiet for a minute. Then she said, "So she was insane for thinking she was a vampire?" She sounded worried.

"In a way." I stopped packing for a moment and took her hand. "But that was only part of it, really. She also attacked people. In fact..."

I told her about Simon. It hadn't come up at the trial. I suppose I could have told the police, but it didn't seem worth it now. Naomi was spending a lifetime in prison anyway — well, twenty years or so.

Marianne looked shocked. "So she's really a killer, as well as masterminding that cult killing spree?"

"Well, yeah. It was kind of an accident, though. She's not really a bad person, I don't think, just incredibly misguided."

"That's generous of you. I'd say misguided was quite a long way away from joining a mad fundamentalist cult in disguise and giving them the names of your friends so they could kill them."

"You don't understand." It came out too harshly. I paused and rearranged my tone. "She believed that Stefan and the others were in an evil conspiracy. She was trying to do the right thing, not trying to get revenge on anyone. Or not much."

Marianne shrugged in tentative agreement while trying to fit a very large black coat into a small plastic bag. I took it away from her. "We're going to Florida, darling, not Iceland. Pack shorts." I put the coat in the storage pile, which was to be sent to my parents to look after. "Anyway. The important thing is that it's all over, you're not implicated and we're free to go to America and fight against the Christians."

"Or something. I wouldn't mind lying around on a beach for a while first." She pulled out a bikini top from a drawer and placed it meaningfully in the centre of her suitcase.

I smiled at her. "OK, beach first. But then, working to dismantle the malignant global effects of the Resurrected Church."

"Of course." She smiled back.

* * *

Marianne had been needed at the trial, of course.

I went with her to offer support, but stayed very much in the background. I didn't want Naomi or any of the CULT people to see me in court, and I definitely didn't want to have to talk to any of them.

The Cingins were impressive, actually, in a way — dignified and clearly sincere. Though Carol lost a few sanity points by accusing a woman in the jury of being a Satanist because she was wearing paisley. They pleaded guilty, as did Naomi. Pete Matthews opted to plead not guilty, and claimed he knew nothing of what was going on. Not a well-advised move, I thought. He ended up with a longer sentence than the Cingins did, even though he hadn't masterminded the operation or killed anyone personally. But then, none of them had killed anyone, technically. Only David, and he was dead himself.

Marianne was merely called upon to testify that she had opened the door to Carol and Himm on that Friday night. She said Stefan had fallen unconscious after a breath-control sex game, and that when the Cingins had arrived, she wasn't strong enough to stop them taking him away. Then she burst into tears. The lawyer was sufficiently embarrassed by it all not to ask too many questions. Carol and Himm backed her up. They said Stefan had been unconscious when they took him and had died in the fire. Luckily, his body was burnt enough that they couldn't tell what had actually happened to him. Marianne was safe.

We were free.

Unlike Naomi. But then she didn't seem to mind that much. Guilt is a powerful thing. She had looked very quiet in the witness box. But she had answered all the questions without hesitation.

"Yes, I disguised myself in order to join the CULT group, and called myself Ruth. I was afraid I would be recognised, since my father is a high-ranking policeman." The white contact lenses and the black wig had already been produced as evidence, having been found in Naomi's bathroom.

"Yes, I was obsessed with evil. I wanted to destroy Stefan Drayton, who I believed had destroyed my life. I also had a grudge against Justin Wild and Viola Edison, who had previously taunted me and hurt me. But that was not the main reason for my actions."

"Yes, I firmly believed I was doing my Christian duty."

"Yes, I believed Carol Cingin when she said we should hunt down and destroy evildoers."

"Yes, I gave CULT the names of Stefan Drayton, Justin Wild, Viola Edison, James Gray, Ranjit Dhesi and Paul McManus. I believed that they were evil and should be destroyed."

"Yes, I set up the meeting of those six people on the night of October 31st. I emailed them and invited them to the pub."

Marianne had already testified that Stefan had received such an email from Naomi, but had decided not to turn up as he had a date with her that evening.

"Yes, I knew that Carol and Himm intended to kill them."

"Yes. I am an accessory to the murders of Stefan Drayton, Justin Wild and Viola Edison and an accessory to the attempted murders of James Gray, Ranjit Dhesi and Paul McManus."

The newspapers described her as 'disturbed' and 'very pale'.

After hearing evidence about her previous belief that she was a vampire, the court sent her for psychiatric testing before sentencing her to life imprisonment.

* * *

Carol testified more loudly. She used the occasion to promote her brand of evangelism and to publicise Project Rupture, which she insisted was real. The police had found no evidence of any conspiracy apart from CULT's own, but she said that just meant they'd been too clever for them. She said she trusted Ruth/Naomi absolutely and believed that CULT had 'eliminated' the right people. They couldn't shake her beliefs no matter what evidence they produced, even with the proven fact that it had been Ruth who had set up that Halloween pub meeting. She almost got remanded for a psychiatric report too, but in the end they just put her in prison.

The same thing happened with Himm, who repeated more or less exactly what Carol had said. He got a longer sentence though, because he'd actually stabbed people. Plus, I think some of the jury (both male and female) assumed he must have been in charge of the conspiracy, since he was the man and the husband. In fact, it was reasonably obvious that Carol and 'Ruth' had organised the whole thing — though for quite different reasons, of course.

* * *

Joanne had come to watch the trial too, I noticed. I didn't see her to speak to, but I glimpsed her across the courtroom. I didn't think she was that upset about Justin and Viola's death, but I assumed she was upset about Stefan.

So was I, in a way. But the worst thing for me was waking up in the night and hearing Marianne next to me, crying. I always pretended to be asleep. I couldn't offer much comfort, because the truth was, if Stefan hadn't died I might never have gotten what I wanted. And I'd wanted Marianne so much.

I waited impatiently for the trial to finish, so we could book our flights. Once we got to America I knew she'd forget about all this, and Stefan wouldn't matter to her any more. When it was just the two of us — and none of these silly vampires and Christians and Christian vampires and vampire Christians, all busy deluding themselves left, right and centre because they couldn't cope with the world as it was — then we could be ourselves.

You must understand that I didn't hate any of the people who died, or any of the people who were on trial. I felt sorry for them in many ways. But they were wrong. And Christianity was wrong, whether it was the Resurrected Church or the CULTists or the Jesus' Blood Church — factually wrong and morally wrong. And I was right.

Everything followed from that. I'd been over my beliefs and my actions again and again in the last months, and always ended up at the same conclusion: that everything I'd done was justified.

The trial, therefore, had me in high spirits much of the time. Despite Carol and Himm's best efforts and despite their impressive sincerity — or rather, because of it — they came across as insane homicidal maniacs. And, most importantly, *evangelical Christian* homicidal maniacs. Britain, which normally followed the US whenever possible, was going to have a lot more trouble becoming a fundamentalist theocracy now that the public had *this* image in their heads. Which was, of course, precisely the reason I'd masterminded it all.

(Mistressminded? Anyway.)

And of course all the vampire stuff and the other stuff came out — James's mosquito delusions, what Stefan did to Naomi, what Justin and Viola did to her. Not what she did to Simon though, that case was closed. But the stuff that came out was enough to force the vampire community way underground, at least for a while. Probably not a bad idea. Certainly, without Justin, the Church stood very little chance of surviving.

In a smaller way, the weird conspiracy people were undermined by the exposure of James, Ranjit and Paul's bizarre opinions, but because they all believed different things the effect wasn't as strong. The trial was enlivened by Ranjit and Paul's frequent shouting matches. They nearly got prison sentences themselves for contempt of court.

I heard that their government jobs were quietly taken away, but James said they could join him in the psychic business, so they all set up together.

I ran into Ethereal Starshadow during the trial, while we were waiting for the jury.

"Those poor people," she said sympathetically. "I hope they all get good psychiatric care. It's so sad when people just can't accept reality."

"Yes, it is."

"Nice seeing you again," she said. "I'd better go. We're casting an elven spell outside to help the jury."

"Help it do what?" I asked.

"Decide."

"Yes, but which way?"

"Oh, whichever." She shrugged delicately. "We just want to have some influence over the proceedings. After all, the elf folk have a responsibility to use our superior wisdom and our special powers to help you normal people."

"Well, I'm sure we're all very grateful."

"Why, thank you!" That girl's sarcasm filter needed some serious cleaning. "It's nice to feel appreciated — it's a bit lonely sometimes, you know, being the secret power behind everything. Controlling the destiny of mankind and guiding it to the Higher Path."

"I see you have the ability to capitalise spoken words, too."

"I'm sorry?"

"Nothing. Thanks for all your help." She briefly laid a wispy hand on my shoulder and skipped off.

I watched her go with a sense of relief.

Chapter Twenty-seven
The Things We Do For God

Afterwards

The trial was over. The jury went home, and the judge went home, and the court reporters went home, and the journalists went to their offices to file reports, and the four defendants went to prison.

In the women's prison, Naomi and Carol sat in their separate small hard cells, several corridors away from each other, and stared at the walls. They were thinking, idly — if you can think idly in a prison, which possibly you can't, I wouldn't know — about the same person.

Naomi thought about her conversations with Elinor.

"Spiritually you'll be happy every single day from now on, now you've been reunited with your God. A prison cell isn't going to take that away from you."

"A... a prison cell? Do I have to?"

"I think you know you do."

And then a few days later Elinor had seen her again, and told her what she had to do.

"I don't really understand," she had confessed, wanting to trust, but feeling a little confused. *"This doesn't have anything to do with my crime."*

"I know. But trust me, this is the best way for you to serve God and punish yourself at the same time."

"But I'll be punished for things I didn't do." She had tried to curl up in a half-formed foetal position, but she was sitting on a park bench so she couldn't. They were sitting in St James' Park, shivering in the cold October sunshine.

"But you will have been punished. It'll be the same thing in the end. And this way you save me, and I'll be free to go and spread God's word."

"*I suppose so...*"

"*Trust me,*" *Elinor had said again.* "*This is the best way. I promise. Plus,*" *she had added,* "*this way you won't get done for murder, just conspiracy to murder, so you'll get less time in prison.*"

"*Oh.*" *Naomi had felt her spirits lift a bit.* "*I hadn't thought of that.*"

"*There you are, then. It'll be easy, I'll tell you what to say. Plead guilty, look like a victim and you'll be out in no time, forgiven by God for your crimes and ready to live a happy fulfilling Christian life for a change. Or do you want to be miserable and evil all your life?*" *The voice had become a little sharper.*

"*No, no,*" *Naomi had said hastily.* "*I'll do it. I promise. I trust you. I do.*"

And she *had* trusted her — she still did, though it was even more horrible being in prison than she'd imagined. But she prayed, and she repented for her sins, and she talked to the psychiatrist about what it had been like being a vampire, and she waited for her life to start again. Or just to start.

* * *

Carol's thoughts were more upbeat, more self-congratulatory. The prison walls could not dampen her spirits, though she missed Himm. (Himm, however, far away in the men's prison, was finding he missed Carol less than he'd thought he would. Life was certainly quieter.)

Like Naomi, Carol was remembering a conversation.

The flames had hissed behind her in the Halloween darkness. The now-defunct Hannah and Mabel had been poking the fire and giggling. Himm and Pete had been prowling the churchyard like cats, looking out for the police, much good that it had done! And she and Ruth — who wasn't, it turned out, Ruth at all — had conspired in the hall.

"*Police? Here?*"

"*In about two minutes. Listen. I have a plan.*"

Carol was a quick thinker. She adjusted to the fact that the police were on their way. It had always been a possibility. She'd planned a public martyrdom. But Ruth/not-Ruth was suggesting an extra twist.

"*Firstly, my name isn't really Ruth. I had to go into hiding to expose Project Rupture.*" *Carol had nodded, she'd suspected as much.*

"*Secondly, I need to you to save me.*"

"*Save you?*"

The girl's eyes were urgent.

"I'm going to leave in a minute. Tomorrow morning, a girl called Naomi will turn herself in and confess to being me — being Ruth, that is. I've told her what to say. All you and the others have to do is confirm that she's Ruth."

"And why would we do that?"

"Because if you do, I will be free to carry on our work. I'll recruit new believers, and when you get out of prison you can join me again. Otherwise, we'll all be locked away. Right now I'm the only one who has a chance to continue the fight to make England a truly Christian country. You can make it possible."

And Carol had agreed.

She had had no doubts then, and had none now, that she had done the right thing. She'd had just enough time to shout quick instructions to the remaining members of CULT before the police had arrived. When the trial started, that girl Naomi had been so thoroughly briefed that she was word-perfect on the conspiracy.

She had seen the real Ruth in court, watching the proceedings seriously and attentively, even taking notes. She hadn't had the white eyes or the black hair, and Carol didn't think Himm or Pete had recognised her, but she had. She had exchanged a quick glance with the girl, and the expression in both their eyes had been one of congratulation and complicity.

She still thought of the events of that night as a triumph. She could still feel the presence of angels at her shoulder, praising her courage and her determination, whispering promises about her reward in Heaven. (Though since she had been in prison, the angels' voices had started focusing a little more on the material comforts to be found in the afterlife, such as comfortable sofas, freshly cooked food and clean fluffy towels.)

Naomi felt angels at her shoulder too. They spoke of sacrifice and of the salvation to be found in privation and hardship. They comforted her and they promised that she would be rewarded. She believed them.

The two prisoners sat in their cells and dreamed of Heaven, as delivered to them by the miracle of Elinor Rosewood.

Chapter Twenty-eight
Playing Judas

Afterwards

The plane was almost empty, since so few people were allowed to travel to the CUS these days. Marianne and I had three seats to ourselves, but we snuggled together anyway, watching MTV on the small TV screen (since all the films were CUS-approved and featured Jesus in a starring role, we'd decided music was the better option). The stewards fed us white wine, which we drank eagerly — the CUS itself was teetotal. Or so they claimed. I was sure we'd find a drink somewhere. A speakeasy, that you entered through a secret door, with girls dancing in tight black silk shorts and waiters asking how much 'milk' you wanted. Much more fun than normal drinking.

"It'll be great," I said to her. "Once we're in, we can go anywhere we like. We can see San Francisco or New Orleans — they're both very under-populated these days, so we'll have no problem finding somewhere to stay. Or New York, if you like."

"I don't mind," she said, stroking my leg. "I'll follow you. I'd follow you anywhere."

"That's what I like to hear." I smiled down at her.

I needed that devotion, that reassurance. I'd had a shock earlier.

* * *

Six hours before, I had been standing with my luggage at the airport, waiting for Marianne, reading a newspaper. "CUS PRESIDENT SAYS UK EXTREMIST CULT WAS JUSTIFIED IN MURDER". Outrage poured off the page. Excellent, I thought. Perhaps Britain would soon break its ties with America altogether. Maybe form a secular utopia. A girl can dream.

"Murderer."

"Sorry?"

It was Joanne. Standing in front of me. With an expression I'd never seen on her face before.

I hadn't set eyes on her since that glimpse at the trial. I'd been so occupied with Marianne and our plans that I hadn't really bothered to keep in touch with anyone else — I'd barely managed to ring my parents to tell them I was leaving the country. I had remembered to email Joanne to tell her when we were off, but I hadn't expected her to show up.

She looked into my face, sharp and unfriendly.

"I thought I had a handle on you."

"Well," I said, "it turns out I'm hard to handle."

"Apparently."

We paused.

She took a deep breath. "You're quite the onion, aren't you?"

"Um..."

"Layers," she snapped. "Layers and layers of you, and rotten at the core."

"OK," I said, "What have you... I mean, how did you..." I paused, choosing my words carefully. "What makes you think I'm not the person you knew?"

"Just a look, really." She also seemed to be choosing her words carefully, coldly, but almost hesitantly, apparently sure of her facts but afraid of my reaction to them. "I was in court on the day everyone was sentenced — I don't know if you saw me." I nodded. "I was watching that woman, Carol, quite intently, trying to work out exactly what was going on in her head, you know? When Naomi was sentenced, everyone else looked towards Naomi to see her reaction, obviously. But I was still looking at Carol. And Carol... Carol looked at you."

"At me?" I said. "Did she? I don't remember."

"How odd. Because when I followed her glance, you were looking back at her. And both of you looked, not *happy* exactly, but... satisfied. As if something you'd both planned had been successfully completed."

"That's a lot to deduce from one look," I said, smiling at her. She didn't smile back.

"Well, after that, you see, I started really *thinking*. The list of people who were attacked by that fanatic group. Three vampires and three people from that weird things group. The one we went to."

"Yes, because Naomi had been there too. They explained that in court. Seems reasonable to me."

"Does it?" Joanne sat down on one of the long silver airport benches and, after a moment's hesitation, I joined her, sliding my suitcase under the bench.

"Would you like a coffee or something?" I said agreeably. "It's nice of you to come and see me and Marianne off."

"No, thanks," she said, deflecting my attempts at amiability. "And I came to see you off because there were a few things I wanted to ask you. Like, why are you going to the States? And why are you taking Marianne?"

"I'm taking Marianne because she's my girlfriend," I said. Joanne looked startled, but didn't say anything. "We got very close after Stefan's death and, well..."

"You never said you were bisexual."

"I never said I wasn't. Your heterosexist assumptions are not my problem."

"Oh, shut up."

"Fair enough," I shrugged. "And I've always wanted to visit the CUS. I'll have to pretend to be a churchgoer, of course, but there's bound to be a subculture somewhere, in one of the big cities. I'll find people who want to get rid of the God'n'Guns lot, and maybe I can make a difference."

"Like you did in London?"

"If you like."

"Is that what you've always wanted? To make a difference?" Her voice had softened slightly, but now it became hard again. "How far would you go to save the world?"

There was a pause.

"I've always been interested," I said neutrally, "in the concept of sacrifice."

"Yes?"

"In which context I feel the whole Jesus thing is very interesting."

"But you don't believe in God."

"No. But it's the kind of unbelief that niggles at you. I mean, so many other people do believe it. You have to wonder why, don't you? What's the appeal? Of the Christian God, I mean?"

"I don't know," said Joanne, sounding as if she was waiting for a punch line. "What is the appeal?"

"Like I said — sacrifice."

"What, as in Jesus sacrificed himself for the world, type of thing?"

"Three sacrifices in one, that's what people don't realise." I made a kind of three-in-one gesture. "Jesus was only one of them. Give up your life to save the world, it's a nice idea. Sweet. If irritating. Don't you just hate it when people do things for you that you didn't ask them for, and then expect lifelong gratitude?"

"Interesting point," said Joanne neutrally. "So, what were the other two?"

"Judas and God. Jesus gives up his life. Judas gives up his soul. And God, of course, gives up his son's life."

"OK. So you can sacrifice yourself, like Jesus, you can sacrifice someone else, like God, or you can sacrifice your... what, your conscience, like Judas?"

"Precisely. Lots of people do sacrifice something, you know. It's just that most of them play God. Not that surprising, it's clearly the most fun role — they'll sacrifice someone else, but not themselves. And then there's a few types who play Jesus and genuinely do sacrifice themselves up for the good of humanity, I applaud that, but it's not me. I decided to play Judas. I'll take on the guilt, I'll do what has to be done, and humanity will benefit."

"Sorry," said Joanne, "could you explain that again?"

I sighed. "Ask not what your country can do for you, but what you can do for your country."

She looked blank.

"The UK was going the way of the CUS. It would have been hell, and sooner or later the whole world would be a theocracy. I had to find a way to stop that happening."

"Why you?"

"Why not me? I had a plan. I carried it out. Some people had to die for it to work. Other people ended up in prison. But overall, on the whole, I did a good thing."

"And escaped scot-free."

"As it happened. Maybe next time I won't end up getting away free and travelling to a new country with a beautiful woman who loves me, but this time, that's how it worked out. What can I do?"

Joanne shook her head as if trying to clear it, or clear me out of it. "I can't talk to you. You don't — I can't talk to you."

"But don't you understand?" I spread my hands out. "I changed the world! A bit, at least. I achieved something! I came from this dull, village life where nobody understood the slightest thing about me or wanted to, and I proved that I'm better than all of them."

except me is real?"

because I'm too much of a psychopath to understand that anyone people around like pawns in my manipulative, destructive game deciding who lives and who dies, who gets to believe what? Moving

"Oh, you mean I'm arrogantly taking on the responsibility of God earlier. There's more than one way to do that."

"You know, Elinor," she said, "you were talking about playing

"Well, more or less, yes."

"So justice is done?"

hospital rather than a prison, I think they said. It'll be good for her."

"Well, twenty years or so. And most of it'll be in a secure mental

after a pause.

"So Naomi spends the rest of her life in prison?" said Joanne

feeling cleared.

only real person in existence. I shook my head impatiently and the after them, protect them. And at the same time, it felt as if I was the tremendous sense of empathy with all of them. I wanted to look faces were blank, stressed, happy, angry, worried, excited. I felt a rushing around it, colliding, avoiding, apologising, meeting; I looked across at the Heathrow concourse. So many people she'd thought about it, surely she would see my side of things.

then? I didn't really think Joanne would turn me in, anyway. Once CUS, we could disappear. Who cared if the UK police were after me talk about it to someone. Anyway, once Marianne and I were in the been stupid of me to tell her, but it had been such fun finally to out the truth, she hadn't really believed it till now. Perhaps it had her hair, and said nothing. I guessed that, though she had worked Joanne put her head in her hands, running her fingers through never been entirely sure. I suppose it doesn't matter that much.

Was that true? I've thought back over and over again, but I've

didn't quite work out."

thought they'd get there in time to stop anyone being burnt. It just what it's worth, I didn't mean for them to die. I called the police. I sighed. "I didn't. I enabled them to be killed, at most. And for

You killed people."

"I thought we'd been over that."

"But you killed people."

I'll find a way."

perhaps I can change that. Or I'll write my memoirs, or something. "That, I must admit, is the only real drawback. But next time

"But nobody knows about it."

She looked at me. "Well, I certainly can't fault your self-awareness."

I grinned. "Of course I've thought of that. But, you know, if someone's going to play God I'd rather it was me than God. I've definitely killed fewer people than he has."

She sighed and said nothing in an 'I give up' kind of way. I decided to abandon the broader moral issues and focus on something I thought we could agree on.

"By the way," I said casually, "Do you know that it was Naomi who murdered Simon?"

"*What?*" Joanne sat upright.

"Yes. We didn't mention it at the time because we didn't want to upset you. She was the one who attacked him. Mad, you know. The vampires sort of turned her sane again afterwards though, and I persuaded her to pay for her crimes. Well, OK, my crimes, but the important thing is, she's in prison."

Joanne was crying. I considered giving her a hug, but somehow it didn't seem like a good idea. Instead I read a magazine for a few minutes while she sniffled herself out of it. She wiped her nose and took a deep breath.

"Why didn't Naomi confess to Simon's murder as well?"

I shrugged. "I thought it was bit unfair to make her to pay for *both*."

She stared at me.

"Really, it's perfect," I said enthusiastically. "This way, everyone ends up with justice done, even if it is a little... indirect. Justin and Viola tortured Naomi and they're dead. Stefan drove her mad, or madder, and he's dead. All three of them were accessories to Simon's murder, too." Joanne looked grim. "Naomi killed Simon and she's in prison. Carol and CULT killed Justin and Viola, and *they're* all in prison, or dead. Ranjit, Paul and James are all innocent, and they're alive. Of course," I added flippantly, "it would have been nice to get Ethereal Starshadow put away too, but you can't have everything."

She couldn't help smiling at that, just for a moment.

Of course, there was one person who had technically committed murder, or at least manslaughter, and wasn't being punished. But nobody's rational about the woman they love, are they? Would you turn *your* girlfriend in for a death she didn't mean to happen? I absolved myself of that guilt without a second thought.

It felt as though we'd been talking for hours, but looking at the clock Marianne was only just due to arrive.

"So, it's been lovely to see you," I said pointedly, standing. I saw she'd given up. Something that had been in her face, some spark of energy, had gone. I felt sorry about that.

"Goodbye, Elinor. I hope one day you'll wake up in the night and realise what you've done."

I opened my mouth to reply, but was halted by a happy cry from behind me.

"Elinor!" Marianne scurried up, grinning widely. "Sorry I'm late! Oh God, I'm so excited!"

"Excitement and adventure and really really wild things," I said, hugging her. "I promise." She grinned even more widely.

"We'd better go and sort out our seats," I said. I retrieved my suitcase from under the bench. "Thanks for coming to see us off." I waved at Joanne. "I'll email you from the States. Maybe we'll come back and visit sometime."

She nodded silently, and didn't get up as we collected our luggage and headed off across the concourse. As we left, I glanced back. Joanne was looking straight at me, and I thought I heard her say something. I turned away and took Marianne's hand.

"So," said my girlfriend cheerfully. "Shall we go and check in?"

"Let's do that."

* * *

The plane dipped and roared, in that reassuring way planes do. Marianne had fallen asleep in the crook of my arm. I sipped my white wine and reflected that I liked being the tall one in a relationship — it made me feel protective. And I did have every intention of protecting her, though I also intended her to fight at my side. Together we would save America from itself, and after that, who knew? The world?

There was one little thing still to be done, though. I took Marianne's hand and, very slowly and carefully, removed the ring Stefan had given her and dropped it under the seat. She didn't wake up. Best if she didn't have any reminders of him, I thought. They'd just upset her. I'd buy her a ring in the CUS, to remind her of me instead.

The plane flew on calmly. My love snuggled drowsily against me. And I went to sleep, dreaming of America.

A Quick Word

If you enjoyed *All Lies and Jest* and feel like helping Kate out a bit, please consider leaving a brief review where you obtained the book, or spreading the word a little. It's genuinely an immense help. You can also find more of Kate's writing in *Red Phone Box*, our darkly magical story cycle, available from the same places that this book is.

For advance notice of upcoming Ghostwoods releases, and special member-only offers, please sign up to our (very) occasional mailing list at:

`http://www.gwdbooks.com/mailing-list-sign-up.html`

We have a very strict policy of not being annoying email jerks. We'll never spam you, sell your details to anyone else, or broadcast any third-party offers.

Marion Grace Woolley

THOSE ROSY HOURS
AT MAZANDARAN

Printed in Great Britain
by Amazon